The Easterly House

Beth Livingston (signature)

Beth Livingston

Christian Drama Publishing

Dedicated to David,
the best son ever,
a man after God's own heart,
and a great editor.

"Let nothing be done through strife or vainglory; but in lowliness of mind let each esteem other better than themselves."

Philippians 2:3

Author's Preface

THE GEORGE EASTMAN House in Rochester, New York, is the setting for this second in the Tour of Mansions series.

I borrowed bits of real history from the life of George Eastman, founder of Eastman Kodak, for my imaginary characters and plot.

George Eastman has become David Easterly.

His secretary Alice Whitney has become Grace Weston.

His housekeeper Molly Cherbuliez has become Miss Donovan.

His chauffeur Billy Carter has become Edgar Hopkins.

His butler Solomon Young has become Solomon Merrick.

His cook Eliza Delea has become Ellen Culligan.

School principal Julia F. Whiton is Miss Whiton.

Although the characters are inspired by real people, their personalities and actions and the plot are purely fictitious.

Part I

Chapter I

Wednesday, June 17, 1908

Rochester, New York

Tears pooled in Julia Bradshaw's eyes.

"Good-bye, Miss Bradshaw," chorused the twenty-one kindergartners, diplomas in hand, as they raced through the playground.

She would miss them all, even prim Theodore, frivolous blond Mildred, and Jack whose naughtiness had almost made her quit her first year of teaching.

Already they had forgotten her as they swarmed through the gate, no doubt dreaming of parks and beaches and lemonade.

Mr. Pratt, the fourth grade teacher, stepped beside her. "We're free!" he said.

"Don't say that. I miss them already."

"You won't for long. How about we go out tonight and celebrate?"

Tall and lanky with a thin red mustache that almost disappeared behind his thick lips, he was relentless in his pursuit of her. Summer would be a vacation from him as well.

"Sorry, I can't. I'm too tired."

"Come on now, I insist."

She shook her head. "I can't." She was looking forward to sitting at home on the porch with a good book.

One boy turned. Was that naughty Jack? She smiled and waved, and to her astonishment, he dashed back.

"Did you forget something, Jack?"

He didn't answer but squeezed her around the waist. She returned the hug, feeling his bony shoulders through the navy blue sailor suit.

He wiggled away as quickly as he had come.

"Thank you," she whispered.

Jack, of all people. She thought Jack hated her for making him toe the line.

"That was touching," Mr. Pratt said.

Touching? It was priceless. It made everything worthwhile.

She pictured those innocent eyes around the story circle. Had she said anything they would remember?

If Jack had learned something, perhaps she wasn't hopeless after all.

A young man sprinted down the street toward the school. His face was red, his eyes wild, his breathing labored.

"Who is that?" Mr. Pratt said.

Julia's eyes widened. It was her eighteen-year-old brother Richard. Never had he looked so frantic.

Something was wrong.

David Easterly leaned over the front seat, "Back to the office, Hopkins."

His chauffeur pulled the Packard onto the narrow residential street as David turned toward his secretary. "Have everything you need now?"

She nodded. "I can't believe I left those addresses home this morning. We'll get those invitations out in today's mail."

It was because of Miss Weston that his life ran so efficiently. Dressed in crisp navy with starched white cuffs, she was smart, efficient, and beautiful with her big brown eyes and low pompadour.

"Oh, look," she pointed as they drove past the two-story brick Francis Parker School. "School's out. Aren't they adorable?" Happy children poured through the gate.

He nodded indulgently.

A little boy ran back. The teacher embraced him, her eyes closed as if savoring the moment. She was stunning, and she obviously loved children.

David hadn't been hugged like that since Mother died two years ago. He wished someone would make him feel loved too.

And not like a boss.

A young man darted in front of their car. Hopkins slammed on the brakes. David and Miss Weston fell against each other.

"Watch out," David said.

"Are you all right, sir?" Hopkins asked.

"I'm fine. How about you, Miss Weston?"

She scooted away, adjusting her wide-brimmed hat. "I'm fine."

"Fool kid. Should look where he's going," Hopkins said.

The young man ran into the school yard and up to the beautiful teacher.

Her hands covered her mouth. Her eyes were tortured.

Some emergency, apparently. He'd like to help, but he couldn't fix all the problems of the world. He had enough of his own at the Rochester Optical Company.

"Back to the office, Hopkins."

⊷⊶

"Come quick," Richard said. "Papa's had an accident."

Julia felt herself falling. Not Papa. Anyone but Papa. Mr. Pratt caught her.

She struggled to stand. "Tell me what happened."

"He fell off a bridge."

A bridge? Her breath whooshed out.

Papa and his brother Charles were carpenters for the New York Central Railroad. They'd had accidents before, but nothing serious.

"Tell me he's all right."

"It's bad. He's been taken to the Park Avenue Hospital."

Her heart seized.

Not dear Papa. Just last night while she had filled out report cards at the dining room table, Papa had played horsy with her youngest siblings, eight-year-old Mary, four-year-old Peter, and three-year-old Annie. Their happy screams and laughter made concentrating impossible. Later, after he'd tucked them into bed, he had massaged her shoulders. "You work too hard, princess."

"I know, but after tomorrow, I'll do nothing all summer."

"You do that."

Mama would never let her, of course, but Papa would.

She needed to see him. Now. She needed his arms around her and his assurance, "Of course I'll be all right, princess."

"Let's go," she said.

"Mama's at the hospital with Uncle Charles. She wants you to stay home with the little ones."

"I'm not staying home. Jenny can." Her fifteen-year-old sister Jenny was more than capable.

"Good luck convincing Jenny."

Not even Jenny could keep her from Papa.

"Mr. Pratt, would you lock up my room and tell Miss Whiton I'll be in tomorrow to clean up?"

He nodded. "Anything else?" He looked concerned.

She shook her head as she grabbed Richard's hand and ran for home, half a block away.

Her students would be alarmed at their teacher running like a mad woman down the street. So be it. Nothing mattered but Papa. *Lord, help Papa be all right,* she prayed with each step.

She couldn't survive without him.

-→=◎ ◎=←-

Four pairs of solemn sapphire eyes stared back at her. Everyone called them the Bradshaw eyes. They each had them, beautiful eyes inherited from Papa's side of the family.

"You're not leaving me home alone with them." Jenny's eyes blazed. "Just because you're the oldest doesn't make you boss."

It was the same old argument.

Julia felt like shaking her. "We don't have time for this. I need to be with Papa."

"So do I."

"Don't fight." Eight-year-old Mary slipped her hand into Julia's. She still wore her flowered, ruffled school dress. Her long dark hair hung in ringlets. A big blue bow on top matched the sprigs in her dress.

Julia looked down at the other little ones. Four-year-old Peter, the only blond in the family, was almost in tears. Three-year-old Annie wrinkled her brow.

It was like looking into the innocent eyes of her kindergarten students.

She squeezed Mary's hand. "You're right. I'm sorry. Jenny, let's not fight. Please agree to stay. You're so much better at running things than I am."

Jenny had helped Mama all four years while Julia studied at the University of Rochester. Julia's housekeeping skills had grown rusty, to say the least, but no one minded. Everyone was proud to have a teacher in the family. After all, she was the first to graduate from college except for cousin Lee who was two years older.

"You always get your way," Jenny said.

"Just do it, Jenny," Mary pleaded.

"Oh, all right."

"Thank you." Julia felt the tension release only to be replaced by a sense of urgency. They needed to leave now.

She gathered little Annie into her arms. Annie's mop of short dark curls tickled her chin. "Be good for Jenny, all right?"

Annie nodded. "When's Mama coming home?"

"Not until tonight. But don't worry. Jenny will fix supper and put you to bed."

Peter hung back, shy as usual.

"Come here, honey. Give Julia a hug." She didn't need to remind him to be good. He always was.

"When's Papa coming home?" he asked.

She swallowed a lump in her throat. Maybe never. No, she couldn't think that way. Of course he would come home. "Just as soon as he can," she said.

She squeezed Mary's shoulder. "Help Jenny, all right?"

Mary nodded.

"And everyone pray for Papa."

Papa wasn't the only one who needed it. They all needed help for what was ahead.

–›‡◉ ◉‡‹–

Julia and Richard breathlessly leaped up the steps of the hospital which was across the street from their church. Ordinarily it took fifteen minutes to walk to church. Today it had taken five.

She had never been inside the Park Avenue Hospital. It was the smallest hospital in Rochester with only forty beds. Four narrow stories high, it looked like a red brick apartment building.

They opened the front door into a small marble-tiled foyer. A black iron staircase with marble steps led to upper floors.

They approached a receptionist behind a desk.

"Where can we find Mr. Alver Bradshaw?"

The woman's face sobered. Not good. She knew about Papa. "Are you family?"

"Yes, I'm his daughter and this is his son. Please tell me how he is."

"He's in surgery. You can wait with your mother across the hall."

Surgery? At least he was still alive.

The waiting room looked like home with its flowered chintz curtains and comfortable furniture.

Mama, seated on a sofa, pressed a handkerchief to her eyes. She looked tiny and shrunken and pale.

Beside her sat Uncle Charles, Papa's older brother, his hair parted down the middle, his mustache and beard neatly trimmed. His eyes were mournful as he patted Mama's hand.

On a nearby couch sat his son Lee, her favorite cousin. No unmarried woman at church could resist his striking blue Bradshaw eyes or his bushy mustache.

"How is he?" Julia asked.

Mama burst into tears.

Julia trembled. "Someone tell me he's alive."

Lee leaped up and drew her close. "Yes, he's alive. He's in surgery."

"How bad is it?"

"Bad."

"But how bad?"

"Ask my father."

She slipped out of his arms and faced Uncle Charles. "How bad is he? Tell me what happened."

His face contorted. "We were repairing the trestle on a downtown bridge when he just fell. I don't know why. Maybe he lost his grip because of sweaty hands, or maybe he passed out from the heat, but he landed face-first on the road beneath. I've never seen anything so awful in my life." He shuddered.

Julie's eyes flooded.

"I yelled for help as I scrambled down. His legs were at strange angles. Thankfully, he was conscious, and I prayed with him before the ambulance arrived."

At least the fall hadn't killed him.

"Do we know how much longer he'll be in surgery?" she asked.

Uncle Charles shook his head.

Lee motioned her to sit beside him. She sat and leaned her head on his shoulder.

"I'm so sorry," he said.

"What are we going to do?"

"Trust God."

It was what she would have advised someone else. But did she even know how to trust? It was one thing to trust God to help her pass an exam. It was quite another to trust Him with Papa's life.

Lord, let him live, please.

What if Papa died? Or what if he was crippled and never went back to work? How would they survive? Her teaching salary wasn't enough to provide for six kids and two parents. Besides, after her last paycheck, she wouldn't have another until September. What would they live on? How would they pay the hospital bills?

God had promised to provide for their needs. She hoped He meant it.

Chapter 2

Waiting was excruciating.

An hour passed with no word. Mama had stopped crying. She looked like a marble statue, cold and distant. Richard on one side looked terrified. Uncle Charles dozed on the other side.

Julia had chewed off four fingernails. If they had to wait much longer, all would be gone. Her toe tapped the floor over and over.

"Can't you sit still?" Lee said.

"No. I can't stand this much longer."

"You're making it harder. Just relax."

"You'd be like this too if it were your father."

Or maybe not. Lee was strong and stoic. She had never seen him ruffled.

She stilled her foot and continued her prayers for Papa.

"Anyone hungry?" Lee asked.

Food was the last thing on her mind.

"I am," Richard said.

"I'll get us something to eat," Lee said. "Want to come, Julia? I'll need help carrying everything."

A breath of air, warm as it was, might feel good. She nodded.

They walked past the receptionist and into the dazzling sunshine. A trolley rumbled by filled with people returning from work.

"I envy them," she said as they headed up Park Avenue toward the grocery, past a variety store and a barber shop.

"Why?"

"They're having a normal day. I may never have a normal day again."

"You will, Julia."

"Thanks for being here. I needed you."

"That's what family is for."

"Thanks for taking time off from work." Lee worked as an accountant at Sibley's Department Store downtown.

"Actually I didn't go to work today."

"Why not?"

"I resigned."

She gasped. "Why? I thought you liked it there."

He smiled. "I did, but I have a new job, a better one. I start tomorrow."

"Where?"

"At the Rochester Optical Company."

Her eyes widened. "Really?"

The Rochester Optical Company was a premier place to work. Founded fifteen years ago by bachelor David Easterly, it had grown into a multi-million dollar endeavor.

He grinned. "A friend told me about the job opening, and I applied. I was interviewed last week by Mr. Easterly's secretary and the head of the accounting department."

"Why didn't you say something sooner?"

"I was afraid I wouldn't get the job."

"You must be so excited."

"I am. Thankful too."

"You'll have to tell me what Mr. Easterly is like. You know I've always been fascinated by him."

"Fascinated? Come on, Julia, you're obsessed."

"I am not. Just with his house."

His ivy-covered, pillared colonial mansion on East Avenue was a ten-minute walk from home. Six years ago she had watched the foundation being dug and the concrete walls erected. As the vast rooms were framed in, she waited until the workmen left at night and then snuck in and wandered around. The lofty ceilings, pillars, and spacious rooms amazed her. Unfortunately, once the doors and windows were installed, she had been locked out, but she had never stopped dreaming about it.

Suddenly she felt guilty. For a moment she had forgotten Papa. *Sorry, Papa. I'm still here. I'm still praying for you.*

No matter how exciting Lee's news was, it didn't change anything for her. Her family was in trouble.

→⟫⟪←

"Please, Mama, take a bite. See this wonderful sandwich Lee made for you," Julia said.

Mama shook her head, her mouth tight.

"You have to keep up your strength. Papa will need you when he wakes up."

"What if he doesn't wake up?" Mama said.

Julia's breath caught. Mama wasn't allowed to say that, not when she had tried so hard not to think it herself.

"Now, Louise, don't talk like that," Uncle Charles said. "Alver is going to be fine. He has an excellent doctor and a powerful God."

"Then what's taking so long? Shouldn't he be done?"

"He had extensive injuries. We must be patient."

"What if they can't fix him?"

"Here, Mama, please take a bite." Julia tried again.

Mama opened her mouth. Julia felt like the mother feeding the child. It was not a good feeling.

Someone knocked. The doctor, wearing a white coat, stepped in. "Mrs. Bradshaw?"

Julia's pulse quickened. The moment of truth was here. Was the news good or bad? The doctor's eyes were bleary yet calm.

"Your husband made it through surgery."

Tingles raced up Julia's arms. *Thank You, thank You, thank You, God.* She jumped up to hug Mama and found herself wrapped in a family hug.

Uncle Charles was the first to speak. "So, Doctor, how is he?"

"He has compound fractures in both legs, a sprained right ankle, lacerated nose, dislocated shoulder, fracture of the sternum, and three broken ribs."

Poor, dear Papa. Perhaps they shouldn't celebrate yet.

"What's the prognosis?" Uncle Charles asked.

"None of his injuries were life-threatening, but it will be a long recovery."

"How long?" Julia asked.

"He will be here at least two months."

Mama's hand went to her mouth.

How would they survive without Papa for two months? Who would make them laugh and tuck the children in at night? Who would pray with them? And how would they afford a two-month hospital bill?

"How is he now?" Mama asked.

"He hasn't come out of the anesthesia yet, but you are welcome to sit with him."

"All of us?" Julia asked.

He hesitated before nodding. "Follow me."

He led them up the marble steps to a pleasant room with two white iron beds. One was neatly made with a white bedspread.

Surely that wasn't Papa in the other bed.

His right leg was encased in a plaster-of-Paris cast from hip to ankle. The left leg cast extended from the middle of his thigh to his ankle. His ribs were wrapped in adhesive bandages. His nose was also bandaged. His eyes were bruised and swollen. His curly dark hair stood out in all directions. If it weren't for his handlebar mustache, she wouldn't have recognized him.

Mama stepped tentatively toward him.

"It's all right," the doctor said.

Mama kissed his hand before dissolving into tears.

Julia was afraid to touch him. "Love you, Papa," she whispered. He didn't move.

It was horrible seeing both Mama and Papa so helpless.

Who would take care of them now?

Not me.

Her plans were to sit on the porch all summer and read.

But she would willingly do what she had to, for Papa's sake.

If only she knew what that was.

→═◎ ◎═←

Across the kitchen table, Mama's eyes were vacant. Exhaustion painted her face. Richard sat next to her, solemn. Jenny looked sullen and uncooperative, as usual.

Julia's brain felt foggy and her eyes heavy. She yearned for bed.

It was too late to make major decisions, but before tomorrow, they needed a plan.

The image of Papa lying so broken in that hospital bed would haunt her forever. When he had finally awakened, it was only to squeeze Mama's hand before the doctor shooed them out and told them to come back tomorrow.

"What are we going to do?" Julia said. "We need money to pay the bills for the next two months. Mama, do you know how much money Papa has in the bank?"

Mama shook her head.

Julia wasn't surprised.

"Do we have to talk about this tonight?" Jenny said. "I just want to go to bed." She stood.

Julia yanked her back down. "If you want food on the table, yes, we have to talk about this tonight. We all need jobs, even you."

"I'll look tomorrow," Richard said. "Maybe they'll hire me as a day worker in the Easterly House gardens. I'd love to work there."

Richard was good at gardening. He had been mowing the lawn and puttering in the yard for years.

"Where will you look for a job, Julia?" Jenny sounded snide.

"I don't know yet. Maybe a store downtown." Perhaps working in a store wouldn't be so bad, as long as it wasn't some smelly little grocery on Park Avenue. "I have to clean out my kindergarten room tomorrow, but I'll look on Friday. How about you?" she asked Jenny.

"Jenny needs to stay home with the children," Mama said.

"Lucky me." Jenny's tone was sarcastic.

"I'll be at the hospital with your father," Mama said. "Someone needs to watch them."

Julia wondered if Mama now regretted having three children so many years after her first three. It was partly Julia's fault. She had begged for a baby in the house. She hadn't expected Mama to give her three.

Papa's rationale was that they needed playmates.

Julia wondered if it was Papa who needed the playmates.

"Every day?" Jenny said. "I'll be home with them every day?"

"Yes, every day," Julia said. "Be thankful you can stay home. The rest of us wish we could."

Oh, how she wished she could.

Chapter 3

Thursday, June 18, 1908

LEE BRADSHAW FELT like a traitor as he exited the streetcar and looked up at the six-story Rochester Optical Company. No one who had experienced such a family tragedy yesterday had a right to be this excited.

But he couldn't contain it. Working for David Easterly was the job of his dreams.

He banished thoughts of Uncle Alver lying so pale in his hospital bed, of Julia trembling in his arms. He prayed that God would grant them courage today. *Give me courage, too, Lord.*

Employees streamed through the front door. He could hardly believe he was one of them.

He joined the flow into the bustling vestibule. He hoped he appeared more confident than he felt.

At least he looked professional in his three-piece striped black suit, white shirt with a crisp round-cornered collar, red cravat with a gold scarf pin, and black silk derby. He nervously smoothed his bushy mustache.

Since his office was on the sixth floor, he opted against climbing the marble stairs with brass railings and instead strode to the elevator where others waited.

Several women ogled him. His cheeks flushed. He hadn't expected so many young women working here. He felt like fish bait.

He gazed up at the dial and watched the elevator descend from the third floor to the second to the first. With a clang, the lattice gate and mahogany doors swung open. He motioned for the ladies to precede him. It was a tight squeeze. The scent of perfume made him dizzy. He hoped he didn't smell like perfume when he walked into his office. The doors swung shut. Rumbling, they ascended, the shaft visible through the windows. They stopped at each floor until only he was left. He exited on the top floor.

A man walked toward him. He recognized Mr. Easterly from pictures in the newspaper. He didn't know what to do. Bow? Salute?

Close up, Mr. Easterly looked surprisingly ordinary. He was shorter than Lee, in his thirties, with dark, side-parted hair and a neatly trimmed mustache and beard. He wore a conservative navy pin-striped suit and waistcoat with a yellow flower tucked into his buttonhole.

"Good morning, sir," Lee said.

Easterly didn't acknowledge him as he boarded the elevator.

Of course he wouldn't.

Feeling snubbed, he strode down the hall to his office. Beyond a wall of windows was an enormous room. Roll-top desks formed five long rows. Perhaps fifty worked here, slightly more men than women.

He entered self-consciously. The smiles and nods of the men welcomed him. But the dreamy eyes of the young women were unnerving.

His throat felt dry as he walked toward his desk. These were important people with important work. And he had no idea what to do.

His roll-top desk was next to Miss Kramer's, his secretary, whose desk was next to Mr. Crosby's, the senior accountant. He had met them at his interview last week.

"Good morning," he said as he laid his derby on his desk.

Mr. Crosby stood and shook his hand. Middle-aged with a balding head, glasses, and mustache, he had kind eyes. "Welcome. Glad to have you here, Bradshaw. I've plenty for you to do."

"Good. Just show me where to begin."

"Miss Kramer, we'll need the ledger."

Miss Kramer was a plain-faced young woman with her hair in a top bun. She pulled a book from a cubbyhole and handed it to him.

After Mr. Crosby's instructions, he plunged into the paperwork. He lost track of time until a feminine voice said, "Excuse me, Mr. Bradshaw?"

He didn't want to be interrupted by some simpering female.

When he looked over his shoulder, his pulse quickened. It was Miss Weston, Mr. Easterly's personal assistant. Rumor was that she ran the company better than he.

Her professional navy blue skirt and white shirtwaist with starched cuffs contrasted with her beautiful big brown eyes and her soft, poufy hair. She was intoxicating and alluring, and entirely out of his league, besides being older by perhaps five years.

In his haste to stand, he shoved back his chair, narrowly missing her.

With an intake of breath, she looked down at the hem of her skirt caught under the leg of his chair.

"Um, sir..." She gently tugged. Was that a twinkle in her eye?

His face flushed. "I'm so sorry." He lifted the chair and freed her skirt.

"Sorry to bother you," she said. "But I need a few more forms filled out at your convenience."

As he took them, his hand brushed hers. A jolt raced up his arm. His face felt warmer. "How soon do you need them?" he asked.

"Any time today would be fine, thanks." Her long skirt swirled as she spun away. He watched her glide to the door.

He heard a chuckle behind him. Turning, he saw a row of staring secretaries.

"Don't dream about her," someone said. "She's taken."

He cringed. Was he that obvious?

"Mr. Easterly has staked his claim."

"Oh, come on now, Cora, you know that's not true," someone said.

"She's with him all the time, even at social events, or so I'm told."

"And he picks her up every morning for work," someone else said. She was obviously off limits to him.

"Thank you, ladies, for your astute observations," he said.

They tittered as he sat and looked over the forms, acutely aware that her delicate hands had touched them.

-→⊨◎ ◎⊨←-

David Easterly raked his fingers through his hair. "Have I had my lunch yet, Miss Weston?" He hated becoming so immersed in his work that he couldn't remember the time of day.

She smiled indulgently. "Yes, your chauffeur brought your lunch at noon. Remember?"

"Oh, that's right." He looked at the dining table where the Minton china still held crumbs. "Thanks."

"Now that you've come up for air, I need your signature on this letter to Mr. Willoughby." She passed it from her roll-top desk to his.

Their desks were side-by-side, facing the room, with the windows behind them. To one side was the dining table surrounded by Georgian paneling and carpeted with an Oriental rug, his home away from home. Since his mother's passing two years ago, he didn't have the heart to spend evenings alone in his lovely colonial mansion on East Avenue.

With a flourish, he signed the letter and passed it back.

"And have you decided yet about Camilla Wentworth's coming-out party?"

"I told you before that I don't want to go."

"Is that your final answer?"

"You don't approve, do you?"

"Some relationships are worth cultivating."

"But I can't stand those insipid parties and having to mingle with people I don't care about. Just send a nice gift and a kind refusal. You're good at that."

In fact, she was good at everything. He didn't know what he would do without her.

Someone knocked on the door. "Come in," she called.

In walked a young man with striking blue eyes and a thick mustache. "I signed the forms," he said.

"Oh, thanks." Miss Weston stood to take them. "Mr. Easterly, have you met Mr. Bradshaw, our new accountant?"

David stood and shook his hand, impressed with his iron grip. "Welcome, Mr. Bradshaw. Glad to have you."

"Thank you, sir." The young man's eyes sought Miss Weston's before he exited.

"Handsome man," David said when they were alone. "He'll have all the young women in the office swooning."

Miss Weston didn't answer. She slid a paper into her typewriter and vigorously tapped the carriage return lever.

"No comment?" he said.

"No."

"You're blushing."

"I don't blush."

"You do now."

Pity that she never blushed for him.

Chapter 4

DONE.

Julia surveyed her first-floor kindergarten room with satisfaction. It had taken all day, but every toy, art supply, and book was neatly packed in boxes on the shelves under the windows. The chalkboards were spotless, the sand table covered, and the little desks, chairs, and tables scrubbed clean.

The four windows that reached to the high ceiling were opened wide, the air sticky and humid. Her face was shiny, her hair droopy, her hands filthy, and she smelled.

As exhausting as it had been, she would rather do it all over again than look for a job tomorrow.

She did not want a job. She wanted to rest and relax. Yes, just be lazy.

But she would do her part. If only she could find a job that was not terribly demanding.

Clerking seemed best, but she dreaded waiting on cranky customers. If she had to give up her summer on the porch, she hoped she would be given the respect her college education deserved.

Now to go home for a bath before she returned to the hospital tonight.

She had already taken two boxes home. Only one was left. She slid it into the hall, closed the windows, locked the door, and headed toward the office, her heels clacking on the dark hardwood floor. The hall felt bare with the empty bulletin boards and display cases. Outside the office, the wooden bench had no children waiting on it. It was rather sad.

Light streamed through the windows surrounding the office door. She entered. The principal, Miss Whiton, talked with the secretary.

"Miss Bradshaw," she greeted.

"I'm finally done," Julia said. "Here's my key."

Miss Whiton sorted through a stack of envelopes. "And here's your paycheck. I was so sorry to hear about your father. How is he?"

"Not good. He broke both legs, some ribs, his nose, and his sternum. The doctor thinks he will recover fine, but he'll be in the hospital for at least two months."

"I'm so sorry." Miss Whiton sounded sincere. "Let me know if there's anything I can do."

Julia nodded. "Thank you. See you in September."

In the hall, she almost collided with Mr. Pratt.

"There you are," he said.

"I was just leaving." She headed toward her room.

"Is that your box in the hall?" He walked beside her.

She nodded.

"Let me carry it home for you."

"That won't be necessary."

"I insist." He swooped up the box of books as if it weighed nothing. Perhaps she should let him.

They walked toward the door. "How's your father?" he asked.

"Both legs are broken as well as some ribs, his sternum, and his nose."

"I'm so sorry. What can I do to help?"

"Nothing, thanks." He could help by leaving her alone.

"Maybe a diversion would help. How about some ice cream and a walk on the bridge?"

Was he crazy? She had no time for frivolity. Besides, she needed a bath more than a walk.

They stepped past the playground fence and onto the shaded sidewalk.

"I can't. I'm going to the hospital tonight and looking for a job tomorrow. My life has become one of survival, Mr. Pratt. I will have time or energy for little else."

As they crossed the street, her brother Richard bounded up the sidewalk with grimy hands and a radiant face.

"There's my brother. He can carry the box from here," she said.

"I can do it."

"No need."

As Richard caught up, she introduced them and asked Richard to take the box.

"Have a nice summer, Mr. Pratt," she said as she propelled Richard down the sidewalk.

"But, wait. Can I come see you?" Mr. Pratt asked.

She looked over her shoulder and shook her head. "No time."

Mr. Pratt looked deflated.

"Does my sister have an admirer?" Richard teased as they walked on.

"Absolutely not." All she needed was the family pestering her about Mr. Pratt. "Now tell me about your day. Did the Easterly House hire you?"

He beamed. "They did, and they told me to come back tomorrow."

"Wonderful. What did you do today?"

"I trimmed the boxwood hedge in the Terrace Garden. Arthur Poole, the head gardener, said it has never looked so fine."

"Good for you."

"You should see that place, Julia. It's amazing. Boxwood paths between thousands of flowers, a lily pond, a pergola, four big greenhouses, vegetable gardens, and fruit trees."

With the outside of the house so grand, she could only imagine the inside.

"But I have even better news. I found a job for you."

Hopefully not in the gardens. She didn't like being dirty. "What?" she asked warily.

"You're the new laundress."

Her eyes bulged. "Are you crazy? I can't be a laundress."

"Why not?"

"I have a college degree, for goodness' sake. I'm not a servant."

"I already talked with the head housekeeper. Miss Donovan said to come tomorrow."

"You did that without asking me?"

"I thought you'd be thrilled."

"But I don't know how to do laundry." She had never done laundry in her life.

"Anyone can do laundry."

"Not me."

"Learn then. You can't pass this up."

"Why do they suddenly need a laundress?"

"Their laundress had an accident today."

"What happened?"

"After the noon meal in the servants' hall, the laundress was flirting on the back porch with Alan Pierce, the painter. When he tried to grab her, she fell backwards down the steps and broke her arm. They need someone to replace her for a couple months. My first thought was that God provided this just for you."

It did seem coincidental. But why couldn't God have provided something not so demeaning? Something she knew how to do?

How hard could it be, though? David Easterly lived all alone in that big mansion. How much laundry could one man generate? A few shirts, handkerchiefs, and undergarments?

Maybe she *could* do it.

At any rate, she'd see inside the house. That alone might be worth it.

⭑⭑

She couldn't believe it. She was going to be a laundress.

Visions plagued her of cracked hands, a perspiring face, and bedraggled hair. Not her. She would be the classiest laundress ever.

But first Mama had to teach her.

"Slow down," Richard said as they rushed down Park Avenue toward the hospital. "Papa isn't going anywhere."

"No, but Mama is. Home with me, I trust."

"What if she won't come?"

"She's been at that hospital all day. Surely she can sacrifice a few hours for me."

"Let's hope she feels that way."

When Julia entered the hospital room, thoughts of laundry disappeared when she saw Papa. He looked even worse. His face was puffy and purple. One eye was fused shut.

Mama knit beside him. A warm breeze ruffled the curtains.

"Oh, Papa." Julia rushed to his side. "How are you?" She kissed his forehead, one of the few places not bandaged or in a cast.

He squeezed her hand. "I feel better already just having you here." His voice was raspy.

She smiled. "How are you really feeling? Are you in pain?"

"The laudanum keeps the pain down, but it makes me groggy."

"Groggy is good. You need to sleep to help your body heal."

"I've been doing plenty of that. So tell me, how are you? All done with school?"

She nodded. "But Richard is the one with news. He has a job gardening at the Easterly House."

Richard beamed.

"Good for you," Papa said.

"But we have a problem. Richard volunteered me to be the laundress."

"Sounds like a blessing to me."

"But I don't know how to do laundry, and I need to learn before tomorrow morning. Mama, can you come home right away and teach me?"

Mama looked up from her knitting. "I can't leave your father."

"Go, dear, and help her," Papa said. "I'll be fine. Richard and I can talk about his job."

"Are you sure?"

He nodded.

"Let me finish this row."

Julia fidgeted. Mama didn't have time to finish the row. Every minute counted.

Chapter 5

Friday, June 19, 1908

"You're wearing THAT?" Jenny poked her head out from under the covers.

"What's wrong with this?" Julia leaned closer to the mirror as she pinned a sapphire-colored brooch to the high neck of her silk shirtwaist with the embroidered yoke.

"You're dressed for school, not laundry."

Julia pinned on a wide straw hat trimmed with pale pink roses and mossy green leaves.

"Just because I'm the laundress doesn't mean I have to look like one."

"Well, la-di-da. I'm sure you'll impress them."

Julia whipped around. "Are you making fun of me?"

Jenny sat up. "Who, me?"

"Maybe you should be the laundress instead."

"I'd rather do that than slave away and get paid nothing."

"Be thankful you can stay home and not have to humiliate yourself."

"Julia, you coming?" Richard called from downstairs.

She was late. No time for breakfast or reading her Bible. Not a good way to start. *Lord, please help me today.*

"Close the door," Jenny mumbled as she plopped back onto the bed.

Julia slammed the door as she hurried down to Richard.

He twisted his hat in his hands as he frowned up at her. "You don't look like a laundress."

"That's the point."

"I don't understand."

"Oh, never mind. Give me a minute to grab something to eat."

"There's no time."

She hurried into the kitchen. Mama plopped scrambled eggs onto the plates of the three little ones.

Mary looked up, her eyes still crusty with sleep. "You look pretty today."

"Thanks, honey." She felt pretty.

"Is Jenny up?" Mama asked.

"Not yet."

Julia grabbed a warm biscuit from the counter. "This is all I have time for. I'm late."

"You should have gotten up earlier."

She'd been up early enough. It was all the primping that had taken so long.

"Thanks for all your help, Mama."

"I'll be praying you remember everything."

"Thanks, I'll need it."

She dashed back to Richard. "Let's get this over with."

She bit into the flaky, warm biscuit as they stepped onto the wide front porch. The summer morning was cool and dewy, trilling with bird songs.

She strode beside silent Richard. As they passed her school, she looked at the four end windows on the first floor. Her room. Oh, to be there now.

Instead she was going to be a laundress. How ridiculous. As a little girl she had imagined being a fairytale princess with servants waiting on her hand and foot. Never in her wildest dreams had she imagined being a servant herself.

Last night she had stayed up late listening to Mama's instructions. First she had to sort the colored things from the whites. Next she had to treat stains. She wrote down remedies for removing milk, meat, tea, fruit, grass, and grease.

Everything soaked in tubs, collars and cuffs with their old starch in a separate one.

Mama showed her how to melt shavings of leftover soap on the stove. One gallon of water was added to a quarter pound of soap.

The cleanest things were washed first, covered in cold water with the soap solution, and boiled for ten minutes before rinsing. Clothes were hung on the line to dry and then dampened and rolled until ironing. Irons heated on the stove were ready when a drop of water on the bottom skittered around.

She went to bed with her head spinning.

There hadn't been time to do a wash, but everything was recorded in a notebook in her pocket. Could she do it? That remained to be seen.

Her stomach churned. The biscuit wasn't sitting well. Or perhaps it wasn't the biscuit. Maybe it was nerves. Or panic.

They crossed Park Avenue. Continuing up tree-lined Barrington Street, the homes were charming, each one different. Babies cried through open windows. The milk wagon was parked in the street, the milk man making his rounds. Men read the morning paper on porches. She wished she were reading on the porch too.

"Nervous?" Richard asked.

"Terrified. I can't believe I'm doing this."

"You'll be talking to Miss Donovan, the head housekeeper."

"What's she like?"

"Old. Stern. Not very friendly."

"How encouraging."

"You'll do fine."

They reached East Avenue, the most prestigious street in the city. Beneath a canopy of elms, automobiles and horse-drawn carriages rumbled toward the city in a steady stream. Broad lawns made the Avenue feel like one big park. The houses were majestic and enormous.

Across the street, the Easterly House, a center-entrance Colonial Revival of ivy-covered cream bricks, rose three stories high. Four two-story limestone pillars sheltered a porch with two rockers and conical boxwood shrubs in pots. The driveway swooped under a porte-cochère to a side entrance.

Her breathing quickened. She felt lightheaded.

Who was she kidding? She couldn't pretend to be a laundress. Not even to see inside the Easterly House. Not even for Papa.

"I can't do this," she said. Her stomach roiled. "I feel sick."

"You can't turn back now. They're counting on you."

Counting on her? They would be mightily disappointed, especially when she ruined one of Mr. Easterly's expensive shirts. Better to go home now and divert disaster.

She needed to sit down. She truly was ill.

Suddenly she heaved all over the sidewalk.

"Julia!" Richard jumped out of the way.

The toe of one shoe was covered with slop, but it had missed her black skirt. Her mouth felt thick and sour.

She wiped her shoe clean on the dewy grass.

"Forget it. I can't go like this." If her lack of skill didn't get her thrown out, her breath would.

"You're not sick. It's just nerves. I won't let you go home."

"But I'll make a fool of myself. I can't be a laundress."

"You *can* do it, I know you. Look at how you put yourself through college. You're the most resourceful person I know."

Yes, when she wanted to be. When she had a worthwhile goal.

But wasn't helping her family a worthwhile goal?

He dragged her across the street.

She shook her arm free. "All right, but don't be surprised if I lose the job. I'm not qualified."

As they walked up the shaded driveway, she was desperate for a drink of water. She opened her mouth to air out the smell.

Closer, the house was massive. Why did one man need all this? She remembered reading in the newspaper that his mother had lived with him until she died two years ago. But even two people didn't need all this. What David Easterly needed was a wife and a houseful of children.

"Where do we go?" she said.

"Through that side door." He pointed at the porte-cochère entrance. "We have to sign it at Miss Donovan's desk."

The porte-cochère extended over the driveway, four limestone pillars on each side. They walked underneath and up three steps. Richard opened the window-framed door.

"You just walk inside? You don't ring the doorbell or anything?"

He shook his head. "This is the servants' entrance."

They stepped into a small foyer with marble floors. To the right rose a narrow burgundy-carpeted staircase. Left was a yellow office with a bay window. Straight ahead a blue velvet curtain framed a light-filled room with marble floors and huge ferns and palms. Organ music played. The beauty pulled her like a magnet.

Richard grabbed her arm. "Not that way. We have to sign in."

He led her into the office.

Behind a roll-top desk sat a stately, elderly woman with wavy white hair fastened in a bun. She wore a white shirtwaist and white skirt.

"Miss Donovan, my sister Julia has come for the laundress job," Richard said.

Time to make a good impression. Julia flashed a smile.

Miss Donovan stood. She glowered at Julia from behind her wire-framed glasses, sizing her up from head to toe. Julia shriveled. What fault could Miss Donovan possibly find in her appearance?

Perhaps she had smelled her breath. She clamped her lips.

"Tell me of your experience," Miss Donovan said as Richard signed in and disappeared out the door.

"I graduated from the University of Rochester a year ago, and I just finished my first year of teaching kindergarten at the Francis Parker School." A sour smell wafted beneath her nose. She stepped backward.

Miss Donovan's lips tightened. "Degrees mean nothing here. Tell me of your laundry experience."

"My only experience is helping my mother at home." Even that was a stretch. She had once hung clothes on the clothesline.

"That does not qualify you to run the laundry in this large household."

"All I need is instruction. I learn quickly, and I'm a hard worker. I will not disappoint you."

Miss Donovan's jaw clenched. Julia was certain a dismissal was imminent.

"Since I'm rather desperate, I'll give you until tomorrow to prove yourself."

That wasn't much time, but more than she deserved.

"Katie Kelly, who assists the laundress when she's not working on the third floor, will get you started. Fill out this application while I retrieve your uniform." She disappeared through a back door.

Julia didn't know whether to feel relieved or disappointed. Miss Donovan was a fool for hiring her.

She answered the questions regarding her name, address, and former employment, giving her school principal and pastor as references.

Miss Donovan returned with a folded stack of white clothes and white shoes. "You may change in the bathroom across the hall." She pointed toward the door at the bottom of the stairs.

Julia entered the elegant powder room, beautifully appointed in silver and marble. Her uneasy blue eyes looked back from the ornate mirror.

Her flowered and beribboned hat framed her pretty face. Princess Julia, that's what Papa called her.

Who was she kidding? She wasn't a princess, but she *was* a respected schoolteacher.

She unpinned her hat and looked again. Already she felt less respectable. She unbuttoned her lace shirtwaist and donned the plain white one. Off came her long black skirt for the white one. She slid on white stockings and ugly white shoes with white laces. She tied on a white apron, slipping her notebook with Mama's instructions into the pocket.

She cringed. She looked like a servant. And she felt like one too.

Impulsively, she fastened the sapphire brooch to the plain neck. That was better. It intensified her eyes. She felt pretty again.

Now to get rid of her wretched breath. She leaned down to the sink and drank deeply.

Refreshed, she looked at herself again in the mirror.

She was a laundress, ready or not.

Chapter 6

SHE RETURNED TO Miss Donovan. "I'm done."

Miss Donovan's eyes pierced her neck. "What is that?"

Julia fingered the brooch. "My father gave it to me for Christmas."

"Take it off."

"But...."

"Now. It's not allowed."

Julia unpinned her last shred of dignity.

"Follow me." Miss Donovan strode toward the light-filled palm room.

Julia's heart quickened. Even if she only worked one day, at least she would have seen it.

But instead, Miss Donovan opened a door to the cellar.

Julia paused, unable to take her eyes off the beauty beyond the curtain. Past a white pillared marble hallway was a cavernous room of plants, tall windows, green wicker furniture, and Oriental rugs.

"What are you doing?" Miss Donovan asked.

"I've dreamed of seeing this place."

"The laundress is to stay in the cellar and the servants' wing and nowhere else. Do you understand?"

"Yes, but can't I just look from here?"

Miss Donovan whipped the curtain closed. "No, you are not allowed. Mr. Easterly is in there eating breakfast. If you do it again, you will be dismissed."

At least she'd had one glorious glimpse.

They descended narrow steps, past the wine cellar, to a hallway of white brick walls. Miss Donovan flung open a door on the left and turned on the light. "Here you are," she said.

The laundry room was equipped with the most modern conveniences. She saw stationary tubs with faucets, galvanized iron tubs on a workbench, two washing machines, wringers, mangles, tables, electric irons, drying racks, and a wood-burning stove.

This wasn't like Mama's cellar.

"You can start while I summon Katie Kelly." Miss Donovan left.

Start? Where?

Five baskets overflowed with white linens. This was more than a few of Mr. Easterly's shirts, handkerchiefs, and undergarments.

She needed to be calm and organized and not panic. After all, Katie Kelly would be here soon.

She opened Mama's notebook. Number one: sort the laundry. She could do that.

She separated five sets of sheets, dish towels, and bath towels into separate piles. Then she pulled out a white damask tablecloth as big as Mama's kitchen floor. Sweat beaded her forehead at the thought of washing and ironing something so huge. She added matching napkins to that pile.

Another basket was filled with chemises, petticoats, and white skirts and shirtwaists, identical to her uniform. She didn't understand. This looked like servants' laundry.

Was she was a servant to the servants, washing their underwear, no less? Could anything be more humiliating?

Her bottom lip quivered.

Lord, why?

He must be trying to teach her something.

She didn't want to learn. She should quit now for a job in an upscale department store, something more suitable.

But perhaps God wanted her here. Was she brave enough to discover why?

She reached into the last basket. The white shirts, collars, cuffs, silk nightshirt, undershirt, and drawers had to be Mr. Easterly's.

She blushed. She really didn't want to look at that famous man's underwear. She'd rather glimpse the man himself.

Enough of this daydreaming. Miss Donovan would make sure she never saw him.

She pulled out her notebook. What next? Remove the stains.

The damask tablecloth had a nasty red spot. What was it? She had Mama's list of remedies, but she couldn't treat it without knowing.

The door flew open. A young woman lugged in another overflowing basket.

"Hi, I'm Katie," she said.

She was petite and child-like. Adorable freckles smattered her pert nose. Her animated hazel eyes seemed too large for her face. Her curly hair was arranged in a disheveled bun. Her white uniform swallowed her.

"I'm so glad you're here. I'm Julia."

"Need help?"

"Oh, my, yes. I don't know where to begin."

"Miss Donovan told me to help you for the rest of the day so we can catch up."

"Thank you. I'm looking for stains. Any idea what this red stain is?"

"Wine."

Oh, dear. Mama hadn't put that on the list.

"How do we treat it?"

"Cover it with salt and pour boiling water through it. It should come right out."

"I see you've brought more laundry." She wrinkled her nose.

Katie plunked the basket on the floor. "Just finished changing all the beds. Never-ending it is, but you'll get used to it."

"Were there guests last night?"

"Oh, no, this is from the servants' wing. Be thankful that only four board."

It *was* the servants' laundry.

"Why don't they do their own laundry?"

"They're busy with other things. Rose Hamilton is the parlor maid, responsible for the dusting and polishing on the first floor. Bridget Maddigan and Jane Johnson are the second and third floor maids, and Miss Donovan, of course, keeps everything running smoothly. They would just be in our way if they tried to do their own laundry."

"You don't live here?"

"No, I take the trolley in every day. I live with my mother downtown. Ever since my father died, I'm all she has."

"And what are your responsibilities?" Julia asked.

"I change the maids' beds, straighten their rooms, clean their bathrooms, and in my spare time help in the laundry and churn the butter in the dairy."

She was a servant to the servants too.

"We best get to work," Katie said. "Miss Donovan will be furious if we don't catch up. The first thing we have to do is record all these pieces of laundry."

"You're not serious."

"Unfortunately, yes. Rose, the parlor maid, counts everything upstairs. We then count it down here and record it." She picked up a book on a table. "When we send the clean laundry upstairs, Miss Donovan compares both books."

"But why?"

"Mr. Easterly is persnickety. He even requires Miss Donovan to keep track of the amount of milk each cow gives and the pounds of butter churned."

Julia puffed out her cheeks. This job was becoming worse and worse. Impossible was more like it.

"Teach me everything I need to know. Miss Donovan gave me until tomorrow to prove myself."

Katie frowned. "That hardly seems fair."

"She doesn't think I'm qualified."

"Are you?"

"No."

Katie's eyes widened.

"Actually I'm a kindergarten teacher."

Katie's eyes bulged.

"I need this job because my father was in an accident this week and will be in the hospital for two months. But I'm a quick learner, so show me what to do. Fast."

Katie grinned. "All right, then. We'll show Miss Donovan."

→►● ●◄←

"Time for lunch," Katie announced several hours later.

Julia's hands were crinkled and red, her back ached, her toes pinched, and sweat trickled down her forehead and back. She'd never worked so hard.

"Where do we go?"

"To the servants' hall upstairs. There are about thirty of us."

Thirty people would see her looking like this? Her face was shiny. Strands had loosened from her bun and tickled her face. Her white uniform was ugly and shapeless.

"I'm not fit to be seen." She smoothed her hair.

Katie giggled. "Don't worry about it. You should see the men who work in the barn and gardens."

"At least let me wash my hands." She ran water in one of the stationary tubs, soaped up, and splashed cool water on her face. "Ready," she said.

But she didn't feel ready. Not only was she not presentable, she had nothing in common with thirty servants.

She followed Katie up a second staircase into the kitchen.

It felt twenty degrees hotter, even with the two tall windows open at the far end of the big room.

On one wall was a long counter with oak cupboards and a mahogany refrigerator with mother-of-pearl handles. Beyond the center marble-topped work table were more oak cabinets and a gas stove with two ovens, a double warming shelf, and metal hood.

A red-faced, portly cook lifted a steaming pan from the black stove. Maids dressed in white flitted into a hallway carrying platters.

"This way." Katie said.

At the end of the hall was a spacious room, surprisingly elegant with yellow floral wallpaper above an oak chair rail. Two sparkling chandeliers hung over a long oak table surrounded by uniformed men and women, all talking.

As Katie led her to two empty chairs, Julia felt all eyes on her. She held her head high, hoping her sophistication and college degree shone through the white uniform and sweaty face.

As she sat, she spotted Richard between some other young men. He looked embarrassed.

Embarrassed? She wanted him to be proud of her.

"Meet Julia, the new laundress," Katie said.

A good-looking young man with a thin mustache whistled, and the other men laughed. Richard squirmed.

Her face flamed. One pretty maid scowled at her.

Julia wished she could say to her, "Don't worry. I'm not a threat. I'll just do my job and leave in two months."

Two months? She'd probably be gone by tomorrow. She scanned the room. Miss Donovan wasn't here. That was a blessing.

When every chair was filled, the platters were passed. Only at church suppers had Julia seen so much food. She filled her plate with fried chicken, potatoes in jackets, string beans, cucumbers, lettuce, and radishes. No one asked the blessing, so Julia prayed silently before cutting her chicken.

Several of the young men continued to ogle her. She ignored them.

"Tell me who all these people are," she said to Katie.

"That man at the end is the butler, Solomon Merrick." He was an imposing man with ebony skin and black hair peppered with gray. "The man beside him with the bushy mustache is Edgar Hopkins, the chauffeur. He and his family live on Russell Street in a house owned by Mr. Easterly. If you see some children in the gardens, they are likely his.

"Those three young ladies are Rose Hamilton, the parlor maid, Bridget Maddigan, the second floor maid, and Jane Johnson, the third floor maid, all who live here. And on the other side of the table is the head gardener, Arthur Poole, his staff, and the engineer, carpenter, houseman, and dairyman. The one who whistled is the painter, Alan Pierce."

He winked at her. She averted her eyes.

"Where is Miss Donovan?"

"She's too superior to associate with us. She eats alone in her office. She has her own suite of rooms on the third floor."

Soon the young men pushed back their chairs.

"Where are they going?" Julia asked.

"To smoke on the porch."

Her mouth slackened when Richard followed. He knew better than to associate with that riff-raff. She had to caution him. She stood.

Alan Pierce caught her eye and winked. "Are you joining us?"

"No, that's not what..."

He left.

Katie nudged her. "Don't mind him. He flirts with all the pretty girls. He's the reason Sally fell and broke her arm yesterday."

"Perhaps she *would* like to join him," said Rose, the pretty parlor maid. "It's what I would expect from someone like her." Her eyes challenged.

"No, you don't understand. I just need to speak with someone."

She fled out the screen door to a wide porch that overlooked the driveway and garage. The men lounged in rockers or clustered around tables in hard-backed chairs. Several had lit cigarettes. Richard distanced himself, leaning against a railing.

"Well, look who decided to come after all." Alan Pierce bounded from his chair, a cigarette dangling between his lips.

Julia stiffened. She shouldn't have come.

"Have a seat." Alan pulled up a chair next to his.

"Thank you, but I just need to speak to my brother."

"Your *brother*?" Alan looked confused.

"Richard."

Every head turned toward Richard. His Adam's apple bobbed as his color heightened.

"Quite a sister, Richard."

"Why didn't you tell us you had a sister like her?"

The comments rolled fast and furious as Richard and Julia escaped down the steps.

"What are you doing?" His teeth were clenched.

"I'm so sorry. Just get me out of here."

They disappeared around the corner of the garage to the poultry yard. Julia leaned against the fence. "I am an utter fool."

"What's going on?"

"I just wanted to tell you not to hang out on the porch with all those smoking men."

"Where else am I supposed to go? I'm not staying inside with the ladies."

He had a point.

"Just don't let their bad influence rub off on you."

"I'm being careful. Now go and leave me alone."

"You don't have to be nasty about it."

"You're embarrassing me."

"How?"

"You put on airs. You act as if you're better than everyone else."

"Maybe I am. No one else has been to college."

"Going to college doesn't make you better. Look at Arthur Poole, the head gardener. He has researched estate gardens in Newport, Rhode Island, and he knows more about gardens than anyone. He documents and catalogs his gardens in more detail than any lesson plan you ever wrote. See, you don't have to go to college to be smart and respected."

"No, but it certainly helps."

"Not when you're so dumb about most other things in life."

"I am not."

He rolled his eyes.

"I need to go. How can I get back in without going on the porch?"

He shrugged. "Use the porte-cochère entrance."

"And run the risk of seeing Miss Donovan?"

"So what?"

"Let's just say that we don't see eye-to-eye on some things. She's given me until tomorrow to prove myself."

"Then what are you doing out here?"

What, indeed?

"See you after work, and I'm sorry for embarrassing you." She hurried back up the driveway, ignoring the whistles from the porch.

She cringed at the loud creak of the porte-cochère door. She tiptoed across the marble hall toward the cellar door, this time not even tempted by the beautiful vista beyond the curtain.

She heard a swishing skirt.

"What are you doing?" Miss Donovan's voice was brittle.

Julia turned. Miss Donovan's arms were folded across her chest.

"Just returning to work."

"Where have you been?"

"Talking briefly outside with my brother."

"You're not paid to socialize."

"It was my lunch break."

"Don't challenge me."

"I'm sorry. That was not my intent."

"I will be down later to inspect your work."

"Yes, ma'am."

She leaped down the stairs. What had just happened? Had she been accused of doing wrong? It felt like it.

She burst into the laundry room. Katie looked up as she carefully fed a towel through the wringer. She oozed disapproval. "Who were you talking to?"

"My brother."

"Your *brother*?"

"Richard. He's a gardener."

"The one with the blue eyes. That's your brother?" Katie blushed.

Julia nodded.

"Here I thought you were talking with Alan Pierce."

"No, Mr. Pierce is not someone I care to associate with."

"I didn't think so." Katie looked relieved.

And so was she. She wanted Katie to like her.

"Miss Donovan said she'd be down to inspect later. Do you think we'll finish?"

Thanks to the multiple washing machines and wringers, they had almost completed the washing. With the slight breeze and the hot sun, the clothes on the line outside wouldn't take long to dry.

"Maybe not all the ironing, but we'll make a good show of it."

"We must finish. My job depends on it."

The clothes yard smelled sweet from the crimson roses rambling along the fence of the neighbor's property. Julia couldn't imagine anything more wonderful than having sheets smell like roses.

She unclipped them from the clothesline, being careful not to let them drag in the grass as she folded them.

The fresh air and sunshine were amazing, a welcome relief from the steamy laundry room.

"I wish we could stay out here forever," Julia told Katie.

"You and me both. Now if you were an inside maid like Rose, you'd have a few hours free this afternoon to walk the gardens."

"Really?"

"They have the afternoons off, but often work in the evenings instead."

"Do you ever wish you were a parlor maid?"

"All the time. My goal is to work my way up. I don't expect Rose will stay here long. She's the pretty one, if you noticed."

"I noticed her." And she'd try to avoid her from now on.

"When she finds a husband, she'll be gone. Then probably Bridget, the second floor maid will take her place, and Jane will take Bridget's place, and hopefully I can have the third floor maid position."

Third floor maid didn't seem like much of an aspiration. "Haven't you ever dreamed of being something else?"

"Sure. The head housekeeper."

Julia almost laughed out loud. She couldn't imagine spunky, tomboyish Katie Kelly as an austere housekeeper.

"How about a nurse or a teacher? Didn't you ever want to go to college?"

Katie took down a pillowcase. "No, I had no money for college. I was good in school, though. Real good." Her voice was wistful. "My teachers all had high hopes for me. I'm sure I disappointed them."

"It's not too late. You could still go to college."

Katie shook her head. "I give my earnings to Mama to pay the rent. She couldn't make it without me."

Nor could Julia's family make it without her this summer. But it hadn't always been like that. Last year she had frittered away her teaching money on pretty things for herself.

"So you want to be head housekeeper. How much longer do you think Miss Donovan will stay? She seems terribly old."

"She won't leave until the day she dies."

"But certainly a time will come when Miss Donovan can no longer perform her duties."

"She's a feisty, stubborn woman. Believe me, she'll perform her duties until the bitter end."

⤜⊚ ⊚⤐

The clickety-clack of high-heels echoed in the cement hall.

Julia looked at Katie. "Miss Donovan?"

Katie nodded.

Her eyes flitted to the piles of ironed linens. She couldn't believe what they had accomplished. But some napkins were still dampened and rolled. "I wish she had waited until the end of the day so we could have finished."

Katie nodded tersely as Miss Donovan entered.

Miss Donovan appeared winded. She leaned against the wall to catch her balance and her breath.

"Hello, Miss Donovan," Katie said.

"I've come to inspect."

"Please look around," Katie said. "I think you'll be impressed. Julia has done a wonderful job."

"I'll be the judge."

Julia held her breath as Miss Donovan traversed the room. The thirty-two-foot damask tablecloth, rid of its wine stain, was rolled on a large tube to prevent creases. It had taken both of them to stretch and fold it so the selvages were even before ironing it on two large padded tables. The damask had been as soft as a satin wedding gown.

Julia liked the electric iron. Within four minutes, it had heated up and remained hot with no rushing back to the stove to replace a cooled one. Mama would love it.

Miss Donovan unrolled the tablecloth. She squinted. She seemed disappointed not to find any imperfections.

She rolled it back up crookedly. Julia cringed as creases formed.

"I'll do that." Katie jumped forward. Julia was thankful. She didn't want to iron that again.

The sheets and pillowcases had gone through the mangle. It had taken several tries before she had folded the sheets smoothly enough to go in straight and not be pulled out of shape. Now they were stacked neatly.

Miss Donovan shook one open. After scrutinizing it, she handed it to Julia to re-fold.

She inspected the bath towels and the kitchen towels.

"There's a stain on this kitchen towel," she said.

"Those stains are permanent," Katie said. "Ellen doesn't mind. In fact, she likes using old towels as rags."

"And what's all this?" Miss Donovan pointed to the basket of napkins.

"We haven't finished the napkins yet. We don't need them again until Sunday night, so they weren't a top priority."

"Everything is a top priority, young lady."

"Yes, ma'am."

She found nothing wrong with the servants' clothing, but when she unfolded Mr. Easterly's shirt, she pointed to a wrinkle on the center plait. "Look there. This is unacceptable." She looked directly at Julia. "Ironing Mr. Easterly's shirt is the most important task of all. If you cannot do it correctly, you are worthless to us. You are dismissed."

"But..." Julia started.

"No, buts. This was the ultimate test, and you failed."

"Miss Donovan," Katie said, "Julia didn't iron that shirt. I did."

Miss Donovan' chest heaved.

"I'm so sorry," Katie said. "I'll fix the shirt right away. It won't happen again. Julia has done an excellent job today. We need her. Please don't dismiss her."

Miss Donovan nodded curtly and left.

Julia's heart raced. "Does that mean I can come back tomorrow?"

"I think so."

"Oh, Katie, thanks for your help." She wrapped her arms around the petite girl.

"You're welcome. You're going to do just fine."

Papa would be so pleased, and so was she.

Chapter 7

WHEN RICHARD STOPPED by at day's end, Julia was too tired to change into her own clothes. Instead, she draped them over her arm.

"How was your day?" Richard asked as they headed down the driveway.

"Exhausting, but I did it. Miss Donovan said I could come back tomorrow."

"I knew it."

"It was only because of Katie."

How ironic. That sweet little thing with no college education was a fabulous teacher. "I still don't like being a servant, though."

"It won't hurt you for a few weeks. It might even be good for you."

Yes, it probably would.

"How was your day?" she asked.

"Great. I mowed the lawn in the Vista."

"The Vista? What's that?"

"The long grassy side lawn."

"That looks like a park?"

He nodded.

"It must have taken you all day."

"Almost."

"Papa will be proud of us for working so hard."

"Are you going to visit Papa tonight?"

"I guess so." She'd rather soak her feet in Epsom salts on the porch. But no, she wanted to tell Papa about her day.

When they were almost home, they saw their neighbor, Mrs. Thornton, weeding her flower beds. Now Julia regretted not changing out of her ugly white uniform.

"Look at you two." Mrs. Thornton grunted to her feet and pressed her hand to the small of her back. "Where are you coming from dressed like that?"

She swallowed her pride. "We're working at the Easterly House this summer."

"You don't say."

"I'm a gardener," Richard said.

"And you, Julia, what are you doing?"

She didn't want to admit it. Once Mrs. Thornton knew, the whole neighborhood would. "I'm the laundress." Her voice was a whisper.

Mrs. Thornton cackled. "You, Julia Bradshaw, a washerwoman? I don't believe it."

Julia's face burned. "I'm not a washerwoman. I'm the head laundress."

Mrs. Thornton smirked.

What did it matter after all? No fancy title would help.

--⊶⊷--

Saturday, June 20, 1908
Early Saturday morning Julia snuggled with her Bible under a blanket on the front porch rocker, inhaling the steam from her coffee.

How would she survive another day at the Easterly House? She had barely the energy to crawl out of bed this morning. Her feet and back and arms still ached. Her hands were red and chapped, her nails jagged.

She dreaded starting all over today, on a Saturday, no less. She had never worked a Saturday in her life.

Today she needed time in God's Word.

She flipped to where she had left off in Philippians. When she reached verses three and four of chapter two, her heart grew still. "Let nothing be done through strife or vainglory; but in lowliness of mind let each esteem other better than themselves. Look not every man on his own things, but every man also on the things of others."

Vainglory described her, no doubt about it. Boastful. Proud. Trying to make a good impression. Thinking too highly of herself.

But she had graduated from college, the first in her family along with Lee. She *deserved* to be proud.

She was pretty too. That wasn't thinking too highly of herself. It was just being honest.

She read the verse again. It didn't seem to matter if she were pretty or smart. Instead she had to treat others as if they were better than herself. Even if they hadn't been to college. Even if they were servants.

How could she do that?

She read further about Christ's attitude, who, even though He was God, did not cling to His rights as God, but made Himself a servant.

She jolted. A servant. Jesus was a servant too.

Jesus had humbled Himself even though He was the King of kings. Could she do any less?

-->==⊙ ⊙==<--

As they walked through the porte-cochère door, Julia saw the blue curtain closed. No peeking today.

Yesterday Julia hadn't noticed the padded window seat in Miss Donovan's office, a wonderful place to curl up with a book.

Miss Donovan sat behind her desk.

"I was just admiring your window seat," Julia said. "This is a lovely office." She would try to bridge the gulf between them.

Miss Donovan blinked but didn't smile.

Richard left after signing in.

"Any special instructions today?" Julia asked.

Miss Donovan stood. "Let's get one thing straight. Just because I let you return, doesn't mean I want you here."

She didn't want to be here either, so there. But she needed this job. "I'm sorry if I offended you yesterday."

"I have the distinct impression you think you're better than everyone else, even me."

Oh, dear. "I sincerely apologize."

"I expect you to be subordinate, to not question how things are done."

"Yes, ma'am."

"Now get to work."

As she passed the closed curtain, she heard organ music and the clink of china. Mr. Easterly was eating breakfast again in that beautiful, bright room. What a shame to be this close and never see it. But she would not peek. She would be obedient.

Downstairs when she turned the corner, Alan Pierce was huddled with two other men. As she approached, they leered at her.

Her heart pounded. Why were they here? It felt like an ambush.

"What do you want?" She feigned bravery.

"We're waiting for our instructions from Henry. The carpenter shop is here." Alan nodded toward the door across from the laundry.

These men worked so close? Not good.

She stepped toward the laundry. "Well, have a nice day then."

"Wait a minute." Alan blocked her path. "How about going out with me after work tonight?"

It was like Mr. Pratt all over again.

She had perfected her excuses. "I'm sorry, but my family needs me at home."

His ears reddened. Perhaps Mr. Good-Looking had never been turned down before.

She skirted past him into the laundry and slammed the door shut.

Trembling, she leaned against it, hoping Alan wouldn't follow.

He didn't. He was too busy fielding the guffaws of his co-workers.

It was his own fault. He should have known better than to think she would associate with someone like him.

→∙═● ●═∙←

Wonder of wonders. She actually did most of the washing herself while Katie worked in the dairy.

Julia lugged the heavy basket of wet laundry up the steps into the sweltering kitchen.

Ellen Culligan, the cook, looked up from where she hulled strawberries on the marble-topped table.

"Right on time," she said.

"Can you believe it?" Julia said. "I did this without Katie's help."

"Excellent."

She went down the hall, out the delivery door, and across the driveway to the clothes yard.

She closed her eyes and inhaled the scent of roses as the breeze caressed her face. She hoped the warm sun dried out her water-logged raisin hands.

As she clipped the clothes to the line, she looked up at the majestic cream-colored brick mansion. She felt dwarfed by the three stories, so many windows looking down on her.

A week ago she never dreamed she would have successfully done laundry at the Easterly House.

Thank You, Lord, for helping me.

A motor car chugged up the driveway. She peeked through the hedge.

A long, shiny, green Packard with chrome running boards and huge tires stopped by the door. The top was down. Sitting in it were Edgar Hopkins, the chauffeur, and Mr. Easterly whom she recognized from the newspapers.

Mr. Easterly stepped down. He was of average height with broad shoulders under a tailored suit, a red flower tucked into his buttonhole. His brown hair was side-parted, his beard and mustache neatly cropped. He had a pleasant, rather ordinary face.

He strode up the stairs under the porte-cochère and disappeared through the door, looking focused and distracted.

So that was the famous Mr. Easterly. Her knees felt shaky. She had finally seen him. In spite of Miss Donovan.

Enough of this spying. She had work to do. Picking up the empty basket, she slipped through the hedge. The chauffeur, Edgar Hopkins, saw her and waved.

"Beautiful day, isn't it?" he said.

She smiled and nodded.

"What did you say your name was?"

"Julia Bradshaw."

"You're quite a nice addition to our staff."

Somehow coming from a married man with children, the compliment felt sincere, not flirtatious.

"Thank you." A movement in the bay window drew her eyes. Miss Donovan watched with crossed arms. Oh, dear.

"Where are you from?" Edgar asked.

She dared not linger. "Just a few blocks down on Barrington Street."

He raised his eyebrows. "You don't say."

He probably wondered why someone who could afford to live on Barrington Street was working as a laundress at the Eastman House. But she didn't have time to explain.

"I really must get back to work." She hugged the basket as she hurried toward the delivery door.

Mr. Easterly stepped out of the porte-cochère door with a large manila envelope. "All set, Hopkins."

Julia slipped inside. Miss Donavan had made it clear that Mr. Easterly should not see her. But how she wished she could meet Mr. Easterly, not as a laundress, but as a schoolteacher who lived on Barrington Street.

→——◎ ◎——←

At lunch Alan avoided her, much to Julia's relief. As the men retreated to the covered porch, Julia and Katie lingered at the table with the other maids.

Time to improve her relationship with them.

"How long have you been here?" she asked Rose Hamilton, the pretty parlor maid.

"Why do you want to know?" Rose asked.

"Just curious."

Rose hesitated before answering. "I came four years ago when Mr. Easterly moved in. My aunt recommended me. She worked for his mother in their old home."

"And do you like it here?"

Rose shrugged. "It's a job."

"When the house was built, I used to walk through it after the workmen left," Julia said. "I've always wondered what it looked like now."

"It is a beautiful place," Rose said, "but be glad you don't have to dust it. It takes a whole day just to dust the books in the library."

And all those plants in the conservatory need to be dusted too. It's a nightmare."

"Is that the room I saw through the curtain?"

Rose nodded.

"It's breath-taking."

"It's where Mr. Easterly eats. A private organist plays for him during meals."

"So that's what I heard this morning."

"I can show you around sometime," Rose said.

"Oh, I dare not. Miss Donovan told me I wasn't allowed beyond the curtain or she would dismiss me."

Rose's lip curled. "The Dragon Lady wields her power again."

Julia turned to another maid. "And what is your name and what do you do?"

"I'm Bridget Maddigan." She had piercing brown eyes in a heart-shaped face. A curl had escaped her bun and rested on her forehead. "I clean all the bedrooms and bathrooms on the second floor."

"She's the lucky one," Rose said. "Mr. Easterly doesn't have many overnight guests, and now that his mother is gone, only his room is occupied."

"Just because the rooms aren't occupied doesn't mean I don't clean them," Bridget said.

Rose shrugged. "You still don't have much to do."

Julia turned to the third girl. She had a narrow, homely face and kinky dark hair.

"And what do you do?"

"I'm Jane Johnson. I clean the third floor."

"What's on the third floor?"

"The four servants' bedrooms which I clean," Katie said.

Jane added, "Also four more guest bedrooms and Mr. Easterly's laboratory and playroom."

"Playroom? What does he play?"

"It's where he stores his fishing equipment and his hunting trophies."

"And what does he do in the laboratory?"

"It's his carpentry shop and his photo-developing room."

"A man of many talents, I see. You've met him, I suppose."

They all nodded.

"What's he like?"

They answered one after another.

"He's nice."

"Thoughtful."

"Honorable and upright."

"Organized and wants everything done a certain way."

"He's distracted a lot. He doesn't notice when we're around."

"He's shy."

"Shy?" Julia was surprised.

"He doesn't like being around people."

That was odd, considering he was such an important man.

"He likes music. He hosts a concert every Sunday night."

"He's lonely."

Julia said, "If he's so lonely, why hasn't he married?"

Rose shook her head. "He's too busy. He's just not interested."

Bridget elbowed her. "Rose should know. She's tried everything."

Rose shook her off. "I have not."

"You're a hopeless flirt."

Rose rolled her eyes.

"Well, he sounds interesting," Julia said. "I wish I could meet him, although it's not likely with me being down in the laundry."

"No, probably not," Rose said.

Julia couldn't help but feel disappointed.

Chapter 8

Sunday, June 21, 1908

GOING TO CHURCH Sunday morning, they walked along Park Avenue, peering into the closed shop windows. Richard carried three-year-old Annie with her mop of dark curls like Papa's. Four-year-old blond Peter gripped Mama's hand. Walking beside Mary, Jenny looked exhausted. Caring for the house and children was taking its toll.

Mama looked like a widow, dressed in black. Julia wished she had worn something bright and cheerful to celebrate Papa's recovery.

Julia walked by herself, twirling a parasol in the already-warm sun. It felt heavenly wearing a five-gored apricot skirt and matching shirt-waist with see-through embroidered sleeves instead of that ugly white uniform.

After fifteen minutes, they passed the Park Avenue Hospital.

"That's where Papa is," Julia told the children.

"Is Papa very sick?" Mary asked.

"Not sick, just hurt. But he's getting better, so don't worry."

The worry was how they would pay for it.

They crossed the street. Their church was on the corner. It was an imposing Tudor Revival reminiscent of a medieval English manor home with its stucco and half-timbering, diamond-paned mullioned windows, and arched double front door.

Inside they were surrounded by concerned friends.

"Oh, Julia," one young woman said, "we just heard about your father's accident."

"How is he?" someone else asked.

"He's doing as well as can be expected, but he'll be in the hospital all summer."

They gasped. "What will you do?"

"Richard and I are working at the Easterly House to make ends meet."

More gasps. Were they impressed or horrified?

"Doing what?" someone asked.

"I'm the..." Julia looked at the eager faces of the girls she had so often bested. "I'm the washerwoman," she said.

Julia told Lee about her job before they entered the sanctuary.

"I can't picture you doing laundry, but good for you. I'm proud of you."

"It's been humbling, but as Richard says, it's probably good for me. Tell me about your new job. Do you like it?"

He nodded. "It's a great place to work."

"It's ironic that we're both working for Mr. Easterly. Have you met him yet?"

He nodded.

"What's he like?"

"Nice but aloof."

"The maids have some interesting opinions of him. They say he's lonely."

"I doubt it. I think he has a romantic relationship with his attractive secretary, Miss Weston."

"Well, someday I'd like to meet him."

"Maybe you will. You're bound to run into him."

She shook her head. "I'm not allowed anywhere near him."

"That's a shame. It would be special for you," Lee said. "Come, let's get a seat before they're taken."

They slipped in beside Richard and Jenny. Mama was in the middle with the little ones. Lee's parents, Uncle Charles and Aunt Lillian, sat at the other end with their nine-year-old daughter Pearl next to Mary. Uncle Charles had married the much-younger Lillian after his first wife died in childbirth. Pearl had been a welcomed later addition and much spoiled. She and Mary were a year apart and best friends.

During the announcements, Pastor said, "I'm sure you've all heard about the terrible accident our brother Alver Bradshaw had this week. Please keep him in your prayers. He will be in the hospital all summer. We, as his church family, would like to help relieve their tremendous financial burden, so next week we will take a love offering for them. Pray about what the Lord would have you give, and please be generous."

Julia's face grew hot as people looked at them. She didn't like being on the receiving end.

She felt humbled again.

→→■◎ ◎■←←

"Be quiet," Mama said. "We don't want to disturb the other patients."

They climbed the marble steps of the Park Avenue Hospital to the second floor. The little ones held onto the shiny brass railing, taking one step at a time. The woman at the desk below watched with a smile.

Mary looked about to burst into tears. Julia wrapped her arm around her shoulder. "It's all right, honey. Papa has two big casts on his legs, but he'll be fine. You don't have to worry."

"But what if he forgot me?"

"Oh, he would never forget you. You're his special girl."

Mama waited for them at the top. "Papa's room is right there." She pointed.

The children huddled close. Mama stopped in the doorway. "Alver, look who's here."

Julia peeked over Mama's shoulder. Papa was propped up, looking rested and clean-shaven except for his drooping mustache. He opened his arms.

"Papa!" Mary ran to his side.

He drew her into a one-armed hug and kissed her forehead. "How's my little Mary?"

"I missed you."

"I missed you too, honey."

"Where's Annie?" Papa said. "Lift her up onto the bed."

"Are you sure?" Mama said. "She might hurt you."

"Oh, no, I need my Annie."

Richard swooped the little curly-topped girl onto the bed. Annie giggled and nestled into Papa's arms.

"And where's Peter?"

Peter hid behind Mama's skirts.

"Come to Papa."

Peter shuffled toward the bed. Papa grabbed him with one arm and tickled his neck. Peter giggled.

"Me too," Annie said.

Papa tickled her too.

"Alver, you're going to hurt yourself," Mama said.

"Nonsense. This is the best medicine I've had all week."

Mama closed the door so the ruckus wouldn't travel down the hall.

When the laughter subsided, Julia said, "How are you feeling, Papa?"

"I'm coming along. Wanting to come home something fierce. I miss you all."

"Guess what Pastor announced in church today," Richard said. "They're going to take a love offering for us."

"Really?" Papa looked sober. "That will help."

Julia suspected she wasn't the only one worrying about paying the bills.

Chapter 9

Wednesday, June 24, 1908

LEE HAD TO escape. The weather was too pleasant to be trapped in the lunch room with the starry-eyed secretaries.

He grabbed his lunch and sprinted down the six flights to the ground level. He had a destination in mind.

He waited until the automobiles and buggies passed before dashing across the street. At the corner he turned left and walked two blocks, past a machine shop and some unsavory taverns, to the Platt Street Bridge crossing the Genesee River. A steady stream of traffic rumbled alongside the pedestrian walkway.

Off to the right was the Upper Falls, a ninety-six-foot waterfall in the heart of the city. Mills and factories on either side harnessed the water's energy. Just above were the elevated New York Central tracks. He was thankful Uncle Alver hadn't fallen off that bridge, for he couldn't have survived a tumble down the falls.

He took bites of his cheese sandwich as he walked toward the far end of the bridge for the best view. A rainbow shimmered in the mist. He wished he could bottle the iridescent colors.

After finishing the sandwich, his cookies, and his apple, he glanced at his watch. Time to return.

Nearby stood a tall woman also admiring the rainbow. She turned suddenly and looked directly into his eyes. It was Grace Weston, Mr. Easterly's secretary. She smiled.

He swallowed hard. He could think of nothing to say. He nodded as he walked by, pondering what he could have said.

"Lovely day, isn't it, Miss Weston?"

"Have you ever seen such a beautiful rainbow?"

"How long have you been standing there? If I'd known, we could have eaten together."

"Would you like to meet back here tomorrow?"

Dream on, Bradshaw. He was a new employee, younger than she. She would have no interest in him. He was surprised she even recognized him. Or maybe she didn't. Maybe it was just a polite smile to a stranger.

He would come back tomorrow anyway on the remote chance she returned.

No harm in dreaming.

⋆⟶◉ ◉⟵⋆

As Julia ironed a doily, she heard footsteps in the hall, not the clump-clump of the men's boots but the clack-clack-clack of high heels.

Miss Donovan appeared in the doorway.

Julia's heart skipped a beat. Now what?

"Hello, Miss Donovan. May I help you?"

Miss Donovan glanced around. There were no unwashed piles, just a stack of beautifully ironed linens. She looked disappointed.

"We need a tablecloth for the dinner tonight."

"It's all ready." Julia handed her a tablecloth rolled around a long tube.

Miss Donovan took it and left.

Julia sighed. She would have liked some commendation.

"Thank you so much, Miss Bradshaw."

"We're never had such wonderful service."

"You are a great addition to our staff."

"What did we do without you?"

Amazingly, she didn't hate the job. Yes, the work was exhausting. Yes, her hands were probably ruined for life. But as the pile of ironed linens increased, she felt a sense of accomplishment.

She wondered if Mr. Easterly appreciated his starched collars and cuffs and perfectly ironed shirts. She wondered if he enjoyed the scent of roses on his sheets as he crawled into bed. Did he ever think about the hands that made his life so easy? She wished she might see him face-to-face someday and say, "I did it."

Oh, well. She shouldn't be doing this for praise. Her paycheck was reward enough.

As Julia unrolled another damp doily, she heard a different step.

"Hello there," said a masculine voice.

Alan Pierce leaned against the doorjamb.

Her heart skittered. She did not want him here.

"How're doing?" he asked.

"Fine." She turned back to ironing. "I'm really busy."

"I can see that. I hear you're a schoolteacher."

"Yes, I teach kindergarten."

"What's a fancy lady like you doing down here then?"

"My father had an accident and broke both legs. We need the money."

He stepped into the room. She felt panicky.

"I'm really busy. I don't have time to talk."

"Looks to me like you can talk and work at the same time."

"I prefer being alone."

"You're one handsome woman, Julia Bradshaw."

Her face felt hotter than the iron. "I'm sure you have better things to do."

"Nope. Just finished up a painting project. I'm looking to kill time."

"Well, I'm sorry, but you'll have to kill it somewhere else."

Lord, make him go away.

"Anything you need help with here?" He lifted a rolled-up damp pillowcase from her basket."

"Get your dirty hands off."

He dropped it and raised his hands in mock surrender. "Sorry."

She heard more clackety footsteps in the hall. Hopefully Katie was coming to her rescue.

Instead it was Miss Donovan again. Her nose flared as she glared from one to the other. "What's going on here?"

Allen sidled toward the door. "I was just leaving."

"You most certainly are." She grabbed him by the ear and dragged him into the hall.

Julia was embarrassed for him.

"If I ever catch you in here again, you're done, do you understand?"

He disappeared through the carpenter's door across the hall.

Miss Donovan advanced. Julia took a step back. "The same goes for you, Miss Bradshaw. You're being paid to work, not socialize."

"Yes, ma'am." At least she wasn't dragged out by her ear too.

"We need a tablecloth for the dinner tonight."

"But I just gave you one ten minutes ago."

Miss Donovan looked confused. "Of course." She spun around and left.

How odd. Perhaps Miss Donovan was upset by the altercation as well.

In any case, God had come to her rescue. Just not the way she would have chosen.

-⊶⊷-

Friday, June 26, 1908

His first paycheck. Lee ripped open the white envelope.

He was thankful for his increased salary over his job at Sibley's. Living at home, he paid a small rent to his parents, and the rest was deposited in the bank for his own house someday.

Slipping the paycheck from the envelope, he frowned. This was more than he expected. Far more. Almost double.

He turned to Mr. Crosby, the senior accountant. "I have a problem, sir. I think I was overpaid."

Mr. Crosby chuckled. "And that's a problem?"

"Where do I go to fix this? Payroll?"

"No, they just use the figures from Easterly's office. Go see Miss Weston."

"Thanks."

He didn't want to. Yes, he did. He wanted to see her lovely face and hear her voice. If only he wasn't such a tongue-tied fool.

But he was too honest to let this mistake stand.

"I'll be right back," he told his secretary.

He strode from the room and down the hall to Mr. Easterly's office. He knocked.

"Come in." It was her voice.

He entered. Mr. Easterly was not there. Just her. With the sunlight shining from behind, she looked like a beautiful angel. Even her face glowed.

His face heated as he approached her desk.

"Mr. Bradshaw, what can I do for you?"

She remembered his name.

"I was overpaid in my first paycheck."

She frowned. "Really?"

After checking it, she pulled a paper from the file cabinet.

"You are absolutely right. It was my mistake. I'm so sorry. I'll take care of it."

"No problem."

"Thank you for being so honest. Not everyone is."

"God wouldn't let me do otherwise."

Her eyebrows rose. "God? Is God a part of your life, Mr. Bradshaw?"

"God is my whole life."

She smiled. "I see we have something in common. It's a pleasure to have you working here."

"Thank you."

As he left, he wished he'd had the courage to ask more. What exactly *did* they have in common?

Chapter 10

Ontario Beach Park, Charlotte, New York

Saturday, July 4, 1908

THEY HAD FINALLY arrived at Ontario Beach Park, her family's traditional Fourth of July destination. Julia felt like a giddy child again, thankful for a paid day off.

With clanging bells, the New York Central train curved along the Lake Ontario shoreline before hissing to a stop near the boardwalk.

Passengers stood.

"What do you need up here?" Uncle Charles looked into the overhead luggage rack.

"That bag there." Mama pointed. She had brought changes of clothing if the little ones wanted to swim.

"Grab my bag too," Aunt Lillian said.

"Hurry, Mama," begged nine-year-old Pearl. She wore blond ringlets with a large white bow pinned to one side. Her pale blue eyes were like Aunt Lillian's, different from the deep sapphire blue eyes of everyone else. In her lacy white knee-length dress with a bow around her dropped waist, she looked like a dainty princess.

Mary, right behind her, jumped up and down in her eagerness to alight. Her hair was braided and she wore a plain blue dress, evidence of Mama's practicality.

Peter clung to Mama's hand. Richard swooped up Annie, her face like sunshine.

Even Jenny looked happy today as she peeked out the windows.

As Julia descended the steep steps, she didn't know where to turn first.

Across a grassy lawn loomed the Hotel Ontario, a three-story Queen Anne painted dark red with a green roof, its shady lower veranda wrapping around three sides. The second-story porch was open and sunny.

To its right was the Life Motion Pictures building where Julia hoped to watch a half-hour moving picture later. She also wanted to go on Chubbuck's wheel swing. She didn't care so much for the Scenic Railway roller coaster along the river. She had ridden it last year and had been scared witless, especially when they dipped into a darkened corridor alive with growls from fake lions and tigers. She wouldn't let Peter ride, or he would have nightmares forever.

"Where shall we go first?" Uncle Charles asked.

"The carousel," the little ones chorused.

"Of course," Mama said. Mama looked relaxed. She needed this day away from the hospital. At first, Julia feared Mama wouldn't come, but Papa had insisted.

They walked on the wooden sidewalk crowded with ladies wearing ground-sweeping skirts and feathered hats, and men in dark suits and straw boater hats, past the hotel and the auditorium.

At the carousel, Lee bought nickel tickets for all except Mama, Uncle Charles, and Aunt Lillian who preferred to watch.

"Which one do you want to ride?" Julia asked Mary as the colorful wooden animals spun past.

"I want a horse," Mary said.

"I want an ostrich," Pearl said. It figured. She always wanted to be different.

"How about you, Peter?" She lifted him up to see.

He watched for awhile before answering. "I don't want to go up and down."

"How about the giraffe on the outside then?"

His eyes shone as he nodded.

When the carousel stopped and the passengers exited, they dashed for their chosen animals. Julia stood beside Peter on the giraffe.

Clinging to the pole, Peter caught his breath as the music started and the carousel turned. Julia circled him with her arm. "I won't let you fall off, honey."

But she wondered if she could keep her promise. As they spun faster and faster, views of the sparkling lake blurred. She felt dizzy and nauseous.

She closed her eyes. She hoped she didn't throw up.

On and on it spun. She hugged the pole, praying she wouldn't fly off.

Would this thing never stop?

Finally the bells rang and the carousel slowed. She lifted Peter off, grabbed his hand, and unsteadily hurried for the exit. She collapsed onto the grass.

"What's wrong, Julia?" Mama asked.

"Why's your face so white?" Mary asked as she dropped beside her.

"I'm just dizzy, that's all," Julia said.

"No more rides for you," Lee said.

Julia wanted to protest. What was a day at Ontario Beach Park without rides? But yes, she'd had enough spinning for one day.

Lee dug into his pocket for money. "Tell you what. I'll stay here with Julia until she's feeling better, and the rest of you go on the pony ride. We'll meet you at the German Village in the midway in half an hour for lunch."

When they'd left, Lee said, "What would help? Something to drink? Something to eat?"

"Just some fresh air. How about a walk on the Pier?"

He pulled her to her feet. "Are you sure you're up for that?"

"I'm feeling a little better already."

They crossed the railroad tracks to the boardwalk along the shoreline. Red, white, and blue banners snapped overhead in the lake breezes above the wall-to-wall promenaders.

On the east end, the Genesee River flowed toward a bustling port downriver. Extending far out into Lake Ontario, a cement pier separated the river from the ocean-like lake. Cawing seagulls perched on the posts.

A breeze threatened to snatch Julia's hat as they stepped onto the pier. She hoped her hatpin held.

"How're you feeling now?" Lee asked.

"Much better, thanks."

"Do you want to walk to the end?"

"Sure, why not?" It was a ten-minute walk to a small lighthouse.

The breeze whipped the waves onto the pier. Julia lifted her skirt as they walked around puddles.

"So how was work this week?" Julia said.

"Great. I love my job. How was your week?"

"Not bad. If it weren't for Miss Donovan and Alan Pierce, it would be fine."

"Any more run-ins with Miss Donovan?"

She shook her head. "I'm obeying her every command. She won't find any reason to complain."

When they reached the lighthouse, they turned back.

Ontario Beach Park looked miniature from here. On the eastern end were the roller coaster and Ferris wheel. On the far right were the Virginia Reel ride, the water toboggan, and the flying swings. In between was the massive Hotel Ontario. A red-roofed bandstand was closer to the water. The midway with games of chance and food vendors was barely visible.

A stiff breeze blew Lee's hair straight back and plastered her skirts against her legs.

More people walked toward them.

Suddenly Lee yanked her toward the railing.

"What's wrong?"

"I don't want someone to see me."

"Who?"

"Someone from work."

"Who?"

"Miss Weston and Mr. Easterly."

Her heart tripped. "Mr. Easterly is here? Where? I want to meet him."

"Don't you dare."

She turned around anyway. A tall, graceful woman had her hand in the crook of Mr. Easterly's arm.

So this was Miss Weston. No wonder Mr. Easterly was enamored with her. She was beautiful with tender brown eyes and soft brown hair peeking out from under her flowered straw hat. She walked confidently and looked perfect next to Mr. Easterly.

Mr. Easterly was only slightly taller. Up close, his deep-set eyes were blue. He had a broad forehead under his straw boater hat. He looked more relaxed than the first time she had seen him.

They passed by without a glance.

"I can't believe I was close enough to touch him," she said. "I should have asked how he liked his laundry."

Lee groaned.

"What's wrong with you? Why didn't you want him to see you?"

"Not him. Her."

"Miss Weston?"

"Yes."

"But why didn't you want her to see you?"

The blush on his face was telling.

"You like her, don't you?"

He grunted.

She latched onto his arm and leaned into his face. "Come on, admit it. You like her," she teased.

He nodded.

"Finally. I've been waiting for this day. But Lee, you were holding out for a woman who loved the Lord."

"I think she does."

"Well, then, that's perfect. Except she's taken, isn't she?"

He shrugged.

"They looked so good together."

"I know. That's what makes it so hard. Besides that, she's older than I am, and she is so important. I'm practically a nobody. It's hopeless."

"Nothing is hopeless with God. You should know that."

"Until God opens a door, I won't pursue her."

"I'm going to pray for some open doors."

"Don't you dare."

She smiled. She was going to pray, all right. And she wanted a front row seat when the sparks flew.

They sat at a picnic table in German Village with their mouths around Zweigle hot dogs.

Lee still felt unnerved after seeing Miss Weston and Mr. Easterly. He was embarrassed that Julia had guessed his secret. He hadn't wanted anyone to know.

"Guess who we saw on the Pier?" Julia said.

Lee glared at her. Would she tell everyone?

"My boss, Mr. Easterly. I never thought he would come here on his day off."

He sagged in relief. She hadn't told.

"I think all of Rochester has come," his father said.

"Did you talk to him?" Richard asked.

"Of course not. What would I say? 'Oh, hello, Mr. Easterly, I'm your new laundress.' He wouldn't have been impressed."

"But *you've* talked with him before, haven't you, Lee?" his mother asked.

"Only briefly. I don't think he'd recognize me."

"Oh, who could forget a handsome face like yours?" his mother joked.

Time to change the subject. "What would you like to do next?" he asked everyone.

"I wouldn't mind just sitting on a bench and watching the people go by," his mother said.

"Sounds good to me too," said Aunt Louise.

"Would anyone like to see a moving picture?" Lee asked.

"Me," echoed around the table.

"I was hoping we'd do that," Julia said.

After they finished eating, Lee bought them each a big salty pretzel before they headed back. They walked on the sidewalk closest to the Hotel Ontario.

The verandah was packed with diners. White-gloved, uniformed waiters circulated gracefully between the tables. Lee was close enough to see the food on the plates.

Julia walked beside him. "Some day I'd like to have enough money to eat there."

Maybe he would bring her back and make her dream come true.

Actually, he'd rather invite Miss Weston. She belonged in an elegant place like this. No Zwiegle's hot dog for her. He would treat her like a queen.

Stop it, Bradshaw. He had no right to think about her.

But he couldn't stop. He thought of her at work, hoping to run into her. He thought of her on the trolley home. He thought of her while in bed at night, her lovely face imprinted on the back of his eyelids.

Seeing her here on the pier with Mr. Easterly substantiated the rumors. She must care for him.

Julia slowed. "Look, Lee."

Miss Weston sat across from Mr. Easterly at a table near the verandah railing. She lifted a bite to her mouth as she smiled at something he said.

Lee's steps faltered. He stared.

Suddenly she looked at him. Her lips parted in a smile.

He felt like a peeping Tom.

Miss Weston's eyes strayed to Julia. Her eyebrows lifted as she looked back at him.

Lee strode on by, his heart pounding. She had acknowledged him. Smiled even. But she probably thought Julia was his sweetheart.

His chances with her had plummeted.

--->==@ @==<---

Ontario Beach Park was spectacular at night, every building outlined with white lights. David Easterly would rather have been home reading than pressed against the holiday crowds, but he had done it for Miss Weston. She deserved a pleasurable day away from the office.

"Those fireworks were magnificent," she said.

"Glad you came?"

"Absolutely. Thanks for inviting me."

But had she enjoyed it? She smiled and conversed but still felt distant. For once he wished she would drop her guard and let him into her heart.

He was no better. He kept everyone at arm's length. But wouldn't it be nice to feel loved by someone?

His thoughts drifted to that beautiful teacher hugging the little boy. He wanted someone to love him like that.

"I'm ready to go home now," Miss Weston said.

Of course she was. She looked exhausted. She walked as if her feet hurt.

They exited through a Moorish arch near his parked roadster.

"Want a frozen custard before we leave?" Abbott's was across the street.

Anything to prolong starting that car and making a fool of himself. Perhaps he should have brought Edgar Hopkins along after all. But Edgar deserved a holiday like everyone else.

"I just want to go home. It's late, and I have to get up early."

"It's Sunday. You can sleep in."

"My third grade Sunday school class would be disappointed if I did."

"Oh, that's right. I forgot you taught Sunday school."

He wondered why she did. He enjoyed nothing more than a leisurely, quiet Sunday morning at home.

They donned linen dusters. As she tied a chiffon veil over her hat, he jumped out and twisted the crank. After several turns, the motor sputtered and caught. Smiling, he returned to the driver's seat, adjusting the levers to idle. He put on his visor and goggles as the car rumbled.

"It started," he said.

She smiled and nodded, not understanding his relief.

Once it had taken almost an hour of cranking for the fool thing to start. Another time the crank had kicked him against the side of the car, gashing his forehead.

He shifted into gear, and they bounded forward, narrowly missing a parked car.

Grace gasped.

So much for not making a fool of himself.

"I've got it," he said as the car jerked again and again.

Her eyes were closed. Was she praying?

"You can open your eyes now. I have it under control."

"Tell me when we're past Charlotte."

"Why?"

"This place makes my skin crawl."

No wonder. Twenty-eight corners boasted thirty-five saloons. A religious person like Grace would be understandably offended.

Still, sometimes her holier-than-thou attitude disturbed him. Shortly after he hired her, she had said, "Just so you know, Mr. Easterly, ours is strictly a business relationship. I am a Christian, and the Bible forbids me from becoming romantically involved with anyone who isn't."

"I assure you, Miss Weston, I am not interested in a romantic relationship."

More than once he had regretted that comment.

Working at adjacent desks for five years they had discovered how much they were alike. Both worked tirelessly at nine-hour-or-more days. Both were organized, perfectionists, austere, reserved, and commanded respect. Both loved flowers and music. She was a female version of himself, someone he trusted implicitly.

Ironic, wasn't it? He was one of the wealthiest men in the city, respected by all. Anyone would be thrilled to be his wife. Anyone but her.

They exited the unsavory town.

He reached over and touched her hand. "You can open your eyes now," he said.

Her eyes remained closed. She had fallen asleep. He didn't wake her. She needed her rest.

But his hand lingered on hers, liking how it felt.

->=◎ ◎=<-

Sunday, July 5, 1908

The Bradshaw family filled their pew the next morning. The children, with sunburned noses, still looked sleepy from their long day at Ontario Beach Park.

Julia felt sleepy herself. Hopefully this afternoon they could all nap.

After a hymn, Pastor announced, "As you know, last Sunday we took a love offering for brother Alver Bradshaw. All the money has been counted now, and quite frankly, I am overwhelmed by your generosity. I know the Bradshaws will be too. Mrs. Bradshaw, won't you come up here? Bring your family too. Yes, all of them."

Julia felt self-conscious as she herded the little ones into the aisle behind Mama, Richard, and Jenny. On the platform, it was worse with hundreds of eyes staring at them. Peter hid his face in her skirts. Mary clutched Jenny's hand. Mama looked terrified. Little Annie waved.

"Mrs. Bradshaw, it is with much love that I present you with this gift from the congregation." He handed her a check.

Mama's eyes teared. "Thank you." She was unable to say more. Everyone clapped, their love filling the sanctuary.

Mama stumbled down the stairs, the rest following.

During the next hymn, Mama passed down the check to her.

Julia's eyes widened. She had never dreamed it would be so much.

Her eyes filled with tears, and she couldn't sing. God was providing for them, just as He'd promised.

Chapter II

Monday, July 6, 1908

As JULIA WALKED through the porte-cochère entrance, she noticed a sliver of light shining through the closed curtain. How she longed to whip back the curtain and feast her eyes on that glorious room.

But she would not disobey.

She had read in Colossians chapter three that morning about how servants had to obey and please their masters, not only when they were watching, but all the time, as if working for the Lord.

She was trying.

She stepped into the office to sign in. "Good morning, Miss Donovan. Did you have a nice holiday?"

Miss Donovan glared over her glasses, her mouth pursed.

I guess she didn't. The poor thing probably hadn't gone anywhere. She wondered if she had family.

"Have a nice day." She headed toward the curtain, savoring the glimpse of the white marble floor and the greenery through the crack. Organ music played as she headed into the cellar. No doubt Mr. Easterly was in there. So near but so far.

The curtain was like an impenetrable brick wall. Even if Miss Donovan had not forbidden her to cross, she did not belong in Mr. Easterly's world.

The pile of dirty linens on the laundry floor was twice as high as usual. Having Saturday off might not have been a blessing after all.

When Katie appeared an hour later, she had everything recorded and sorted.

"Good morning," Katie said. "Looks like you're off to a good start."

Katie's cheerfulness always lifted her spirits.

"I am, but I'll need help today."

"That's what I'm here for. Tell me what to do first."

Katie was amazing. Even though she knew the job well, she still let Julia take charge.

"I saved the stains for you. You're so good at getting them out. How was your holiday?" Julia asked.

"Holiday? Oh, we had a holiday?" Katie chuckled. "Washing the dog and scrubbing the kitchen floor wasn't much of a holiday."

"I'm sorry. You didn't have any fun?"

"Just having time to catch up on things was good enough for me."

"Did you see any fireworks?"

"Yes, from our rooftop patio. How about you? What did you do?"

"It's a family tradition to go to Ontario Beach Park. We thought we couldn't afford it this year, but my cousin Lee paid for us."

Katie looked wistful. "Someday I'd like to go."

"You've never been?"

She shook her head. "Money's always been tight."

Julia wished she could treat Katie to a whole day of fun.

"Guess who we saw there? Mr. Easterly and Miss Weston."

"Really? Hobnobbing with the elite, are we?"

"No, I didn't speak to them. It was enough just to see them up close. Miss Weston is gorgeous."

"She's nice too."

"What else can you tell me about her?" Maybe she could snoop for Lee.

Katie shrugged.

"Is Mr. Easterly courting her?"

"I wouldn't know," Katie said. "No one tells me anything. The person to ask is Rose."

All right. She would ask at lunch.

-->==◉ ◉==<--

Katie went up early to set the servants' luncheon table. Julia followed at noon. As she stepped into the sweltering kitchen, Ellen's beefy arms lifted a pan of muffins from the oven. She looked for some place to set it.

"Julia, can you grab me a pot holder? In that drawer there." She pointed with her head.

Julia rushed to the drawer closest to the oven. She snatched a thick potholder and dropped it on the counter. Ellen set down the hot pan.

"Thanks, dearie."

"You're welcome. Anything else I can do?"

"Well, bless your heart. I wish everyone were as willing. How would you like to come work for me once Sally"'s arm is healed?"

It was nice to feel appreciated.

"I'd love to, but I can't. Once September comes, I teach kindergarten at the Francis Parker School."

"My! I didn't realize we had such a star among us."

"Oh, Ellen, stop it. I'm no different from anyone else."

She suddenly realized it was true. These were good people. She was one of them. She liked them better than the teachers at school.

"You most certainly are different, dearie. You have a heart of gold."

Perhaps God had been glorified in this job after all.

In the servants' dining room, Julia sat next to Rose. "I have something to ask you," she said. "I was surprised to see Mr. Easterly at Ontario Beach Park with Miss Weston on Saturday."

Rose raised her eyebrows. "Surprised? Why?"

"Are they courting?"

"Not that I know of."

"Explain their relationship."

"Who knows? She's his assistant at work and his hostess at home."

"His hostess? What do you mean? Does she come here?"

"Every Sunday evening for his concerts. She stands by his side and welcomes people."

"Why would she do that?"

Rose shrugged. "He needs a hostess since he doesn't have a wife."

"Does he pay her?"

"I don't think so. I think she does it as a friend."

It was too confusing. Friend? Employee? She didn't know what to tell Lee.

The room suddenly hushed. Miss Donovan stood at the head of the table.

"Attention, everyone," she said. "Because we all had a day off on Saturday, many of you are behind on your work. I will expect you to work extra hours to catch up, without pay, of course."

When Miss Donovan left, murmurs circled the table.

"I'm not working without pay," Rose said. "It'll get done when it gets done."

Julia would try to work her extra hours cheerfully. After all, hadn't Ellen said she was different from everyone else? It was time to prove it.

→⊨◎ ◎⊨←

Noon. Time for lunch. Lee stretched his arms and stood.

His secretary, Miss Kramer, watched him. "Going for a walk again?"

He nodded.

"We'll miss you in the lunchroom."

Yes, they would. He dreaded when the blustery Rochester weather kept him inside, defenseless against their batting eyelashes and silly giggling.

But walking on the bridge was more than an escape from the ladies. It was an escape for his soul, a time to re-connect with God after being too busy all morning.

Plus Grace Weston might be there.

He had only seen her that once, but every day he looked for her.

His mouth grew dry at the thought of meeting her face-to-face. What would he say?

He had no trouble conversing with the young women at church, probably because he wasn't trying to impress them.

Grace was another matter. He couldn't impress her if he tried. She was so far above him.

It was an impossible dream.

The sun was hot on the bridge. Maybe he shouldn't have come. He didn't need more sunburn.

He looked for her. She wasn't there.

It was just as well. Now he wouldn't have to manufacture a conversation. He leaned against the railing and pulled out his sandwich.

Even without a rainbow, the rushing falls was captivating.

He took a few bites. The sweat trickled down his spine. It was too hot. He needed shade.

He returned his sandwich to the tin and headed back.

That's when he saw her. She came toward him, looking cool and shaded in a large floppy hat. Their eyes met.

"Leaving already?" she asked.

"It's too hot out here. I'm looking for shade."

"Follow me. I know just the place."

His stomach turned over. She had invited him? To go with her? He was actually walking beside her?

If only he could think of something to say.

At the end of the bridge was a stone wall overlooking the river. Some trees provided shade.

"How's this?" she asked.

"Much better."

"So do you come out here often?" she asked as they sat on the grass, facing each other.

"Whenever the weather is nice."

"I can only get out on the days Mr. Easterly goes home. Usually his chauffeur brings his lunch, and he likes me to eat with him."

Of course. Who wouldn't want to eat with her?

That explained why he hadn't seen her.

"Did you have a nice time at Ontario Beach Park on Saturday?" he asked. There. He finally said something.

"I did, although it exhausted me. I'm afraid I fell asleep on the way home. I wasn't very good company."

He should respond, but he would rather enjoy the pattern of the sunlight on her face through the weave of her straw hat.

"I was there with my family," he finally said. "That was my cousin Julia you saw."

"Oh, your cousin?"

Was that relief in her eyes?

"She's lovely," she said.

Silence again.

"Did you get your corrected paycheck yet?" she asked.

"Yes, thanks for taking care of it."

"You're welcome. I'm so sorry for the mistake. Thanks for your honesty."

"As I said, God wouldn't let me do otherwise."

"I've been wondering about that comment. Are you a Christian, Mr. Bradshaw?"

Tingles raced up his spine. Was she one too?

"It depends on what you mean by a Christian."

"Someone who has surrendered his life to Christ."

Joy exploded in his heart. He couldn't have given a better answer himself.

"Yes, I am. I asked Jesus to forgive my sins and come into my life when I was ten years old."

She clapped her hands. "I knew it." She looked radiant.

"You too?"

She nodded.

Suddenly she wasn't the revered assistant to Mr. Easterly but a sister in Christ. It changed everything.

"Tell me your story," he said.

"My story? I was an only child. When my father and stepmother died of tuberculosis when I was six, I went to live with my aunt in Michigan whose husband had died in the Civil War. In spite of her hardships, Aunt Mary had an infectious joy because of Jesus. She helped me accept Christ as my Savior when I was eight years old. She nurtured me for many years."

"How did you end up in Rochester?"

"I went to business school in Niagara Falls, New York. One weekend I visited school friends here in Rochester and heard that Mr. Easterly was looking for a secretary. I walked into his office and asked for an interview. He hired me on the spot, so here I am, five years later."

"Do you ever dream of going back to Michigan?"

"No, this is my home now. Aunt Mary died four years ago. I have no family left."

No family? He couldn't imagine. He wished he could introduce her to his boisterous family.

"I'm sorry," he said.

She smiled wistfully. "My hope is in God. I'm content. Most of the time."

Amazing. He wasn't sure he would be content in her shoes.

"Would you look at the time? We'd better get back," she said.

He had completely forgotten to eat his lunch, but it didn't matter. Feasting on Miss Weston was better any day.

-->==◎ ◎==<--

Tuesday, July 7, 1908

Tuesday morning when Julia entered the porte-cochère entrance, the blue velvet curtain was wide open. Sunlight dazzled. Organ music swelled.

She squeezed her eyes shut. She wasn't supposed to look.

She entered the office. Did Miss Donovan know the curtain was open?

"Good morning, Miss Donovan."

Miss Donovan thrust the sign-in sheet before her.

"Have a good day," Julia called over her shoulder.

She approached the open doorway. It was impossible not to look. She intended to hurry downstairs, but her feet just stopped.

Across a shiny white marble hallway peeked palms and green wicker furniture. Light flooded through the two-story windows.

Oh, she yearned to see more.

She stuck her head through the doorway. To the right a floor-to-ceiling painting of a red-coated soldier was flanked by two blue damask armchairs.

Beyond, white Corinthian pillars framed the spacious entryway. White marble floors. A free-standing staircase with white spindles and dark mahogany railings. An Oriental rug. A grandfather clock. It was breathtaking.

A woman appeared. She was tall and lovely with beautiful brown eyes, a sweeping black skirt, and tailored shirtwaist. It was Miss Weston.

A look passed between them. Miss Weston smiled slightly.

Julia came to her senses. What was she doing? She shouldn't be here. She was not to be seen.

She pulled her head back in just as she heard the clack-clack-clack of shoes on the marble floor behind her.

She'd been caught.

"What are you doing?" Miss Donovan said.

She had no excuse. She knew she shouldn't have looked. Why had she done it?

With a heavy heart, she faced the housekeeper.

But Miss Donovan's eyes were not on her. "Oh, Miss Weston, I'm so sorry. Please forgive the intrusion."

"Not a problem." Miss Weston glided by, entered the powder room, and closed the door.

Miss Donovan's fury unleashed. "Get out!" Her eyes were frenzied. She pointed to the porte-cochère door.

"I'm so sorry. I didn't mean to look. Please forgive me."

"Get out. I warned you."

"Please give me another chance. I'll never do it again."

Miss Donovan's lips tightened. "Get out and never come back." Her finger still pointed toward the door.

"But..."

Miss Donovan advanced. Her intent was clear.

Before she was dragged out by the ear, Julia fled. She yanked open the door and slammed it behind her.

Stunned, she sank on the top step, drew her knees up to her chest, and wrapped her arms around her legs.

Lord, what have I done?

Chapter 12

It was an agonizing walk home. How could she admit to her family she had lost her job because she disobeyed?

She was so embarrassed.

She knew better. She had been trying to apply God's Word about being obedient to her master. How could this have happened? It was beyond humiliating.

What would Papa say? Mama? Lee?

Who would tell Richard when he stopped to pick her up at the end of the day?

Who would tell Katie? Poor Katie would have to do the laundry all by herself.

Who would tell Rose and the girls? And Ellen the cook? Here Ellen had thought so highly of her.

Her testimony was ruined. How *could* she have done it?

She dragged herself up the porch steps and through the front door. Dishes clinked in the kitchen.

"Is someone there?" her mother called.

She wished she could flee up the stairs.

"It's me." Julia walked into the kitchen.

Mama sat at the end of the table, Jenny and Annie on one side, and Mary and Peter on the other. The remnant of breakfast was on their plates.

"What are you doing home?" Mama said. "Are you sick?"

"No, I lost my job."

Mama's chin dropped. Jenny smirked.

"What happened?" Mama said.

She would tell the whole ugly truth and be done with it.

"The housekeeper threatened to dismiss me if I looked beyond the curtain into the house, and I did it."

"Why?"

"I couldn't help myself. It was beautiful beyond words."

"Julia!"

"I'm so sorry."

"What are you going to do now?"

Julia collapsed into Papa's chair. "I don't know." She didn't want another job. "Perhaps I can stay home and help Jenny. That money from church helped, didn't it?"

"Please, Mama," Jenny said, "let her help."

"I'll have to talk with your father," Mama said.

If only Papa didn't have to know. At least she wouldn't be there to see his initial disappointment. She might never be his princess again.

—⟩▰ ▰⟨—

After Mama left for the hospital, Julia helped clear the dishes. "Want help washing these?' she asked Jenny.

"No, you can do the laundry since you're such an expert now."

Jenny's tone had a bite to it.

"Sure." Being as nice to Jenny as she was to Katie would be a struggle.

"Who wants to help with the laundry?" she asked the three little ones.

"Me," all three piped up.

"Come on then." They followed her into the cellar that seemed dark and dingy and small compared to the Easterly House.

"Who wants to sort?"

"Me," they all said.

"Annie and Peter, put the whites here and the colored things here. Mary, pull out the towels in a separate pile."

Having the little ones underfoot was actually fun.

They looked for stains, and she was surprised at how many they found, even more than were actually there.

"Good job. You three are going to be the best launderers when you grow up."

They beamed.

Later they followed her into the backyard and played in the sandbox as she hung the clean clothes on the line.

What a glorious day. The sting of losing her job had faded. It was wonderful being home. It was wonderful being with the children and not worrying if Miss Donovan would come down or if Alan Pierce was peeping through the door.

But she missed Katie and Rose and the girls and Ellen. She didn't suppose she could sneak back some day just to say hello and apologize for her quick exit.

What must they think of her? What would Miss Donovan tell them? She hoped she didn't embellish the truth. After all, she had only peeked into the hallway. What was so bad about that?

Nothing except she had been forbidden to do so. She had disobeyed.

She wondered if Miss Donovan had opened that curtain on purpose, just to tempt her. It wouldn't surprise her.

Why had Miss Donovan despised her so? She was a good worker. She had learned quickly.

But she couldn't dispel Miss Donovan's first impression of her. She was wrong to flaunt her college education and her teaching position. Knowing now how Miss Donovan needed to feel superior, the woman must have felt intimidated and threatened. No wonder she wanted to get rid of her.

Jenny stuck her head out the back door. "Julia, someone's here to see you."

Who could that be? Someone from the Easterly House begging her to return? Already they couldn't do without her.

As she bounded up the stairs, she realized she was still wearing her white uniform. She could leave immediately, if needed. Jenny could finish hanging out the wash.

"Who is it?" she asked as the screen door banged behind her.

Jenny shrugged as she stirred something on the stove.

In the front hall she was shocked to see Miss Whiton, her school principal, looking overheated in her long-sleeved navy suit.

"Miss Whiton, won't you come in?"

"Thank you."

She ushered her into the parlor. Someone had left a *Good Housekeeping* magazine on the horsehair sofa. Books were spread on the ottoman. The floor was scattered with toy blocks. She wished Jenny were a better housekeeper. This was downright embarrassing. After she cleared the sofa, they both sat.

She hoped this wasn't bad news. Perhaps Miss Whiton was here to tell her she had lost her teaching job too. Imagine losing two jobs in one day.

"I came to find out how your father is doing," Miss Whiton said.

Julia was touched. Miss Whiton had always been kind and considerate, but never personal.

"He's coming along," she said. "He's taking less laudanum every day and is awake more. Both his legs are in casts, so he can't get out of bed, but his spirits are good."

"I'm glad to hear that. And how are the rest of you doing?"

"Oh, fine." She decided against telling about losing her job. "Mama goes to the hospital every day, so things aren't running quite as smoothly at home, but we're managing."

"Let me tell you why I've come." Miss Whiton leaned closer. "Word has spread in the neighborhood about the accident, and there has been such an outpouring of concern that we would like to organize a charity carnival to help you out."

Julia didn't know what to think. On the one hand, she was elated. They could use the money, but that word charity made her squirm.

She hoped Miss Whiton hadn't noticed her hesitation. "That would be wonderful. Tell me the details."

"We were thinking of having it Saturday, July 25, less than two weeks away, on the school's front lawn. We'll have games set up for the children, a bake sale, perhaps some entertainment. One of the mothers just finished a quilt we can raffle."

"I'm speechless. Thank you."

"Oh, don't thank me. Thank Mr. Pratt. It was his idea. He's organizing it."

Mr. Pratt, of all people. She didn't want to be beholden to him. But she could hardly refuse now.

"Just tell us the time, and we'll be there," Julia said.

"Yes, we'll want your whole family there, even the children. Seeing them might make the people give more generously."

They truly were a charity case.

On the other hand, how amazing that Miss Whiton would stop by on the very day she lost her job. It was no coincidence. God was providing for them again.

-->==⊚ ⊚==<--

As Julia set the table for supper, Richard burst through the front door.

"What happened?" he demanded.

"I lost my job."

"How could you?"

"I know. It was the dumbest thing I've ever done."

"But to take Mr. Easterly's vase? Why would you do that?"

Julia's heart raced. "I didn't take his vase."

"That's what Miss Donovan said."

She knew it. She knew Miss Donovan would fabricate something. "What exactly did Miss Donovan say?"

"She told us she had let you go because she found you in the house stealing a vase."

Julia's blood boiled. How dare she!

Her reputation was in shreds. If her own brother believed it, surely everyone else did too.

"That's not true. She caught me looking into the hall, but I never stepped in, and I never stole a vase."

Richard looked relieved. "I didn't think you would. You had me worried."

"I'm so embarrassed. What must all those people think of me now?"

"You were the topic of conversation over lunch."

"What did they say?"

"Katie defended you and said that Miss Donovan likely had made it up, but I think everyone else believed Miss Donovan."

Julia winced. "This is terrible."

"Don't worry. Tomorrow I'll tell them what really happened."

She didn't want them thinking so poorly of her even overnight.

"Is Miss Donovan going to hire someone to replace me?"

Richard shook his head. "She said that Sally would be back in a few weeks, and Katie would fill in."

Poor Katie. How could Katie handle the job alone?

Katie must hate her for making her life so difficult.

"How about Katie's other responsibilities?"

"The third floor maid is going to clean the servants' bedrooms. Believe me, she wasn't too happy about that."

So Jane must hate her too.

"And her dairy duties?"

"One of the kitchen maids will fill in."

She felt horrible. Her one little act of disobedience had caused turmoil for everyone.

⤛ ⬤ ⤜

Surprisingly, Mama arrived in time for supper. She looked drained. Walking back and forth to the hospital every day was wearing.

The little ones smothered her with hugs. Mama looked as if she might keel over.

"Let Mama come in and put her feet up," Julia said.

As Mama collapsed onto the sofa, the children crowded around her.

"You're home early," Julia said. "Is everything all right?"

"I told Papa about your job. He wants to see you this evening."

"Oh." For once, she dreaded seeing him.

What would he say? Would he yell at her? Would he force her to find a job tomorrow?

"Tell Mama what Miss Whiton wanted," Jenny said.

"Miss Whiton from school stopped by," Julia said.

Mama looked around the cluttered room. "Here?"

"Yes, and she said the school is organizing a charity carnival to raise money for our expenses. Isn't that wonderful?"

Mama's eyes brightened. "Perhaps there's hope after all."

Hope? She would remember that on the way to the hospital tonight. She was glad she was too big to spank. Or was she?

⤛ ⬤ ⤜

Julia peeked into Papa's hospital room. He was asleep. Good. Maybe she could just leave.

A nurse, wearing a white floor-length uniform and her hair in a bun, cradled a pile of clean sheets in her arms. "Good evening, Miss Bradshaw," she said.

"Good evening." She looked back into Papa's room. His eyes opened.

"Julia." He motioned her in.

She sat by his bed. "How are you feeling?"

"A little better each day. Tell me what happened today."

"I lost my job, and I'm so ashamed."

"What happened?" He took her hand.

The whole story gushed out.

He stroked her hand.

"In the beginning I didn't want to work there. I thought the job was beneath me, but God has been working on my heart. I learned not to think so highly of myself. And I found that I really enjoyed those people. They became my friends. I also learned how to be a good laundress and how to do my job as unto the Lord and not men. And now I've ruined everything. I am so ashamed and sorry. But do you know what Miss Donovan told everyone? That she caught me in the house stealing a vase." Tears welled up in her eyes.

"Come here, princess." He opened his arms. She buried her face against his chest, sobbing.

"There, there." He patted her back.

She cried until no tears were left and then just rested against Papa's chest listening to the thumping of his heart.

Instead of yelling or spanking her, he had shown love and forgiveness, just like her heavenly Father.

God, I'm sorry for what I did. Please forgive me for being disobedient. I was so wrong. Please help this all to work together for good somehow.

She lifted her head. "Thanks, Papa. I feel better now."

"I wanted you to come tonight because I knew your heart would be hurting. Mine was hurting for you. I hate to see my children suffer.

If I could, I would shelter you from all the difficulties in life, but that wouldn't be best for you. God brings trials into your life to draw you closer to Him, to help you grow, and if I sheltered you, you wouldn't become the person God wants you to be. It looks to me as if you're maturing spiritually, princess, which thrills my heart more than anything in the world."

"Thanks, Papa."

"Now about your job... I don't want you to get another one. You're needed at home. Mama is stressed because Jenny isn't keeping up. The money from the church will help."

She was flooded with relief. "Thanks, Papa. But there's more good news. Miss Whiton stopped by today and said the school is organizing a charity carnival for us."

"Well, there you have it," Papa said. "God has made a way for you. Don't fret about this, sweetheart. Losing your job was all part of God's plan."

All right, she wouldn't fret. She would trust that God was working everything together for good.

⇥⊶ ⊶⇤

Thursday, July 9, 1908

Julia felt like a trespasser as she ducked under the window of Miss Donovan's office. Hopefully Miss Donovan sat at her little round table looking at her lunch and not outside.

Yesterday Richard had told the Easterly House staff what had really happened. But it wasn't enough. She needed to make certain they believed him.

She crept past the windows to the storage room and the butler's pantry. At the kitchen window, she stood on tiptoe. Ellen was at the table. Julia knocked.

Ellen looked. Her mouth dropped.

Julia motioned toward the porch and kept walking past the pantry window, the delivery entrance door, and the servants' hall to the servants' porch. The men were out smoking already.

All talking ceased when they saw her. A flush crept across her cheeks as she climbed the stairs. "Hello," she said.

"We're sorry about what happened," Solomon Merrick, the butler said.

"I am too."

The chauffeur, Edgar Hopkins, nodded. "It's too bad. It was nice having a pretty face to look at."

"Why are you here?" Alan Pierce asked.

"I wanted to see everyone one last time and apologize."

She opened the screen door into the servants' hall. The ladies were still seated around the table just as she'd hoped.

"Julia!" Katie jumped up. They embraced. "What are you doing here?"

"I just had to come back and apologize for what happened."

Ellen appeared in the doorway. "Tell us what happened, girl. I'll stand here in the doorway and watch for Miss Donovan."

The other girls gathered around.

"Miss Donovan told me I would be dismissed if I ever looked beyond the curtain. Monday the curtain was open. I just couldn't help looking, and Miss Donovan caught me. I am so ashamed because I fully intended to obey her. But I did not walk into the house, and I did not steal a vase."

"We know. You're too nice for that."

"I'm so sorry that I've made your lives more difficult."

"We'll manage," Jane said.

They all nodded. Julia felt their forgiveness. "Thank you." Her eyes misted.

"Well, I just wanted to see you all one more time and tell you how much I miss you."

"We miss you too," Katie said. "What will you do now?"

"Help my sister Jenny take care of the children while my mother is at the hospital."

Katie sighed. "I'll probably never see you again."

Julia hugged Katie again, knowing she was right. The others lined up for hugs until Ellen whispered, "Miss Donovan's coming."

"Go." Rose pushed her out the door.

Julia fled, closing a chapter of her life.

She'd never be this close to the Easterly House again.

⇥ ⇤

Saturday, July 25, 1908

Julia was overwhelmed. This was all for them?

A banner strung between two trees read, "Help the Bradshaws." Long lines formed outside red-striped game tents on the school lawn. A beautiful Texas Star quilt hung on another line between the trees. A clown rode through the crowd on a unicycle honking an annoying horn. In one corner children stood in line for a pony ride. At the opposite end was the baked goods sale, the goodies going fast if the line was any indication.

Miss Whiton greeted them. "Oh, here are the guests of honor."

Mama didn't smile, but the eyes of Mary, Peter, and Annie sparkled as they observed the fun. Jenny's expression soured after scanning the crowd. Richard was absent, working at Easterly's today.

Miss Whiton took Mary's hand. "Come, children. Play anything you want. It's free for you."

Mary looked at Mama. "Can I, Mama?"

When Mama nodded, she ran off to the beanbag toss.

Julia took Peter and Jenny took Annie. Mama wandered over to the bake-sale table.

"Peter, would you like a pony ride?" she asked.

He nodded. They pressed through the crowd.

"Hi, Miss Bradshaw."

It was pretty blond Mildred from her kindergarten class with a huge bow clipped to her hair.

"Oh, Mildred, how nice of you to come today. Are you enjoying yourself?"

Mildred's dimples flashed as she nodded and dashed off.

Julia spotted Jack and Theodore in the crowd. Everyone had come to help. What a blessing. Humbling, though.

What must these people think? That they were poor? That they had asked for money?

She would rather work in a smelly little grocery than admit their need.

Yet this was from God's hand. She should accept it gratefully. She needed to stop thinking so highly of herself and allow these people the blessing of giving.

As they waited in the pony line, more people greeted them. Julia graciously thanked them for coming.

Peter clung to her hand, his eye on the pony being led around the circle.

When it was his turn, his chin trembled. "No," he said.

"What's wrong?"

"I'm scared."

"I'll walk with you and hold your hand. There's nothing to be afraid of."

He shook his head.

"Come on, you can do it. I promise you won't fall."

His bottom lip quivered as she lifted him onto the pony. He reached for her, trying to get off.

"You're going to love it, Peter. Wait and see."

With one arm around him, she nodded to the trainer who pulled the pony forward. Peter felt stiff for the first steps. Gradually he relaxed. When the ride was over, he smiled as she lifted him down. "Now wasn't that fun?"

He nodded.

"See, it's good to try new things."

Like doing laundry. Like being a servant. She couldn't believe how much she missed it.

"What shall we do next?" she asked Peter.

As she looked around, she spotted Mr. Pratt talking to a man by the fence.

Oh, dear. She really should thank him for organizing this.

The men shook hands, and the other man walked away. When Mr. Pratt looked up, their eyes met.

"Come, Peter, there's someone I need to talk to," she said.

Mr. Pratt looked quite dapper in his white flannel suit and flat-topped boater hat. His red mustache had filled out some.

"And who do we have here?" Mr. Pratt squatted and looked into Peter's eyes.

"It's Peter, my little brother."

He shook Peter's hand. "Nice to meet you, Peter. I'm Mr. Pratt. I teach with your sister." He patted his blond head as he stood. "Cute little boy." He scanned the crowd. "Looks like we have a good turnout today."

"Miss Whiton told me this was your idea. Thanks so much."

"You're welcome."

"It must have taken forever to organize."

He shrugged. "I was glad to do it."

He was being unbelievably nice. She felt ashamed for how she had treated him.

"Why did you do it?" She bit her lip. She shouldn't have asked that. What if he said he was madly in love with her or had been trying to get her attention? She suspected both were true.

"If it were me, I would appreciate the help."

How could he be so nice when she had mistreated him so? Perhaps an apology was in order. Yet she didn't want him to think that she was encouraging him. Still, for the sake of her family, she should be civil.

"Mr. Pratt, I would like to apologize for the way I've acted toward you."

His eyebrows rose.

Oh, my, this was hard.

"You see, the reason I kept refusing you is because I'm a Christian, and I can't go out with anyone who does not share my religious beliefs."

"How do you know what my religious beliefs are? You never asked."

He was right.

"I believe in God," he said. "I go to church."

So did a lot of people. That didn't mean they had a personal relationship with God.

But what if Mr. Pratt were a Christian? Would that make a difference?

She still didn't like that thin mustache, or his fat lips, or his balding head, or his annoying personality, or his lack of refinement. But those things were superficial. Maybe he was a gem inside. Maybe it was time to give him a chance.

Part 2

Chapter 13

Francis Parker School #23

Friday, December 4, 1908

TEACHING WAS SUPPOSED to be fulfilling, not torturous.

Today's devotional was especially for Joey.

He was a handsome boy with big brown eyes and olive skin, his thin lips in a perpetual sneer. Somehow in the three months since school started, he had taken control of the class.

The minute he walked into the room, Julia was on high alert, wondering if he would pinch his neighbor, throw sand into someone's eyes, or pull pigtails.

She was at her wit's end knowing how to punish him, especially since he delighted in standing in the corner.

Julia rejoiced that she was not his mother. At least by day's end she was free of him.

The children sat in their bow-back spindled chairs, looking up at her with eager eyes. "Today's verse is 'The Lord loves a cheerful giver.' Can you say that with me?"

The class repeated the words.

"Good. What does a little child have to give? Raise your hand if you have an answer."

Hands shot up. She called on Katherine with the cameo face, the sweetest little girl in the class.

"Kindness," Katherine said.

Katherine certainly exemplified that. "Excellent, Katherine." Katherine beamed. "Lawrence, what do you think?"

"Love," he answered. Did Lawrence know what it meant to love? He was good-looking, intelligent, fun-loving, but selfish, always looking out for his best interests.

Actually he's a lot like me, isn't he, Lord?

"What else can a little child give?" she asked as she noticed Joey pinching Katherine. Katherine swatted him away. Julia would ignore him and finish the lesson.

She called on Emma. "We can be sunshine," Emma said.

How did she ever come up with that on this gloomy December day?

"Yes, you can either be a sunbeam or a shadow." She stared at Joey, hoping he paid attention. "You can either be good and kind or bad-tempered and selfish. How many of you would like to be good and kind?"

Every hand went up, even Joey's, although she doubted he had heard a word.

"Excellent. One way you can be good and kind is to treat others better than yourself. Let's see if we can do that today, shall we?"

They all nodded their heads.

Pudgy Charlie raised his hand.

"Yes, Charlie?"

"Joey's pinching Katherine."

Charlie was the tattler. Things would be easier to ignore without Charlie. Now she was forced to take action.

"Children, you may carry your chairs back to your desks, and Joey, you may take yours to the corner."

He triumphantly moved to the corner.

"Now everyone stand. Stretch your arms high in the air."

She raised her hands too.

"Miss Bradshaw, you have a hole under your arm," Joey called out. The class tittered.

She lowered her arm. How embarrassing. She would have Mama fix it this evening.

"Now hold out your arm and pretend you're ringing a Christmas bell."

The children did and Joey supplied the sound effects.

"Now pretend you're ice skating." The children glided around the room. Joey swatted anyone who came near.

She felt like giving up. Joey was too much of a distraction.

Obviously he had a long way to go in treating others as better than himself.

As did she.

-->=⊙ ⊙=<--

They were gone. Finally. Every coat had been buttoned, every hat tied, every mitten squeezed on, and every boot buckled.

Julia surveyed the room. Ugh. Scraps littered the floor from pasting Christmas pictures in scrapbooks. The toy shelves were a mess. The desks were sticky. Even her desk was cluttered.

She just wanted to go home and forget about school for the weekend.

She collapsed into her chair.

She had no right feeling discouraged after all God had done. Papa had come home at the end of August, and after several more months at home learning to walk again, he was back to work where he had been assigned to a desk job.

Richard was still a gardener at the Easterly House, tending the greenhouses during the winter. Mama was more cheerful. Jenny enjoyed socializing now that she wasn't tied down.

If only Joey weren't in her class. How could one little boy ruin her life?

She told funny anecdotes about Joey at home, but no one knew how he sucked the life out of her. And she wouldn't tell. She wanted them to think she was the perfect teacher.

"Knock, knock," came a voice at the door.

She knew who it was. Mr. Pratt stopped by every day.

Ever since the carnival where enough money had been raised to carry them comfortably through her father's hospitalization, Mr. Pratt had been friendly, but not obnoxious.

"Tough day?" he asked as he stepped in.

She nodded.

"Joey again?"

She nodded.

He sat on the edge of her desk. "I can hardly wait until he's in fourth grade."

"Maybe I'll have him whipped into shape by then."

"What did he do today?"

"The usual. Tattling, sassing, pinching, shoving, misbehaving."

"Send him up to me next time."

"Seriously? What would you do?"

"I'll show him who's boss. I'll strike fear into him. I'll threaten him with his very life."

She felt a glimmer of hope. "You would do that for me?"

He leaned closer and put his hand over hers. "I would do anything for you."

Oh, dear. She wiggled her hand out and stood. "I'd better clean up so I can go home and enjoy my weekend."

"Need help?"

"No, it won't take long, and I'm sure you have plenty to do in your own room."

"Do you have plans for the weekend?"

Oh, no. He was going to ask her out. Again.

"Yes, I'm going Christmas shopping tomorrow."

"So soon?"

"I like to do it well ahead of time."

"Need help?"

"No, with so many people to buy for, I don't want any distractions."

"So you think I'd be a distraction?" He winked.

Not a distraction. An annoyance.

"Yes. Now I need to clean up, if you don't mind."

He left, looking deflated again.

Since he had shown no further interest in spiritual things, she walked a tightrope, trying to be friendly but not encouraging. She hadn't succeeded today.

The door creaked open again. Mr. Pratt poked his head in.

She sighed.

"May I go to church with you Sunday?"

Her stomach clenched. Had he finally figured out that was the only place she would go with him?

She reluctantly gave him the name of the church and the time of the morning service.

"I'll see you then," he said.

Oh, dear.

-->==◉ ◉==<--

Saturday, December 5, 1908

Julia came down to breakfast wearing a black fitted jacket over a red plaid wool skirt.

Papa looked up from the morning paper. "You look pretty today. Going somewhere?"

"Christmas shopping downtown."

"Oh, can I go too?" Jenny asked.

Jenny tagging along would ruin her day.

"Take her," Mama said. "She deserves a fun day out."

She did. She had to stop thinking only of herself.

"Sure, Jenny can come. Can you be ready right after breakfast?"

Jenny's eyes sparkled as she nodded.

They caught the trolley on Park Avenue and were whisked the few blocks to downtown. They jumped off at Sibley's Department Store at the corner of East Main and North Clinton.

The streets were crowded with Christmas shoppers. They dodged horse-drawn buggies and wagons as they dashed across the street, their shoes wet from the dusting of overnight snow.

"Can we look in the windows?" Jenny said.

Julia didn't want to waste time looking at the window displays.

"If you're quick."

Jenny headed for the first twelve-foot plate glass window filled with a life-size Santa Claus and an assortment of expensive toys, including Steiff teddy bears, china dolls, and a pedal car. The awning overhead gave some protection from the wind but not the cold.

"Wouldn't Peter love that pedal car?" Jenny said.

He would. She could imagine Peter's giggles as he rode it down the sidewalk.

"Not for $4.39," Julia said.

"You make lots of money," Jenny said. "You can afford it."

"Hardly." If she spent that much on everyone, she would have nothing left.

Julia hurried Jenny along. With red noses and cold toes, they were ready for the warmth of the store.

They passed the Salvation Army bell-ringers as they pushed through the front door. The beautiful red, green, and gold garlands wrapping the giant first floor pillars took their breath away.

Jenny's eyes sparkled. Julia had never seen her so animated.

"Where do we start?" Jenny asked. .

"The Book-Hunter's Shop," Julia said.

"Why there?"

"I'm buying Papa a Bible for Christmas."

"He has a Bible."

"Have you seen it? The binding is cracked and the pages are falling out."

She didn't mind splurging on a really fine leather one. He deserved it after all he'd been through this year.

She bought one with leather as soft as butter. Papa would love it. She pictured him reading in his parlor chair in the glow of the lamplight, oblivious to the children playing at his feet. He would treasure her gift.

They spent considerable time in the jewelry department on the first floor. Jenny was enamored with a gold brooch with a sapphire-colored stone, similar to Julia's. Julia knew it would complement the blue in Jenny's eyes, so she bought it when Jenny's back was turned. She found a pocket watch for Richard who never knew the time when he was out in the greenhouses.

She bought Mama a Hotpoint electric iron, just like the one she used at Easterly's.

She found toys for the little ones in the magical toyland after enjoying the wonderful tunnel filled with Christmas scenes of Santa and his elves and children.

It was past noon when they finished.

"I'm hungry," Jenny said.

Perhaps she should treat Jenny to lunch.

"Let's go to the soda fountain," she said.

Jenny's eyes widened. "Really?"

"Sure. I have money left. It will be my treat."

"Can I have a malt? I've never had one before."

"Sure." She had never had one either. With six children, their family couldn't splurge on eating out.

They found seats at the marble counter. They both ordered grilled cheese sandwiches and chocolate malts.

Jenny couldn't stop smiling as they waited for their food to arrive.

"Thanks so much. I never dreamed we could eat here."

"You're welcome." Julia was equally excited.

"This was really fun today," Jenny said.

"It was, wasn't it? And it was more fun because you were along."

"Really?"

Julia nodded, realizing it was true. She was ashamed she hadn't included Jenny more often.

Being eight years older, she didn't have much in common with Jenny. But maybe now that Jenny was fifteen, she should bridge the gap between them.

"It's been a tough year with Papa's accident and us having to work so hard, hasn't it?" Julia said.

Jenny's eyes filled with tears. "It was the worst year of my life."

"Really? Why?"

"Mama expected me to do everything, and nothing satisfied her. I felt so useless."

"Are you kidding? You ran that house single-handedly for two weeks. I couldn't have done that. You did a great job."

Jenny looked skeptical.

"It's true. You were amazing. You're going to make a fine wife and mother some day."

Jenny was quiet. "What if I don't want to be a wife and mother? What if I want to go to college like you?"

"I think that's wonderful. What do you want to be?" Why had she never asked her before?

"A nurse."

"A nurse? I was never smart enough to study all that science."

"Do you think I could?"

"Absolutely."

"When I visited Papa in the hospital, I was impressed with how kind and helpful the nurses were. They made a difference for him. I want to help people too."

"That's wonderful. You know, don't you, that the Park Avenue Hospital has a training program for nurses? You could train right there."

"I know. I live close enough that I wouldn't have to board which would save money."

"I'm proud of you, Jenny. You'll make a great nurse, and hopefully a great mother someday too."

Jenny's eyes flashed confusion. "I can be both?"

"In different seasons of your life, yes."

"Do you want to get married?"

"Yes, when I find the right man."

"Has anyone ever asked you out?"

"Yes." She thought of Mr. Pratt.

"Why didn't you go out with him?"

"He wasn't what I was looking for."

"What are you looking for?"

"Someone like Papa. Someone who loves the Lord with all his heart. Someone who captures my heart. I haven't met anyone like that yet, so I will wait until I do."

"What if you're too fussy? What if no one out there is good enough for you?"

"Then you're stuck with me."

Jenny grinned. "That's not so bad."

Their sandwiches and malts arrived.

Julia smiled too. The time with Jenny was even better than the frosty malts.

⊶ ⊷

Sunday, December 6, 1908

Julia wondered if it was wrong to pray that Mr. Pratt wouldn't come to church. Wrong or not, she had been praying without ceasing.

She filed down the aisle with her family.

"Papa, can I sit on the end today?"

His eyebrows lifted. "Why, princess?"

She shrugged. "Just because." She should probably tell Papa about Mr. Pratt but was too embarrassed. Papa would wonder why she hadn't mentioned him before. He might also be disappointed in her choice of men.

If he did show up, she would have a lot of explaining to do.

She left a little space for him on the end. Good thing he was skinny.

As the pipe organ played, others found seats. She was afraid to turn around and look.

Then there he was, looming over her.

Her heart plummeted.

He looked uncomfortable.

"You came," she said.

His Adam's apple bobbed up and down.

"Have a seat."

He squeezed in. They were shoulder to shoulder, leg to leg. She smelled cigarette smoke on his coat.

Papa scooted down a little, and so did everyone else. She inched away so they weren't touching.

Papa leaned toward Mr. Pratt.

"Papa, this is Mr. Pratt. He teaches fourth grade at my school."

Papa shook his hand. "Pleased to meet you. I'm Julia's father. Welcome."

"Thank you."

Her brothers and sisters stared unabashedly.

Jenny's face was a question mark. What must Jenny think? Especially after her talk yesterday about wanting a man who loved the Lord, someone who captured her heart. *This isn't him,* she wanted to shout. She was glad Jenny was too far away to smell the cigarette smoke.

Little Annie shimmied off the pew and squeezed toward the aisle. She climbed onto Julia's lap. She flashed Mr. Pratt a dazzling smile.

His mustache twitched. He smiled and looked away.

Annie nestled against Julia and sucked her thumb.

"Honey, why don't you sit here beside me?" Julia patted the space next to Mr. Pratt.

Annie shook her black curls.

"Why not?"

Annie wrinkled her nose. "He stinks."

Oh, my. She hoped he hadn't heard.

His attention was on the impressive beamed ceiling and the gorgeous stained glass windows.

She prayed that by the time Pastor preached, he would feel comfortable enough to listen.

→⇒◎ ◎⇐←

Lee loved having the whole family together for Sunday dinner. His Bradshaw cousins surrounded the table, filling the house with noise and laughter and joy.

He plopped mashed potatoes onto his plate before passing the bowl to Julia. Next came the roast, the gravy, the creamed peas, and the homemade bread.

"So what's new?" his mother asked from one end of the table.

"Julia has a beau," Mary said. Beside her, cousin Pearl tittered.

Julia's face flamed. "I do not. He's just a teacher from school."

"I wondered who he was," Lee said. The man hadn't looked like someone Julia would have chosen. "How did he end up at our church?"

"He asked where I went."

He wasn't surprised. Obviously the man was smitten.

He wanted to steer the attention off Julia. "Uncle Alver, how are you feeling?"

"Not bad for an old man who fell off a bridge."

"And how's your job, Richard? Still working in the greenhouses?"

Richard nodded.

"What do they grow there?"

"Orchids, roses, carnations, chrysanthemums, sweet peas. Mr. Easterly likes fresh flowers throughout the house."

"Speaking of Mr. Easterly," his stepmother said, "Lee, tell them your exciting news."

Julia turned toward him. "What? You didn't tell me you had exciting news."

"It's not that exciting." In fact, he was more nervous than excited. "I received an invitation to Mr. Easterly's Christmas Eve party."

Julia squealed.

"Congratulations," Uncle Alver said. "You're coming up in the world."

"Everyone in my office received one."

"Where is it going to be?" Julia asked.

"At the Easterly House."

Julia gasped. "You're going *inside* the Easterly House?"

He nodded. That's what made him nervous. He had no idea how to act in a place like that.

"Oh, I wish I could go," Julia said.

"He can invite a guest," his mother said. "Why don't you take Julia?"

He wanted to take Miss Weston, but he hadn't talked with her in weeks, ever since the weather grew too cold to walk down by the river. Besides, he assumed she would be with Mr. Easterly.

No, he would never invite Miss Weston. Still, he had fantasized so much about her that he hadn't considered inviting anyone else.

Some of the office girls had hinted they needed an escort. That was another reason he wasn't excited about going. He didn't want to be around those girls more than necessary.

Julia latched onto his arm. "Oh, please, Lee, won't you take me? You know I desperately want to see inside."

He did know. He should have thought of her first.

"Sure, you can come." Besides, having beautiful Julia on his arm would discourage all those other girls. They didn't need to know she was his cousin.

Julia whooped and kissed his cheek. "Thank you!"

Everyone laughed.

His father said, "It looks as if you've made one girl very happy."

One girl, yes, but the wrong girl.

→→═◎ ◎═←←

Saturday, December 12, 1908

The kitchen was as white inside as the snowy landscape outside. Flour covered the pine worktable, the floor, the baker's cupboard, the children's aprons, even Annie's curls.

"Roll it nice and thin," Julia told Peter. "That's perfect, Mary. Here's the cookie cutter. Press straight down and up. Annie, don't rub your nose when your hands are floury."

She didn't have the patience for making gingerbread men with the children. But she had no choice.

Earlier in the week she and Jenny had gone shopping for her dress for Mr. Easterly's Christmas Eve party. Nothing in her price range was suitable, so she had come home with ten yards of royal blue satin and asked Mama to sew a gown for her.

Mama's eyes hardened. "You want me to sew with only fifteen days until Christmas? Who's going to do the Christmas baking? Who's going to buy the gifts? Who's going to decorate this house?"

"I will," Julia said.

That wasn't Mama's only complaint about the party.

"What about the Christmas Eve service, Julia?"

The Christmas Eve service was a family tradition. With a pine-scented decorated tree on the platform and candles flickering against stained glass windows, it was the prettiest service of the year.

Unfortunately, Richard was missing it too, much to Mama's dismay. The whole Easterly staff was needed at the Christmas Eve party. Richard would be serving.

She couldn't stop thinking about walking beyond the curtain. Would it be as beautiful as she dreamed? Probably more so, decorated for Christmas.

And this time she wouldn't be disobeying. Miss Donovan couldn't stop her.

She would feel like a princess in her royal blue gown. Probably everyone else would be wearing red or green or white. She wanted to stand out.

Why? She certainly didn't need to impress Lee. But she did want to impress Mr. Easterly with her beauty and elegance and sophistication. She had no intention of telling him she had been his laundress.

Who was she fooling? With all those people there, he would never notice her.

Actually, she would rather catch up with Katie and Rose and the girls than hobnob with people she didn't know. But was it appropriate for a guest to socialize with the help? Probably not.

Just for this one evening, she would be a guest and soak in memories for years to come.

Jenny stuck her hand in the coal-burning oven to test the temperature.

"Is it ready yet?" Julia asked.

"I'm counting."

After thirty-five seconds, Jenny said, "All set."

"And look, Mary has the first pan full. Good job, Mary." Julia swept it into the oven.

Mary beamed. "I like cooking."

"You'll be as good as Jenny some day."

"And as good as you?"

"You'll be better than me, honey. I haven't had much practice."

"It's your own fault," Jenny said.

"But you're so good at it. Why should I bother?" Julia teased.

"Because some day you'll be cooking for your own family," Jenny said.

"Are you going to marry Mr. Pratt?" Mary asked.

"No."

"Do you like him?"

"Only as a friend."

"Does he like you?"

"I suppose."

"Why don't you want to marry him?"

"He doesn't love Jesus."

"Oh." Mary pondered that as she nibbled a scrap of the gingerbread dough. "Good. I don't want you to leave."

Julia squeezed her. "Thanks, honey. I don't want to leave either."

But she didn't want to live here forever. She wanted to get married and have a houseful of her own children.

"Julia," Mama called, "can you try this on?"

"Coming." She couldn't wait to see her gown. Would it be as beautiful as she imagined? She hoped Mama wasn't hurrying just to finish it.

"Jenny, can you take over here? I'll be back soon."

She bounded up the walnut staircase into Mama's little sewing room. Royal blue satin was mounded everywhere.

"How's it coming?" Julia asked.

"Better than I thought. I need you to try on the skirt and the bodice."

Julia slipped off her dress and stood before the mirror in her chemise and petticoat. She lifted her arms as Mama slid the silky satin skirt over her head. It was a twenty-one gored skirt with a slightly rounded train that swept the floor. It hugged her slim hips perfectly.

"It fits, Mama."

"Try the bodice on."

With a rounded neckline, it was smooth and form-fitting, ending in a V at the waist. The sleeves were horizontal shirred tucks that created a puffed look above her elbow and ended in a smooth cuff at her wrist.

It was the most beautiful, elegant dress Julia had ever worn, and the color matched her blue eyes.

"My!" Mama said.

" It's gorgeous, Mama."

"No, you're gorgeous. Look at you. I never realized..."

Julia looked at herself in the mirror. She had always known she was pretty, but she had never looked this stunning.

"You need a silver pendant at the throat," Mama said. "And silver silk gloves and silver shoes."

How did plain and dowdy Mama know so much about fashion?

"See if Aunt Lillian has something you can borrow," Mama said.

She would stop over after church tomorrow.

"I need to put on the finishing touches," Mama said, "and then I'll let you hem it."

"Me?"

"Yes, you."

"But I don't know how to hem."

"Then it's high time you learned. What kind of a homemaker will you be if you don't know how to hem?"

What kind, indeed? It was a good thing she hadn't found her man yet.

⇢⟐ ⟐⇠

Monday, December 14, 1908

Snowflakes danced as Julia walked down the shoveled sidewalk toward school. Her breath puffed out white.

No doubt about it. It looked like Christmas with snowy lawns, holly wreaths on doors, and evergreen garlands on porch railings.

This time of year was magical. She hoped she could communicate not only the joy of the season to her class, but the true meaning of Christmas as well.

And this year, with the Easterly party to look forward to, the season was more joyous than usual.

She did a little skip and then looked around to determine if anyone had seen her.

The sidewalk was empty, thank goodness. It helped that she was earlier than usual. A farmer was delivering Christmas trees for their classrooms, and she wanted to have first choice.

Within minutes she was at school. No wagon was there yet. No other teachers either. She was first, all right.

As she stuffed her hands into her pockets and marched back and forth on the sidewalk to keep warm, a long green Packard chugged across Park Avenue and stopped at the corner house.

It looked oddly familiar.

The driver's door opened and out stepped a man in a long wool coat with a fur collar, gloves, and a top hat. She recognized Edgar Hopkins, Mr. Easterly's chauffeur.

What was he doing here on Barrington Street so early in the morning? She edged closer.

Edgar walked toward the door of a two-story addition behind the large house.

The door opened and out stepped a tall woman swathed in wool scarves.

"Good morning, Miss Weston." Edgar tipped his hat.

This was where Miss Weston lived?

Edgar swung open the back door of the Packard, and she slid inside. Someone else was in the back seat.

Julia stepped closer. The man had a neatly cropped beard and mustache.

She remembered someone saying Mr. Easterly picked up Miss Weston for work every morning. Apparently it was true.

She was glad Lee didn't see them so cozy in the back seat.

As the Packard chugged away from the curb, Mr. Easterly looked at her. She spun around and turned back toward the school, feeling guilty for spying. Fortunately, he wouldn't recognize her now. But in another week, after the party, he just might.

--->==◎ ◎==<---

It was her. The beautiful teacher.

David Easterly almost told Edgar to stop the car. But he didn't.

Instead, he watched her until they turned the corner.

"What's so interesting out that window?" Miss Weston said.

"Oh, nothing." He buried himself in the morning newspaper.

His ears felt hot. Good thing they were hidden by his hat.

--->==◎ ◎==<---

The Christmas tree wouldn't win a prize for beauty, but it didn't matter. The minute her class saw it, she couldn't curb their excitement. It had been bedlam all day.

The short-needled pine was fat, its unruly branches reaching out into the room. At her request, the janitor stood it several feet from the window with room to walk around.

All day they had made decorations, starting with red and green paper lanterns which filled up the tree quickly.

Stringing popcorn had been a disaster. She feared most of the popcorn had ended up in their tummies and the rest on the floor. But there were some sizable garlands on the tree, hung crookedly. Tomorrow they would make red and green paper chains.

With wreaths hanging in the four huge windows, Christmas had definitely come to Miss Bradshaw's kindergarten classroom.

"Class, I want every scrap of paper and piece of popcorn picked up and put in the trash. When you are done, come and stand with me around the tree."

They worked frenziedly with Joey pointing out all the pieces everyone else had missed, ignoring the mess under his own desk.

Julia watched silently. She was learning to pick her battles. She would clean up his desk herself once school was dismissed.

Finally they all gathered around.

"Hold hands and make a big circle around the tree," she said.

They scurried into place.

"Remember the song 'Here We Go Round the Mulberry Bush?' We're going to sing 'Here We Go Round the Christmas Tree.' Ready?"

With beaming faces, their little voices belted it out as they walked around clockwise.

Suddenly there was a commotion behind the tree. Children falling. Screams.

"What's going on?" she said.

More cries. Then the tree tipped forward.

She couldn't believe it. The tree was falling.

"Children, jump back!"

But they weren't quick enough. The tree crashed to the floor, pinning several underneath.

Children screamed. Others cried. Someone yelled, "Joey did it."

She had no doubt.

She had to get those children out. She saw three pairs of thrashing legs.

She tried to lift the top of the tree, but it was too heavy. She hurried to the first leg. It belonged to sweet little Katherine.

"Lawrence and John, get over here."

They ran over.

"When I lift this branch, grab Katherine's feet and pull her out. Understand?"

They nodded.

She grunted as she lifted the heavy branch just enough to slide her out.

Katherine sat up, sobbing. A long scratch marred her cameo face, but the skin wasn't broken.

Julia wanted to fold her in her arms and kiss her tears away, but two more children still needed rescuing.

"Lawrence and John, over here."

Quickly they pulled them out. They didn't appear to be hurt.

Everyone was wailing and crying. She didn't know whom to comfort first.

"Children, sit in your chairs, please."

No one listened.

One by one she gave hugs and guided them to their chairs. Finally order was restored.

The Christmas tree looked like a broken, dead giant lying across the floor.

"Tell me what happened," she asked the class.

"Joey pushed me into the tree," Charlie said.

No wonder the tree fell over. Charlie was heavy.

"I saw Joey do it," Lawrence called out.

No doubt.

How should she punish him this time? Standing in the corner no longer worked.

Lord, help!

She passed out white construction paper. "Children, I want you to draw a picture of a Christmas tree decorated with as many beautiful things as you can imagine. Joey, come with me."

Surprise, fear, and defiance flashed across his swarthy face as he followed her into the hall. She left the door open.

As she squatted in front of him, she almost gagged. He smelled as if he hadn't bathed in a long time.

"Joey, why did you do it?"

He looked down and shrugged.

"This is very serious. You scared and hurt a lot of children."

His stomach rumbled. She paused. It sounded like a hungry stomach.

"Joey, what did you have for lunch?" Joey went home for lunch every day.

He shrugged.

"Did you eat anything?"

He shook his head.

"Why not?"

"Nothin' to eat."

"What do you mean?"

"No food in the house."

"Doesn't your mother fix you something?"

"Mother's gone."

"Where?"

"She left awhile ago."

"Who do you live with?"

"My father, but he's not there much."

Julia pictured it. Joey going home to a cold, empty house with no food in the cupboards and no one to care for him.

No wonder Joey craved attention. This boy didn't need to stand in the corner. He needed love and nourishing food.

She wrapped her arms around him, holding her breath against the smell. "I'm so sorry, Joey. Listen, I have an apple in my desk. Let me get it for you. You can eat it out in the hall. Tomorrow I want you to come early to school. I will bring you some breakfast and lunch. How would you like that?"

He nodded.

She stepped into the room, thankful to see the other students quietly working on their pictures. She brought him the apple, and he wolfed it down.

Joey didn't cause trouble for the rest of the day. When she dismissed them, he actually smiled at her.

Thanks, Lord, for giving me insight. She hoped her troubles with Joey would be much improved.

Shortly after, Mr. Pratt stopped in. He gasped when he saw the tree spread across the floor. "What happened?"

"Joey did it."

"Why am I not surprised?"

"He pushed Charlie into the tree, and the whole thing toppled over. It was mass confusion."

"I can imagine."

"Would you help me lift it?"

"Certainly."

She was surprised at his strength. Between them, they righted the tree. The paper lanterns on one side were smashed. Crushed popcorn and pine needles littered the floor.

"Let me help clean this up," he said.

For once she didn't object.

They worked side-by-side sweeping and straightening. It was actually pleasant having him there.

"Thank you so much," she said when they finished.

"You're welcome. I love rescuing damsels in distress." He took her hand, bowed low, and kissed it.

She withdrew it behind her skirt and wiped it off.

"Julia, go out to dinner with me tonight."

Her mouth gaped.

"I won't keep you long, I promise."

Her usual excuses surfaced. It was Monday. She had tomorrow's lessons to prepare. But he looked so eager, so vulnerable. Would it really hurt to go out with him just this once? After all, he had been so helpful.

"All right."

He blinked rapidly.

She had rendered him speechless.

"All right then," he finally said.

"What time will you pick me up?"

"How's six o'clock?"

"Fine. I'll see you then."

He walked toward the door, but stopped and looked back with shining eyes. "Thanks, Julia."

She had made one man very happy.

-→=⊚ ⊚=←-

They took the streetcar to a little Italian restaurant downtown. It was cozy and dark with flickering candles and red-checked tablecloths. They ordered spaghetti and meatballs and warm, crusty bread.

"This is delicious," Julia said. "New for me. My mother is a more traditional meat and potato cook."

"Mine too. So we have something in common," Mr. Pratt said.

It was a start.

"Tell me about your family," she said.

"I come from a long line of teachers. My father is a teacher, and his father before him. My great-grandfather taught in a one-room schoolhouse in the country."

She chuckled. "So it's in your blood."

He nodded. "I love teaching. How about you? Why did you want to be a teacher?"

"I love children, and I wanted to make a difference in the world."

"Have you?"

"If you'd asked me yesterday, I would have said no. But I had a breakthrough with Joey today." She related the change in Joey's behavior after she gave him something to eat.

"Good for you. I hope it continues."

She found out that Mr. Pratt lived alone in an apartment on Park Avenue above a grocery. Every Friday night his married brothers and sisters gathered at the family home on Somerton for dinner. They seemed to be close-knit.

Julia was impressed. He was more family-oriented than she expected.

"So what did you think of our church?" she asked.

"Quite different from the church I grew up in. Not as formal. But I like it. I'll be back, if you don't mind."

Yes, she did mind.

"So tell me what you believe about God," she said.

He leaned back in his chair, loosening his collar. "That's a hard one."

If he were a Christian, it would not have been hard to answer. She waited patiently.

"I believe God created the world but has pretty much left it alone since then. How about you?"

"I believe God loves me personally and is intricately involved in my life, leading me and guiding me."

His eyebrows lifted. "He guides you? How?"

"Mostly through His Word, the Bible."

"Really? You read it then?"

"Every day."

"How do you find time?"

"In the morning before school. It's what encourages me and gives me strength for the day."

"With Joey in your class, you certainly need it."

And so do you, she wanted to say.

→━◎ ◎━←

"Thanks so much for a wonderful dinner," Julia said as Mr. Pratt stood on her porch.

He twisted his hat in his hands. He looked expectant. What did he want?

Not a kiss, she hoped.

Just go home, she wanted to say. She was tired. She had much to do before tomorrow.

"Thank *you*," he said.

"I'll see you tomorrow then," she said as she opened the door.

He stepped off the porch and turned to wave before disappearing into the darkness.

As she opened the front door, she was assailed by her family.

Peter hugged her knees. "You're home!"

"Did you have a nice time?" Papa asked.

"Yes, we ate at an Italian restaurant downtown. I had spaghetti and meatballs. It was delicious."

"What did it taste like?" Mary asked.

"Tomatoey. Spicy. I liked it. Mama, we should try it sometime."

Mama pursed her lips.

"How was Mr. Pratt?" Jenny said.

"Nice enough, but I found out one thing. He's not a Christian."

"I thought you already knew that."

"Now I know for certain."

"Why did you go out with him if he isn't a Christian?" Mary said.

"I don't know. He has been so helpful at school."

"So you won't go out with him again?" Jenny said.

"No."

"But do you like him?" Mary asked.

"Come on, children. Don't pester your sister. Time for bed," Papa said.

"But I want to know. Julia, do you like him?" Mary said.

"At the beginning I didn't, but he has become a friend."

"If he were a Christian would you go out with him again?" Jenny asked.

Julia shrugged, glad she didn't have to decide that right now.

Chapter 14

Thursday, Christmas Eve, 1908

LEE STOMPED THE snow off his boots as he climbed the Bradshaw's front porch steps. Jenny answered his knock.

"Hi, Jenny. Is Julia ready?"

Jenny, dressed in a white dress with a red sash for the Christmas Eve service, nodded. "Wait'll you see her."

As Lee stepped into the foyer, he inhaled the smell of pine and wood fire coming from the parlor.

"Lee's here," Jenny yelled. The three little ones rushed out to hug his legs.

"How's everyone?" he asked. "Excited for Christmas?"

They nodded vigorously.

Uncle Alver stepped out from the parlor. "Good to see you, Lee. Exciting night ahead."

Lee nodded as he shook his hand. He was more nervous than excited.

He was nervous about using the proper etiquette. He was nervous about knowing how to converse. Most of all, he feared being disappointed. He yearned for a few moments alone with Miss Weston, but he doubted that would happen. She would likely be beside Mr. Easterly all evening. At least he would have the pleasure of seeing her looking like a queen.

"Well, Julia is certainly excited. I've never seen her like this. She's absolutely giddy," her father said.

Lee hoped she wouldn't be disappointed either. She likely wouldn't see as much of the house as she wanted to.

Jenny yelled up the stairs again, "Julia, Lee's here."

"I'm coming," Julia called down.

Satin swished before she appeared on the walnut staircase. He stared. She was breathtaking in a royal blue gown. His mother's silver pendant hung around her neck, and silver shoes peeked out beneath her hem. Her hair was swept up into a pompadour.

When she reached the bottom, she twirled. "What do you think?"

"You'll be the most beautiful woman there."

She glowed.

Her mother followed down the stairs. "Get your coat and boots. You don't want to make Lee late."

Uncle Alver reached into the coat closet behind the stairs and withdrew a white wool cape with a fur-trimmed hood. He draped it around Julia's shoulders. "You sure that's warm enough, princess?"

Her eyes shone. "I don't care if I'm cold. I just want to look good. Where's my muff?"

Mary handed her the muff.

"Don't forget your boots," her mother said.

Julia sat on the chair, slipped the dainty silver shoes into her bag, and thrust her feet into the warm, serviceable boots. "I wish I didn't need these. They're ugly."

As she buttoned them, Lee said, "You'll be glad for them. It's deep out there."

Finally she was ready. It had taken far longer than he anticipated.

"Good-bye, everyone," she said. "The next time I see you, it will be Christmas."

The little ones squealed.

"Have a wonderful time." Papa kissed her cheek.

After hugs and kisses from everyone, she gathered her trailing skirt over her arm, and they were off.

"Look at it out here," Julia said. "It's beautiful."

The street lights illuminated a fairyland of pudgy puffs of snow on every fence and tree branch. All day it had snowed. It had stopped now, but the roads weren't well plowed. Nor were the sidewalks.

"Beautiful but deep," Lee said. "Walking won't be easy." He wished he had a sleigh or an automobile so she could arrive in style.

The snow came above their ankles. He had tucked his suit pants into his boots so they wouldn't get wet. He wondered how long she could hold up her skirts.

The snow didn't seem to bother Julia. She fairly danced down the sidewalk.

"This is the most exciting night of my life," she said. "A dream come true. Can you believe I'm actually going inside the Easterly House? I'll stand in that room with the ferns, and Miss Donovan can't kick me out. Thank you, thank you, thank you for inviting me."

"You're welcome."

He wished she would stop chattering. He needed quiet time to calm himself.

They passed the Frances Parker School. At the end of the block, she stopped. "See that house?" She pointed to the corner house.

"Yes."

"You'll never guess who lives there."

"Come on, we don't have time for guessing games. Who?"

"Grace Weston."

His heart leaped. "How do you know?"

"I saw Mr. Easterly pick her up in his fancy Packard."

Grace Weston lived here? So close?

"She lives in the back end. She came out that door." She pointed.

The house was clapboard, a sprawling three stories high. At the front was a raised porch with white columns and a spindled railing. A bay window separated it from a back addition where Miss Weston's door was on the ground level with what looked like inside steps to a second-story apartment. Beside it, brick steps led up to a first-floor apartment.

"It's all dark," he said as he looked up. Curtains were drawn across a large window.

"She's already at the party, don't you think?"

She was, no doubt, at Mr. Easterly's side, greeting the guests. He suddenly couldn't wait to see her.

He took Julia's arm. "Come on."

He couldn't believe Grace Weston lived so close, close enough that he could stop by any time. Not that he would.

But he would be walking by often, hoping for just a glimpse.

--->=⊙ ⊙=<---

As they crossed slushy East Avenue, the Easterly House shone like a jewel through the frosty winter night. Japanese lanterns festooned the little iron balcony above the front door. Tiny white lights circled the four soaring Corinthian columns on the front porch. Julia caught glimpses of drapes and gleaming tables and fireplaces behind the evergreen wreaths in every lit window.

Her heart fluttered. She could hardly wait.

A steady stream of horse-drawn carriages, sleighs, cabs, and automobiles turned into the driveway.

Self-consciously, Julia continued up the driveway while people stared from the waiting carriages. She felt like a servant instead of a guest, looked down on once again.

"Are we the only ones who walked?" she said.

"I'm sorry. I should have rented a cab."

"It doesn't matter. We live so close."

But it did matter. Tonight she wanted to feel like a princess.

She lifted her chin and breezed past the carriages. They might not have arrived in style, but she would be the first inside. So there.

Edgar Hopkins, in his fur-trimmed coat and top hat, directed traffic to the porte-cochère entrance.

No! She wanted to enter the front door, not the servant's entrance.

"Lee, let's go in the front door."

"I don't think we're supposed to."

"Let's try anyway."

They veered to the right down the circular driveway.

"Stop!" Edgar yelled.

They halted.

"I knew this was a bad idea," Lee whispered. 'Now maybe they won't let us in at all."

"Leave it to me. I know Edgar."

They turned around as Edgar ran up to them. "Everyone is to use the porte-cochère entrance tonight," he said.

"Mr. Hopkins, it's me, Julia Bradshaw."

He looked blank.

"You know. I was a laundress here last summer."

He peered at her in the dim light from the windows. Recognition dawned.

"My cousin, Lee Bradshaw and I are guests tonight, and I have always wanted to enter by the front door. Please can't you make an exception for me?"

"Sorry, Miss Bradshaw. All the guests are entering the side door, going upstairs to the dressing rooms, and then descending the stairs to greet Mr. Easterly. I can't make an exception. It would cause confusion and consternation on the part of Mr. Easterly."

So she would be meeting Mr. Easterly after all. It might be worth following protocol.

"Thanks, Edgar."

He led them back where they climbed the porte-cochère steps. Another man opened the door. They stepped into the narrow well-lit marble hall.

The blue velvet curtain was wide open.

Tall butler Solomon Merritt motioned them upstairs.

She didn't want to go upstairs. She wanted to walk through that curtain.

"Can't we go that way?" she asked Solomon.

He didn't recognize her. "The coat rooms are upstairs, ma'am."

She *did* need some place to hang her cape. She would follow the crowd upstairs.

She glanced into Miss Donovan's office. It was empty. Where was she?

She suddenly didn't feel so confident. Could Miss Donovan even yet drag her out by the ear? Or make some humiliating scene?

Hopefully Miss Donovan wouldn't recognize her either.

She shook off her fur-trimmed hood and climbed the narrow burgundy-carpeted staircase. Lee followed. She ran her finger along the satin-smooth creamy paneled wall.

"Don't touch anything," he whispered.

She just couldn't help it.

At the top of the stairs a wide carpeted hallway looked down into the conservatory milling with guests among the ferns and abundant flowers. She wanted to absorb it all, but a footman motioned them to the right. "The dressing rooms are this way."

Straight ahead was a staircase to the third floor. Beyond was the ladies' dressing room.

"I'll be right back," she told Lee.

The room was crowded with other women removing their coats and boots.

She spotted Katie. "Katie," she squealed.

Katie, in her long white uniform and white shoes, still looked like a little girl. Her hazel eyes stared at Julia without recognition.

"It's me, Julia Bradshaw."

Katie's hand covered her mouth. "Julia?"

Julia flung her arms around her. "It's so good to see you again."

"What are you doing here?" Katie asked.

"My cousin Lee is an accountant for Mr. Easterly. He invited me."

Katie smiled. "Look at you. You're beautiful."

Julia felt beautiful. "How are you, Katie?"

"Fine. I was promoted to second floor maid after Bridget left."

"I'm so happy for you. Where's Rose?"

"She's somewhere with Miss Donovan."

Julia shivered. "Where *is* Miss Donovan?"

"Who knows? Just don't let her see you. She still complains about you."

"So she hasn't forgotten me?"

"Oh, no."

"I think Edgar Hopkins and Solomon Merritt forgot. They didn't recognize me."

"It's no wonder. I didn't recognize you myself. Look at you. You look like a fine lady. I hear you have a beau now."

Julia wrinkled her brow. "Who told you that?"

"Richard. We eat lunch together every day."

How interesting. Richard hadn't mentioned that.

"He's not a beau. Just someone I teach with, so don't get excited. I wish we had more time to talk, but I'd better get out there. Lee will wonder what happened to me."

"I miss you," Katie said.

"I miss you too." Katie had been a friend she admired and respected. She joined Lee at the top of the stairs.

"What took so long?" he asked.

"I was talking with Katie."

"Ready?" He seemed unusually nervous.

As they waited, a footman released one couple at a time down the stairs.

"Mr. Easterly is greeting at the bottom," Lee said.

Her stomach fluttered. She had dreamed of meeting him. Now she wasn't sure she wanted to. Whatever would she say?

"You may go now," the footman directed.

Below, two gorgeous staircases converged on the landing into one wide burgundy-carpeted staircase into the foyer.

Lee held out his arm for her. On the landing she had an unobstructed view of the conservatory behind. Windows covered one wall and the ceiling. Directly beneath, the organ was partially concealed by greenery and poinsettias. Enormous palms and ferns edged the room. Guests mingled. Cigarette smoke and strains of string music drifted up.

Lee tugged her arm. She turned and descended the wide staircase strung with tiny twinkling lights.

Mr. Easterly and a statuesque Miss Weston, in a champagne-colored gown, greeted the guests in the vast white marble foyer.

Straight ahead was the mahogany front door with narrow leaded-glass windows on either side. It was flanked by two tall electric candelabras and two recessed burgundy window seats. A grandfather clock donged the hour.

"Julia, pay attention," Lee said. "Mr. Easterly is looking at you."

She looked below. Warm gray-blue eyes were fastened upon her, one side of his mouth in a quizzical smile. His dark beard and mustache were neatly trimmed, his hairline slightly receding. He was several inches taller than Miss Weston, but his broad shoulders made him seem taller.

She had wondered what it would be like to meet him as a respected schoolteacher and not a laundress. She was about to find out.

->==@ @==<-

From the moment he'd entered the mansion, Lee had looked for Grace Weston. He suspected she was with Mr. Easterly. He'd been right.

She looked like a Greek goddess in her flowing gown trimmed with gold and silver braid. He wanted to bow down and worship her.

Immediately he was ashamed. *Lord, I didn't mean that. You are the only one I worship. Forgive me. Help me get my emotions under control.*

She looked up as he descended. Their eyes locked. Something flashed between them.

She looked impressed. Interested.

Or was it just his imagination?

Perhaps tonight he would be bold enough to find out.

->==@ @==<-

Was that *her*? David's heart raced. He wasn't sure, but it looked like the beautiful teacher. What was she doing here? In his house?

Up close she was even more stunning. Her gorgeous eyes were the same color as her gown. She was slender and graceful and utterly charming.

Miss Weston whispered, "Lee Bradshaw, accounting department."

Was this Lee Bradshaw's wife? Sweetheart? Such a good-looking man deserved this beauty. He felt an ache inside, as if he had lost something precious.

He extended his hand. "Welcome, Mr. Bradshaw. I'm so glad you've come."

Lee Bradshaw's solid grip matched his own.

Then he looked into her dazzling blue eyes.

"And this is...?"

"My cousin, Julia Bradshaw."

His cousin? He was flooded with relief.

He captured her gloved hand. "Miss Bradshaw, it is such a pleasure to meet you."

Was that a tremor in his voice? What was wrong with him?

"It's a pleasure to be here, a dream come true."

"Oh?"

"I live a few blocks away on Barrington, and when your house was being built, I tried to imagine what it would look like inside." Her eyes scanned the room. "It has exceeded my expectations."

"Would you like to see the rest of the house?"

Her eyes glowed. "Could I?"

"I would very much like to see your first impressions."

"Really?"

He had surprised her. He had surprised himself. With a houseful of guests, when could he slip away? But he would. Nothing was more important.

"Tell you what. I'll give you a private tour during the concert after dinner."

"Thank you very much, sir."

"I assure you, the pleasure is all mine, Miss Bradshaw."

-->══◉ ◉══<--

Julia was stunned. A private tour? Unbelievable.

How much would he show her? Just this floor? The second floor too? Or even the third floor? She wanted to see it all. Would it be inappropriate to suggest it?

Or maybe it was all inappropriate. Maybe she shouldn't go on the tour at all. What would Mama think of her being alone with Mr. Easterly? What would Lee think? She would ask him.

She tugged Lee's arm. "Ready?"

He was leaning close to Miss Weston, listening to her every word. She hated to drag him away, but many more were waiting to be greeted.

"Perhaps I'll see you later," Miss Weston said to him.

Julia felt the thrill go up his arm.

They stepped past the staircase and the marble pillars into the long, wide hallway edging the conservatory. On the left was the blue velvet curtain to the porte-cochère entrance.

She was officially beyond the curtain.

She closed her eyes and savored the moment.

They stepped into the crowded conservatory. Footmen circulated with trays of wine. The chatter almost drowned out the Christmas carols from the stringed quartet.

"Did you hear what Mr. Easterly said?" she asked Lee.

"No, I was talking with Miss Weston." He looked flushed.

"Mr. Easterly is giving me a private tour after dinner."

Lee raised his eyebrows. "Why would he do that?"

"I don't know. Do you think it's all right?"

He shrugged. "Why not? Sounds as if God is giving you the desires of your heart."

Why not, indeed? This would truly be a night to remember.

Julia was too excited to mingle.

She crossed the room and dropped onto a window seat. She looked up. The conservatory was like an elegant two-story hotel courtyard with balconies on two sides. The ceiling was coffered with white beams and skylights. At her back were floor-to-ceiling windows framed by long green drapes. No wonder so much light shone in on a sunny day. What a wonderful place for Mr. Easterly to eat breakfast.

The inlaid green and white marble floors were partially covered by an Oriental rug. Lush exotic plants made it feel tropical. Poinsettias added a holiday touch.

She wished the room wasn't so crowded. It was impossible to see everything.

Then she spotted her. Miss Donovan. She walked beside Solomon Merritt, her back ramrod-straight, her head held high, white bun gleaming in the glow of the many lights.

Miss Donovan did not look her way but walked toward a wide, blue-curtained doorway where a table was set with little cards.

Any minute Miss Donovan might see her. She closed her eyes, looked down at her lap, and shielded her face with her hand.

Miss Donovan vigorously rang a bell to quiet the guests.

Solomon announced in his deep voice, "Dinner is served. You may pick up your table assignments here."

She would have to pass Miss Donovan. It wasn't worth the risk. She needed to leave now.

Oh, but her tour. She couldn't leave.

Lord, make me invisible, please!

She found Lee talking with a middle-aged gentleman with glasses.

"Julia, I'd like you to meet my boss, Mr. Crosby, and his wife."

With her back toward Miss Donovan, she smiled and shook their hands.

"Shall we go in?" Mr. Crosby said.

"I hope we're at the same table," Lee said.

After the Crosbys left, Julia held Lee back. "Miss Donovan's here. Don't let her see me."

"Where?"

"The white-haired lady passing out table assignments. What shall I do?"

"She won't recognize you."

"Yes, she will. She'll throw me out."

"Don't be so paranoid. I'm sure she's forgotten you."

"Not according to Katie."

"She won't recognize you dressed like that."

Yes, she would. Miss Donovan didn't miss anything.

"Hide me."

"Don't be ridiculous."

"I'm serious. Let me walk right behind you." They inched toward the dining room, Julia's face hidden by Lee's broad shoulders. Only the top of her hair was visible, and surely Miss Donovan wouldn't recognize that.

When they reached the table, as Lee searched for their place cards, Julia averted her face and scooted into the next room. Miss Donovan did not notice her.

Safe. For now.

She was in the dining room. High-backed blue leather chairs surrounded an enormous table covered with a white damask tablecloth she had probably once ironed. The centerpiece was red roses, orchids, lilies of the valley, and maiden-hair ferns. At each place setting were smaller matching bouquets. The china gleamed, the silver and crystal sparkled. Over the table hung a chandelier of blue shirred silk rimmed with silver and blue fringe.

A fire blazed in a white marble fireplace. The andirons, fireplace tools, and sconces on the mantel were silver.

The walls were a whitish-gray, the ceiling plastered with medallions and scrollwork. A blue and rose Persian rug partially covered the parquet floor.

The beauty was too much to absorb.

Round tables filled a bay window. More tables circled the room. Each had a number.

When Lee joined her, she asked, "Which number are we?"

"Ten."

They weren't in this room. They passed through another door into a long latticed corridor whose walls and ceiling were covered with English ivy and white lights. A wall of paned windows looked onto a snowy garden lit with more white lights. It looked like a fairyland.

The corridor was lined with tables. So many tablecloths. Even more napkins. She felt sorry for the laundress.

At number ten, Lee shook hands with others from the accounting department, including Mr. and Mrs. Crosby. He introduced her simply as "Julia," not as his cousin. When she saw all the single women, she understood why. Let them think she was his sweetheart.

At her place was an orchid surrounded by rose buds, grown no doubt in Richard's greenhouses. She had never had an orchid before.

In the candlelight, she read the gilded menu card near her plate. Nine courses? That would take forever. Would there even be time for her tour?

Staff wearing black tuxedos entered carrying silver trays. She spotted her brother Richard. He looked self-conscious and awkward. No wonder. This was much harder than tending plants. She prayed he would do well. He caught her eye but didn't smile.

She recognized the other servers. Henry Wilder, the middle-aged carpenter, looked clumsy and bumbling. And there was Arthur Poole, the head gardener, and William McKay, the valet, and Alan Pierce, the handsome painter.

Alan approached their table. Oh, no. Was Alan their server? She cringed. Would he recognize her? Embarrass her?

He flashed a smile. "Good evening, ladies and gentlemen. I have some caviar and vodka for your first course."

He served without noticing her.

He placed before her a pile of black slimy balls in a glass bowl on ice.

"What is it?" she whispered to Lee.

"Caviar. Fish eggs."

She gagged. "I can't eat this."

"Don't make a scene."

"I won't eat it. Nor can I drink the vodka."

"I know. Neither can I."

Alan watched from the shadows. Julia knew the moment he recognized her. His eyes widened, and he looked again. A smile crept across his face. Then he winked. Julia quickly averted her eyes, heat creeping into her face.

She needed a diversion. Someone to talk to. But Lee was deep in conversation with Mr. Crosby. Well, then, she needed to eat something, but she couldn't eat the caviar or vodka. Instead she moved the caviar around with her spoon, making herself sick just looking at it.

When Alan cleared the table, he whispered in her ear, "Well, well. Never expected to see you here. You look ravishing."

Although no one else heard, her heart nearly thumped out of her chest. Ravishing? That sounded... indecent.

During the next course of clear bouillon, marrow balls, hearts of celery, and cheese straws, he never took his eyes off her.

As he served the third course, his arm purposefully brushed hers. She recoiled and nearly had the Halibut Timbals with Truffle Sauce in her lap.

Why, oh why, were there so many courses? She was ready to be done with Alan's flirting. She wanted her tour now.

She ignored him during the Breaded Sweetbreads with Peas. He rested his hand on her shoulder as he placed the plate of Tenderloin of Beef with Mushrooms, lima beans, and Parisian Potatoes in front of her.

Her chest heaved. How dare he? She shook him off.

That was a mistake.

"Do you know him?" Mrs. Crosby asked from across the table after he left.

Everyone looked at her.

"He's a friend of my brother's." She didn't add that her brother was serving one table over or that she had once been a laundress here.

As they ate, Lee whispered, "What's going on?"

"Our waiter is bothering me. He's someone I tried to avoid when I worked here."

"I'll take care of it."

Lee protectively draped his arm around her shoulder when Alan served the Partridges with Bread Sauce and the lettuce salad. Alan took the hint.

She was too full to eat much of the pumpkin pie and Nesselrode pudding.

Finally they finished. Surely now she could escape and have her tour. She hoped Mr. Easterly hadn't forgotten.

But now the thought of having a private tour seemed preposterous. Maybe she had only imagined it.

Alan cleared their plates. "When you're ready, please adjourn to the conservatory for the concert."

Her heart raced. Mr. Easterly had said he would give her the tour during the concert.

"Let's go, Lee."

They exited the garden-like room and stepped up into the dining room. Mr. Easterly stood by the conservatory door, greeting guests.

As she approached, he said, "There you are, Miss Bradshaw. Ready for your tour?"

He remembered!

"Mr. Bradshaw, I wonder if you would do me a favor," he said. "Would you mind keeping Miss Weston company while I steal your cousin away?"

Lee's face turned scarlet. "It would be my pleasure, sir."

"She's in the conservatory saving a seat for you."

The conservatory was now set with folding chairs facing the organ. As Lee strode away, Julia prayed, *Bless him with a wonderful evening. Me too.*

→►═◉ ◉═◄←

David had been impatient for dinner to end. He couldn't stop thinking about the beautiful, tenderhearted schoolteacher with the striking eyes. He could hardly believe she was under his roof.

When was the last time a woman had affected him so? Never. He had become callous to their charms and flirtations. He didn't need a woman. His business and home were more than enough. Why, then, were his palms sweating and his heart racing?

"We'll start the tour here," he said. "Tell me what you think of my dining room."

She looked at the table which had been cleared except for the centerpiece and some crumbs.

"It's beautiful. I can just picture my little brothers and sisters and cousins sitting here for Christmas dinner. We wouldn't even need extra tables."

He had expected her to comment on the sterling silver sconces, the grand mahogany furniture, the priceless Oriental rug.

Children? Here? What would this room be like echoing with children's voices? Not good. He would worry about an expensive bowl being broken or spills on the tablecloth.

On the other hand, he wistfully imagined family around the table. Tomorrow it would sit empty for Christmas.

"I need to say a few words to my guests before the concert begins," he said. "Wait in the hallway by the large painting of General McDowell, and we'll continue the tour."

"All right."

"See you in a few minutes, then."

Perhaps this tour was not a good idea. If her impressions of the first room had shaken him, what other surprises would she have?

→>═◉ ◉═<←

As Lee looked for Grace Weston, his stomach knotted. God had answered prayer. He would have time alone with her. How amazing was that? Now he needed to trust God to keep him from being so nervous.

He spotted her in the front row studying her program.

Self-consciously he strode toward her. He imagined every eye watching him slip into the empty chair beside her.

"Mr. Easterly said you were saving this for me."

Her face lit up. "I am. He hated leaving me unattended while he gave your cousin a tour. I hope you don't mind."

"It's my pleasure."

She handed him the program. "Looks like some good music tonight, a string ensemble. I'm in the mood for some Christmas music."

"Me, too. I need something to make it feel like Christmas Eve. I'm missing our candlelit service at church."

"I tried to talk Mr. Easterly out of having it tonight, but he insisted. I suspect others have family traditions too."

"Maybe next year."

"What are your Christmas plans?" she asked.

"We always go to my aunt and uncle's for dinner. Lots of people and food and Christmas cheer. How about you?"

"I'll be alone. I think I told you my family is gone. My parents died when I was young, and I was raised by an aunt. She's gone now too."

"You won't get together with Mr. Easterly?"

"Oh, no. We don't usually socialize outside of work."

Now that was good news.

But no one should have to be alone for Christmas.

⇥═◉ ◉═⇤

Julia settled into the blue damask high-backed chair in front of the large painting of the red-uniformed soldier. She felt like a queen on a throne.

Oh, the stories she would tell at Christmas dinner tomorrow.

Her view was straight down the vast, marble, columned hallway. Guests' voices buzzed in the conservatory, but she couldn't see them through the greenery.

The voices quieted as Mr. Easterly spoke. "Welcome and thank you for coming. I want you to know how much I appreciate your dedication to the Rochester Optical Company. Each of you is necessary for the success of our company, and I value you." Everyone applauded. "Tonight we welcome the Herman Dossenbach Quintet. I hope you enjoy it."

Suddenly Miss Donovan stormed through the curtain full speed and turned in the opposite direction toward the dining room.

Julia barely had time to react. She jumped up and ran to the nearest open door, a bathroom. She closed the door and leaned against it, her heart racing. Oh, my, that was close. What if Miss Donovan had turned in her direction instead?

She couldn't stop shaking. Miss Donovan could have grabbed her ear and thrown her out, and once again she would have missed seeing the house.

And what would Mr. Easterly have thought when she wasn't there?

She faced the room as she waited for her heart to still. It was the fanciest bathroom she had ever seen with polished oak paneling, a marble floor, marble sink, and silver towel racks. She peeked through another door to the toilet.

But what was that? It wasn't like any toilet she had ever seen.

Then it dawned on her. She was in the men's bathroom.

Oh, dear!

She heard footsteps. Mr. Easterly's or Miss Donovan's?

She poked her head out. Mr. Easterly stood by the blue damask chair, looking in all directions.

Goodness gracious.

She sheepishly slid out.

"There you are," he said. "What were you doing in *there?*"

"My mistake. I didn't realize it was the men's room."

His eyes twinkled. She imagined he was trying not to laugh out loud.

She was mortified. She should go home now before she embarrassed herself further.

"No harm done. Let's begin. Come through this portière."

She followed him through a burgundy velvet curtain with gold fringe. So that's what those curtains were called.

"Welcome to my billiard room," he said.

It was a spacious, wood-paneled, masculine room. At this end, three shirred and fringed burgundy silk lamps hung over a billiard table. Tufted sofas and comfortable chairs clustered before a fire crackling in the fireplace. Velvet burgundy drapes hung at every window.

"It's beautiful. What do you use this room for?"

"I relax here, listen to the gramophone, make phone calls."

A black candlestick telephone was on an end table.

Wouldn't her brothers and sisters love it here? Room for everyone to spread out. Why, both their parlor and dining room would fit into this one room.

"I often bring guests in before dinner for billiards. Care to play?" he said.

"Oh, no. I don't know how."

"I'll have to teach you some day."

Some day? Would he invite her back? Certainly not. All she expected was one tour of the house.

"Do you like to read?" he asked.

"I love to."

"Then you'll enjoy this next room. Come."

It was a snug green library with three walls of floor-to-ceiling books. Two wing chairs faced a roaring coal fire in a small white marble fireplace.

The coziness was irresistible. She dropped into a chair and held her hands out to the flame. He sat in the chair beside her.

She closed her eyes and inhaled the pleasant mustiness of the books. "I could stay here forever."

"Please do. You look as if you belong."

Her eyes popped open.

Whatever did that mean?

⇥═ ═⇤

What was wrong with him, saying such things? David watched her freeze up and knew he had transgressed.

But what if she did belong? To him?

He would have a home. A real home. With love. Imagine spending evenings side-by-side before this cozy fire. No more late nights at the office.

On the other hand, he would lose his peace and quiet. Women chattered, didn't they? Could he tolerate it?

Maybe, though, it would be nice to talk with someone.

She looked ready to bolt. He had to put her at ease again.

"Do you read much?" he asked.

"Whenever I can. I'm a kindergarten teacher and busy preparing lessons. I wish I had more time."

So she taught kindergarten. He flashed back to when he had first seen her hugging that little boy, oozing kindness and love.

"What do *you* read?" she asked. She leaned back against the chair.

"Biographies, westerns, mysteries, classics, self-improvement books. I also subscribe to the *London Times*, several New York papers, and five Rochester papers."

She looked impressed, as he intended.

"How do you find time to read them all?" she asked.

"Over breakfast and dinner."

"You must eat alone then."

"I usually do, yes."

"Don't you get lonely?"

His breath stopped for a moment. That was a mighty personal question, far beyond the boundaries of a first-time acquaintance. "I beg your pardon?"

A flush crept across her cheeks. "Forgive me. I was just thinking of myself. I would feel lonely if I lived in this huge house by myself."

Dare he tell the truth? Suddenly he wanted to.

"Well, Miss Bradshaw, since you are the only one who has cared enough to ask, yes, I'm lonely. Ever since my mother died two years ago, sometimes I work until three in the morning just so I don't have to come home to an empty house."

He'd never shared that with anyone. Or admitted it to himself.

But it was true. How often had he wished for some human connection apart from work? Someone who would take the time to penetrate his crusty shell and truly know him.

He felt the first layer of that shell peel back.

"In a way I envy you. Sometimes I wish for some time alone," she said. "I live in a small house with my parents and five brothers and sisters. I have little time to myself. I crave peace and quiet. I have to keep reminding myself that people are more important than my agenda."

He was stunned. In one sentence he had learned her essence. People were important. Not things or accomplishments.

Exactly the opposite from him.

⇥⟫ ⟪⇤

Julia was no longer intimidated by him. Instead she felt a connection, as if she had glimpsed into his soul.

She liked him.

How odd. She had been obsessed with his house. Now she wanted to know more about him.

"Can I coax you away from the fire to show you another room?" he asked.

"Of course."

She followed him across the marble entrance hall and through another portière.

"Welcome to my living room," he said.

Under a center crystal chandelier was an enormous round mahogany table with a centerpiece of fresh flowers. At the far end was a green-and-white marble fireplace beside a grand piano. The walls were green silk damask with white wainscoting. The drapes and rug were also green. Two walls of bookcases edged a reading table and chairs. Large sofas and easy chairs were artfully scattered. A desk in a bay window overlooked the lit garden.

Julia moved closer. "This is beautiful. So big."

"Thirty-five by forty-two feet."

"You know what I love about it? Even though it's big, it's homey. In fact, your whole house feels homey."

A smile spread across his face. "It pleases me to hear you say that. Most people comment about the priceless paintings or the plaster ceiling medallions, or the Steinway grand piano. You are different, Miss Bradshaw. I love seeing my home through your eyes."

"These are very plain, ordinary eyes, Mr. Easterly. I don't know enough about artwork or pianos to appreciate what you have here. I just know I like it, and it is more beautiful than I imagined."

"Believe me, there is nothing plain and ordinary about your eyes. They are the most beautiful and captivating eyes I have ever seen."

Her cheeks heated. My! She hadn't expected that.

He looked at his watch. "It's later than I expected."

Oh, dear. Was her tour over?

"I'd like to show you more, but first I must give a change of plans to my housekeeper." He pressed a wall buzzer.

His housekeeper? That was Miss Donovan. Was she coming here?

She had to hide. Her eyes darted around the room. Where?

"Let me show you this picture of my mother," he said.

The large picture was over the bookcases between two doors, both leading into the marble foyer. Miss Donovan would be coming through one of those doors. She would spot Julia immediately.

She had to hide.

Julia glanced up at the painting. Mrs. Easterly looked austere in her black dress and lacey white shawl.

She had to hide.

"I loved her dearly," Mr. Easterly said.

She had to hide.

Footsteps click-clacked in the marble foyer.

"What's over here?" She turned around and walked toward the desk in the bay window just as she heard Miss Donovan's voice. "You called, Mr. Easterly?"

"When the concert is over, please invite the guests to the fireworks. And pass out their Christmas gifts as they leave."

Julia felt Miss Donovan's eyes boring into her back.

"You're not returning at all?" Miss Donovan's voice prickled.

"I may not."

My goodness, what did Mr. Easterly have planned? Julia's palms sweated as she stared into the illuminated garden. She had thought the tour was over.

"And please post a note in the ladies' dressing room that says, 'When you leave, it's not necessary to say good-bye to Mr. Easterly.'"

"Yes, sir."

Julia's stomach fluttered. How long was he going to detain her?

Miss Donovan's footsteps retreated.

He joined her at the desk.

"Is this your desk?" she asked. It was neatly arranged with a lamp, a black candlestick telephone, and some stacked books.

"I don't use this much. Most of my work is done at the office. Would you like to see upstairs now?" he asked.

Warning bells clanged in her mind. Upstairs meant bedrooms.

"Perhaps not. It's late. I should leave."

"Nonsense. The concert isn't over yet."

"Quite honestly, Mr. Easterly, I do not feel comfortable going upstairs alone with you."

"I can ask Miss Donovan to accompany us."

"No!" She hoped terror didn't show on her face.

"I respect your reservations, Miss Bradshaw, but I assure you that my only motive is to show you the rest of the house, the places most people don't see."

Could she trust him? Instinctively she knew she could. And if she was wrong, hundreds of guests were within screaming distance.

"All right."

He led her back through the foyer and up the grand staircase. The stringed music had ended. Organ music blasted from the pipes on the second floor. She felt as if she ascended into heaven.

He took her into a suite on the right. "This was my mother's room," he said. "I had the house built for her, but unfortunately, she didn't live long to enjoy it."

Twin beds wore white coverlets. Rose-flowered chintz drapes matched a chair, ottoman, and sofa in front of a white fireplace.

It was a room Julia would have liked for herself, feminine and beautiful. Perhaps his mother wasn't as austere as that picture downstairs portrayed.

"What was your mother was like?" By understanding the mother, she would better understand the son.

"She was sweet, dainty, and tiny," he said. "And I loved her more than anyone. She was my best friend. I miss her so."

His mother was his best friend? Incredible. Julia's mother certainly wasn't her best friend.

"She had a hard life. My father died of a brain disorder when I was almost eight and left my mother with very little. She was forced to take in boarders. I have tried all my life to make it up to her."

"I would say you succeeded."

"Thank you." He looked pleased. "She loved flowers. Her room has the best view of the gardens."

"You've left her room intact, haven't you?" On the dressing table were her brush, comb, mirror, and vials of perfume. Family pictures graced the tables and mantel.

"I have." He looked sheepish. "Sometimes I come in here just to remember her. Now let me show you my room."

Julia's heart hammered. Mama would have a conniption.

As they entered the wide hallway, Katie and Rose emerged from the ladies' dressing room. Their eyes bulged when they saw her with Mr. Easterly.

Mr. Easterly ignored them as he passed.

Julia shrugged and rolled her eyes. She wanted to say, *It's not what you think*, but she didn't know what to think herself.

Her head barely poked into his large room. It smelled of cigars and leather. A massive bed was centered before a fireplace. "Very nice," she said.

Katie and Rose still gaped as he said, "I want to show you one more room on the third floor."

The gossip mills would churn tonight.

At the top of the stairs he took her into another room.

"This is my playroom," he said.

Playroom?

Stuffed animal head trophies decorated the walls. Fishing gear abounded. She never would have guessed he was an outdoorsman.

In a corner was the only Christmas tree in the house, a long-needled white pine. It wasn't grand, like what she would have expected, but childish, with colored glass balls, carved and painted figures of Kris Kringle, his sleigh and reindeer. A Lionel train circled through tunnels and bridges.

"I love your tree," she said.

He looked embarrassed.

"Why do you have it up here and not downstairs?"

"It's for my pleasure alone."

She understood. Underneath his polished, commanding exterior, was a boy at heart. If his father died when he was eight, he had carried the burden of being man of the house for a long time.

She suddenly wanted him to experience a real Christmas, like a child again.

"What are you doing tomorrow for Christmas?"

"Nothing. My staff has the day off, so I'll be here alone."

"No one should be alone for Christmas. Come to our house."

She didn't consider what Mama would say. She just wanted this lonely man to have some Christmas joy.

"I couldn't intrude," he said.

"You wouldn't be. But let me warn you, we're a noisy bunch. I'm the oldest, then Richard is eighteen, Jenny is fifteen, Mary is eight, Peter four, and Annie three. Come early so you can watch the children open their gifts and then stay for dinner at one o'clock. I want you to experience a real Christmas. Please come"

She watched him struggle. *Lord, make him say yes.*

Just why she wanted this so badly, she had no idea.

David Easterly stared at his distorted reflection in a glass ornament.

His whole life seemed distorted and meaningless.

She was offering him a gift. The gift of Christmas. The gift of family.

A lifetime of lonely Christmases stretched before him. Suddenly he wanted one real Christmas more than anything.

"I would be happy to accept," he said.

Her face was radiant. "I'm so glad. Come at eight o'clock."

"Eight o'clock in the morning?"

"I know it's early, but you won't want to miss the fun."

No, he didn't. Not a minute of it.

He needed gifts for those little ones. All stores would be closed now. He would have to be creative. He was up for the challenge. He wished his guests were gone so he could get to work.

Suddenly a boom shook the house.

Julia flinched."What was that?"

"The fireworks. Let's go downstairs. We can watch them from Mother's bedroom window."

At the window overlooking the Terrace Garden, they saw the guests peering from the conservatory, dining room, and loggia windows.

The twelve men stationed throughout the rose gardens shooting off the fireworks were invisible. Just as planned. He heard a whistle, and the sky exploded with color.

Julia gasped. He stepped closer to her, distracted by her nearness. He wanted to put his hands around her waist, to bury his face in her soft hair.

Now that definitely hadn't been in the plan.

-->=◦ ◦=<--

Lee pressed his nose against the paned window of the loggia, the long corridor where they had eaten dinner. Beyond the pond, a pergola draped in white lights overlooked the snowy gardens. It was the most romantic setting he could imagine.

Miss Weston snuggled against him, pressed in by the crowd. As more fireworks exploded overhead, she smiled up at him. "Wasn't that beautiful?"

She was more beautiful. Her brown eyes were luminous. Her soft hair smelled like lavender. He felt intoxicated by her nearness.

It was the best night of his life. They had talked, savored the concert, and talked some more. He wished the night would never end.

Chapter 15

Friday, December 25, 1908

"MERRY CHRISTMAS!"

Julia bolted upright at Peter's voice.

Morning already?

It was after one o'clock when she'd crawled into bed, too excited to sleep. She had reenacted every conversation in every room, remembering more of Mr. Easterly than his beautiful house.

Mr. Easterly. Was coming. Here. Her heart hammered.

Lord, have mercy. Why had she invited him? Was she crazy?

What would Mama say? Mama wouldn't want the wealthiest man in the city in their humble home.

She'd have to convince her to see beyond his money. To see his lonely heart. To want to make this his best Christmas ever.

Was it even possible?

She was crazy.

But excited too. Mr. Easterly was coming! She would see him again. What would he think of their simple Christmas?

Wait a minute. What was Christmas without a gift? What could she give a man who had everything?

The one thing he needed was the Lord.

She'd give him the expensive, soft leather Bible she had bought for Papa. Papa would understand. She would replace it after Christmas.

The bedroom door flew open. Mary burst in, dressed in her white flannel nightgown. "Get up!" she said.

"It's Christmas." Peter crowded in front of her. Sleep still crusted his eyes.

"Presents!" Annie said. Her black curls were tangled.

Julia swung out of bed. "Go downstairs, children. I'll be there in a minute."

Their footsteps pattered down the stairs as she tied on a robe. Jenny was still buried under the covers.

"Get up, Jenny. I have a Christmas surprise you won't want to miss."

Jenny sat up. "What?"

"Come downstairs. You'll be shocked."

Jenny jumped up.

Together they hurried downstairs. Smells of coffee wafted from the kitchen.

Papa lit a fire in the parlor fireplace, the lumpy white stockings hanging overhead. The children were mesmerized by the gifts under the tree.

"Merry Christmas," Papa said.

"Merry Christmas. Where's Mama?" Julia asked.

"In the kitchen."

Julia headed for the kitchen. She wanted everyone present.

In the kitchen, Mama, with a calico apron tied around her ratty bathrobe, stirred the oatmeal. "Mama, can you come into the parlor? I have something to tell everyone."

Mama's brow wrinkled. "Now?"

"Yes, please come."

When she rejoined the family, Richard was there too, looking sleepy and rumpled.

Julia took a deep breath. "I have an announcement to make. I invited a guest. He's coming at eight o'clock to watch us open gifts."

Mouths slackened. Eyes widened. Mama shook her head. Papa raised his eyebrows.

"Who?" Mama asked.

"Mr. Easterly."

They collectively gasped.

"Not *the* Mr. Easterly," Jenny said.

Julia nodded.

"You're joking, right?" Richard said.

Julia shook her head. In the light of day, it did seem preposterous, but it was too late to renege now.

"Why did you invite him?" Papa asked.

"I felt sorry for him. He was going to be alone for Christmas."

"We can't have Mr. Easterly here," Mama said.

"Please, Mama. I want him to experience a real Christmas, a family Christmas where God is glorified and people love one another."

"If that's the case," Papa said, "the clock is ticking. We have less than an hour to get ready."

As the others dashed upstairs to change, Julia lingered with Papa. "I hope you don't mind, but I want to give Mr. Easterly your gift."

Papa's mustache twitched.

"It's a Bible, the one thing Mr. Easterly needs. I'll buy you another after Christmas."

Papa nodded. "Yes, give it to him. That's a great idea. He doesn't know the Lord, does he?"

"I don't think so."

"Tell me, princess, how did you happen to invite him? How did you know he would be alone today?"

Julia was certain guilt radiated from her eyes. "He knew how much I wanted to see his mansion, so he gave me a tour."

"Just you?"

"Yes, but he was a perfect gentleman."

"Be careful, Julia. Mr. Easterly is a powerful man. He could easily take advantage of you."

But he hadn't, even when he'd had opportunity. Instead, he had opened his heart.

"I'll be careful. I have no ulterior motives. I just want to give him a wonderful Christmas."

Papa squeezed her hand. "All right, but I will be praying all throughout the day."

That was exactly what she wanted him to do.

-→━◉ ◉━←-

David Easterly rumbled down the street in his roadster, checking addresses through the lazy snowflakes. His excitement mounted. He could hardly believe he was having a real Christmas.

He had expected to spend Christmas reading in the library with an occasional stroll through the greenhouses. A Christmas like any other. A Christmas that perfectly suited him.

Instead he felt daring, bold, nervous, exhilarated, and crazy. He rather liked the feeling.

But who spent Christmas with a family he didn't know, even if they did have a beautiful daughter?

"Me," he shouted to his empty car.

He'd awakened early to round up gifts. In the greenhouses, he cut bouquets for Julia, her sister, and her mother. He found two unopened boxes of imported German chocolates for her father and brother. For the children, he emptied the Christmas candies from dishes around the house into little purple boxes with purple tissue paper he used for his guests' orchids.

He was only a few minutes late. He had driven the smaller motor car instead of the Packard, giving Edgar Hopkins the day off with his family.

As he passed Grace Weston's apartment, he wondered what she was doing today. He hadn't seen her after the concert. He hoped she didn't mind being with Lee Bradshaw. He didn't think so, for it had been her suggestion.

He passed the Frances Parker School where he had first glimpsed Miss Bradshaw. Forevermore this school would invoke pleasant memories.

Halfway down the next block, he spotted the number on a square, two-story white house with black shutters and a spacious porch.

A man shoveled the driveway.

David pulled against the curb. The road was not well plowed. He stuck too far out into the road, but it would have to do. He did not want to pull into the driveway.

Not many knew of his phobia for backing up. In his garage, he'd had a turntable installed so he could always pull forward.

The man in the driveway motioned him to drive in.

David shook his head and indicated he wanted to stay here.

The man walked toward him. David opened the door.

It had to be Julia's father. He had the same vivid blue eyes. His handlebar mustache was icy, his cheeks red.

"Welcome, Mr. Easterly. I'm Alver Bradshaw." They shook hands. "Pull your car right in."

"The street's fine."

"No, I've made room for you."

Which was worse? Becoming stuck in the driveway and looking like a fool, or offending Julia's father? He chose the path of least resistance and pulled the car into the driveway.

He gathered the bouquets.

"Need help?" Mr. Bradshaw asked.

"Can you grab those little boxes there?"

"Sure thing."

As they walked up the porch steps, Julia's father said, "We're happy to have you join us today."

"Thank you. I can't tell you how excited I am to be here."

Julia swung the door open. She looked Christmassy in a long black and red plaid taffeta skirt and a white shirtwaist with a red bow around her neck. Her eyes sparkled.

"Merry Christmas," she said. "Come in." She pulled him into the warm foyer.

He handed her an extravagant bouquet. "Merry Christmas."

"Thank you. How beautiful." She buried her face in the soft petals.

She raised her voice. "Everybody, come meet Mr. Easterly."

Soon he was surrounded by more striking blue eyes, except for Mrs. Bradshaw's whose brown eyes regarded him warily.

"Mrs. Bradshaw, these are for you." He handed her a bouquet.

She looked surprised. "Are these orchids?"

"Yes, from my greenhouses."

"Thank you."

He thrust the third bouquet at the adolescent girl. "These are for you."

"This is Jenny," Julia said.

Jenny was a lovely girl with the potential of being as beautiful as her older sister.

Jenny blushed and thanked him.

"Mama, why don't you find vases for our flowers while I introduce him to the rest of the family?"

Her mother disappeared with the flowers.

"This is my brother Richard."

He had a seriousness in his face like his mother, yet something was familiar about him. He reached out to shake his hand.

"Perhaps you know Richard," Julia said. "He is one of your gardeners."

Now he felt awkward. He never socialized with his staff.

"And this is Mary." She was a sweet girl with long ringlets topped by a huge red bow.

"Here's Peter." Peter ducked his blond head as he shook his hand.

"And our little Annie." Short, dark curls covered her head. Her eyes flashed mischievously at him.

"I have gifts for all of you," he said.

"Thank you so much. Bring them in here," Julia said.

As he stepped into the parlor, his breath caught. This was the Christmas he had always dreamed of.

In one corner a cedar tree dripped with strings of raisins, popcorn, and cranberries. Gold-painted nuts and pinecones hung beside gingerbread men, popcorn balls, and candy canes. White flannel underneath looked like snow.

Hickory logs crackled in the fireplace where seven lumpy white stockings, all sizes, hung.

"I hope you don't mind sitting on the floor to open gifts," Julia said.

How long had it been since he'd sat on the floor? He felt like a child again.

Peter sat on one side, Annie on the other. Julia was across the circle.

"Who wants to pass out the stockings?" Mr. Bradshaw said.

Mary volunteered.

"We saved the stockings until you arrived," Julia said. "Usually the children empty them first thing."

Soon a lumpy white stocking was in his lap. He looked up in surprise. He hadn't expected anything. Julia smiled at him.

He pulled out an orange, gumdrops, and peppermint candies.

Annie tried to unwrap a peppermint candy.

"Not until after breakfast," her mother said.

"Oh, Louise, it's Christmas. Let her have it," Mr. Bradshaw said.

Annie struggled with the paper.

"Would you like help?" David asked.

He unwrapped it and popped it into her mouth. Her face looked like sunshine.

He never expected her to crawl into his lap. But there she was in the circle made by his crossed legs. She looked up at him and grinned.

He instantly fell in love.

When the presents were distributed, he was surprised one had his name. A stocking could be assembled at the last minute, but a gift?

They took turns opening. He would have been content just to watch. Mary was thrilled with a green tufted sofa for her dollhouse.

Peter glowed when he unwrapped Noah's Ark and twenty painted animals.

Annie hugged a new rag doll. "Would you like to hold it?" She held it out to him.

He couldn't remember when he had last held a doll, if ever. It felt small and soft. Its embroidered face was crude but endearing. It had black yarn hair in loopy curls like Annie's.

He held it against his shoulder and gave it a big hug. She beamed.

This was fun. He gave it a big sloppy kiss with sound effects.

Annie giggled and giggled.

Across the circle, Julia smiled.

"You can be her daddy," Annie said.

"I'm honored." This might be the closest he would ever come to being a daddy. Daddy to a doll. He'd take it. It was better than nothing.

What would it be like to be a real daddy to a darling daughter with black curls and rosy cheeks? It might be the most wonderful thing in the world.

"Your turn, Mr. Easterly," Julia said.

He gave the doll back to Annie. "I wasn't expecting a gift."

"Open it," Peter said.

Before he had a chance, Peter ripped off the paper. Annie lifted the box lid. He felt equally as excited and almost wished they had let him open it himself.

"It's a Bible," Peter announced.

David lifted out the soft leather Bible. "Thank you."

"You're welcome," Julia answered. Their eyes connected.

So it was from her. But he didn't need a Bible. He had enough to read already. It would just sit on a shelf.

"How come you got a Bible?" Peter asked. "Don't you got one already?"

Somewhere in his library was a Bible. "Not as nice as this," he said.

"Papa has a Bible." On the end table by Mr. Bradshaw's armchair was a well-worn Bible, not tucked away on a library shelf.

When the last gift was opened, Mr. Bradshaw reached for his Bible. "Before breakfast, let's read the story of the first Christmas from Luke chapter two."

The words were hauntingly beautiful. Perhaps he would read them himself tonight when he was all alone. It would be a good reminder of this wonderful day.

⸺⋇⸺

Mama bustled around the kitchen looking more harried than usual.

"How can I help?" Julia said.

"This bacon just won't crisp up," Mama said.

Julia peeked over her shoulder. "It looks fine to me."

"But it's not perfect."

"It doesn't have to be perfect."

"Yes, it does. Mr. Easterly is here."

Mr. Easterly was ruining Mama's Christmas. Hers too. She was more nervous than she'd expected, watching his every reaction.

She loved how he'd responded to Annie's doll. So playful and fun. Who would have thought?

Her goal was being realized. He was experiencing Christmas like a child.

But when he had opened the Bible, she hadn't missed the flicker of disappointment.

She prayed that in time he would appreciate its value; that it might change his life.

"Shall I set the table?" she asked.

"Please do," Mama said.

As she carried plates into the dining room, Mr. Easterly was sprawled on the floor beside Peter, standing up animals two by two. Annie straddled his back with her arms around his neck.

Peter giggled at something Mr. Easterly said. Mr. Easterly laughed too. Annie bounced on his back.

No, the imperfect bacon wouldn't be what Mr. Easterly remembered about today.

→═◉ ◉═←

The clock chimed ten as they finished breakfast.

David Easterly had never eaten such a meal. The food couldn't match Ellen's, but the company... oh, the company. Peter and Annie sat on either side of him. He cut Annie's eggs into small pieces and helped Peter butter his biscuit. All the while Julia watched his every move across the table. It was intoxicating.

Now this was Christmas. The thought of sitting alone in his big house made him shudder. He might be spoiled forever.

"Ten o'clock," Mrs. Bradshaw said. "Goodness, Charles and Lillian will be here in three hours. I have so much to do."

"That's Lee's parents," Julia explained. "What can we do to help, Mama?"

"Children, pick up all the paper in the parlor," Mr. Bradshaw said. "Julia and Jenny, help your mother in the kitchen."

"What can I do?" David asked.

Mrs. Bradshaw looked aghast. "Nothing."

"How about if I wash dishes?"

Julia's eyes teased. "Have you ever washed dishes in your life?"

"Absolutely. Lead the way. You can dry."

After the table was cleared, Julia tied an apron around his waist. "This will protect your suit," she said.

He didn't care about the suit, but having her hands around his waist was priceless.

Julia filled the big porcelain sink with sudsy hot water and handed him a dishrag. He dug in.

"Thanks so much for inviting me," he said. "This is the best Christmas I've ever had."

"I'm glad. You had fun with the little ones, didn't you?"

"I did. I had no idea what I was missing."

"Maybe you need some little ones of your own."

"Are you volunteering?"

Her face flamed. "No... that's not what I meant... I'm sorry..."

He enjoyed teasing her. "We could fill my table with children. That was your idea, right?"

Her eyes widened. "No... I meant my brothers and sisters...if you thought..."

"Relax. I'm teasing you."

But a table surrounded by his own children sounded like a splendid idea.

-->==() ()==<--

As Lee walked with his family toward his uncle's home, he wondered if Christmas would be spoiled this year by having Mr. Easterly there.

On the walk home last night, Julia had said, "Guess what? I invited Mr. Easterly to come for Christmas, and he said yes."

"You what?"

"He was lonely. He didn't have anywhere to go for Christmas."

"He's used to it, I'm sure. He likes being alone."

He couldn't imagine Mr. Easterly with their family. He was so disciplined, so orderly. Wouldn't he be annoyed by the noisy confusion?

He would find out.

He couldn't stop thinking about Grace Weston being alone today. As much as he loved Christmas with his family, he would choose to be with her in a heartbeat. Last night was magical. He wanted more of her.

"Lee, carry me," his little sister Pearl said. "My feet are all wet."

"You're too big to carry."

"Pul-lease."

With her fur-trimmed wool coat, she would weigh twice as much. "Sorry, kiddo. Look, we're almost there. Only two blocks to go."

"Daddy, will you carry me?" she said.

"No, Pearl."

"Sweetheart, think about something other than your wet feet," Mother said. "Try to guess what Mary received for Christmas."

It couldn't compare to what Pearl had opened that morning, he was sure. Poor Uncle Alver had six children to buy for, whereas Father only had two.

They listened to Pearl's whining until they arrived at Uncle Alver's.

"Merry Christmas." Uncle Alver met them at the door and took their wraps.

So was Mr. Easterly here? He heard giggles from the parlor. Probably not, by the sound of it. He expected it to be somber and stiff with such an important guest.

He stepped into the parlor. Was that Mr. Easterly sprawled on the floor with Peter and Annie?

He wouldn't have believed it if he hadn't seen it himself.

"Having fun?" Lee asked him.

Mr. Easterly looked up. "Oh, Mr. Bradshaw. I didn't see you come in." He tried to untangle himself from Annie and Peter.

"Don't get up," Lee said as he reached down to shake his hand. "Good to see you, sir. Merry Christmas."

"Merry Christmas to you too. As you can see, I'm having the best Christmas of my life."

Amazing.

Spotting Julia placing a dish of pickles on the dining room table, he walked over and said "Merry Christmas." He lowered his voice. "How's it going with Mr. Easterly?"

"Better than I dreamed. He's smitten with the children."

"I'll bet he's smitten with you too."

Her cheeks flamed. "Hardly."

He looked at the set table. It was crowded, but could one more squeeze on the end?

"I wish I could have invited Grace Weston for dinner. She's all alone today."

"She is? The poor dear. Of course you must invite her."

"It's too late."

"No, it isn't, not if you go right now. Dinner isn't quite ready."

"I should ask your mother's permission."

"I'll do that." She pushed his arm. "Just go. Look, I'm setting another plate already."

He grabbed his coat from the closet, slid on his boots, and was out the door.

⋯⊷⊙ ⊙⊶⋯

"Mama, I just set another plate at the table," Julia said as she entered the bustling kitchen. Mama carved the turkey, Jenny mashed sweet potatoes, and Aunt Lillian sliced the ham.

"Did we count wrong?" Mama asked.

"No, someone else is coming."

"You're just full of surprises today," Jenny said. "Have you come up with another way to ruin our Christmas?"

"This wasn't my idea. It was Lee's."

Aunt Lillian looked up. "I didn't know he had invited someone. Who?"

"Miss Weston, Mr. Easterly's secretary."

Aunt Lillian's eyebrows lifted. "Why would Lee invite her?"

"Last night at the party he heard she would be alone today. When he saw Mr. Easterly was here, he wanted to invite her too. I told him to go ahead. Is that all right, Mama?"

Mama grunted. "I guess so. We have plenty of food."

Aunt Lillian still hadn't moved. "Tell me more. What's she like? Does he like her? Is she a Christian?"

"She's amazing. She loves the Lord, and she's beautiful. And yes, I think he likes her very much."

Aunt Lillian's eyes sparkled. "Well! This is a first." Her knife sliced through the ham lickety-split.

Julia grinned. She had a feeling this might be Aunt Lillian's best Christmas too.

⇥⊙ ⊙⇤

Lee's heart lurched with each jogging step. He was going to see her again! But what if she refused to come? He would never be brave enough to ask a second time.

He was at her door before he knew it. He waited for his heaving breaths to subside before knocking.

Footsteps came down the stairs. His heart raced.

The door opened, and there she was looking soft and vulnerable.

"Merry Christmas," he said.

Her hands flew to her mouth. "Mr. Bradshaw, what are you doing here?"

"I'm kidnapping you for Christmas dinner. Hurry, get your coat."

She looked uncertain. "But I'm not dressed for it."

She was wearing a plain black skirt and white shirtwaist.

"You look fine." He tugged her hand. "Just come. Dinner will be served in a few minutes."

"But where?"

"At my cousin Julia's, just down the street."

"I can't intrude."

"Mr. Easterly is there too. Just come."

"He is? Well... all right."

She looked excited now. "Come in while I grab my coat."

He stepped into the small vestibule as she bounded up the stairs, not like the prim and proper Miss Weston.

She returned minutes later wearing a long wool coat, boots, and a furry hat and muff.

"Ready?" he asked.

Her eyes shone as they stepped into the cold.

"You have no idea what this means to me," she said. "I was sitting there feeling sorry for myself, even crying a little. Then you show up. I still can hardly believe it. You are an answer to prayer."

"I've never been an answer to prayer before."

"Oh, yes you have, believe me, you have."

Now what did she mean by that?

The sidewalks were icy. He offered his arm. She slipped her hand around it.

He trembled at her nearness, her dearness. He couldn't believe the distinguished and beautiful Miss Weston was all his for this moment.

"So who will be here today?" she asked.

He listed everyone in his and Julia's families.

"Quite a houseful. I've never been with such a large family. This will be fun. You're sure they won't mind if I'm there?"

"Of course not. The more the merrier."

Suddenly he realized that no one but Julia knew about his feelings for Miss Weston. What would his parents think when he showed up with her?

Maybe they *would* mind.

Lord, don't let this turn into a fiasco.

By the time they climbed the front steps, Miss Weston's cheeks were rosy. She looked adorable. He wanted to kiss the tip of her little red nose.

Instead, he flung open the door. He heard voices in the parlor and the kitchen. Good, the meal hadn't started yet.

"Let me take your coat." He helped her.

The closet was already stuffed. He hung his coat over hers on the last peg.

Now to introduce her to his family. He rubbed his hands down his pant legs and took a deep breath.

They stepped into the parlor filled with men and children.

At first no one noticed them. Then Mary pointed. "Who's that?" People turned with questioning looks.

"Everyone, I'd like you to meet Grace Weston, Mr. Easterly's secretary. She was alone for Christmas."

Mr. Easterly was the first up. He extended his hand. "Merry Christmas, Grace. You're going to love it here."

Uncle Alver welcomed her. Then his father heartily shook her hand.

"I want you to meet my little sister. Pearl, come here," Lee said.

Pearl slid off the couch, her blond ringlets bouncing as she daintily approached in her white dress with a matching bow in her hair.

"She looks like an angel," Grace whispered. "I didn't know you had a sister so young."

"My mother died when I was born. Father married Lillian twelve years ago."

Grace shook Pearl's hand. "I'm so pleased to meet you," she said.

Annie pushed in and held up a rag doll. "See my new dolly."

Grace squatted and stroked the doll's yarn hair. "She's very pretty, just like you. And your name is?"

"Annie."

Over Grace's head, Father winked at him and smiled. He apparently approved.

-->==◉ ◉==<--

As Julia mashed the potatoes, she wondered how Lee was doing. Had he convinced Miss Weston to come? Oh, she hoped so.

She had poked her head into the parlor a few minutes ago. They hadn't come yet. Time to try again.

She finished mashing the potatoes and covered them with the lid before stepping into the parlor.

Her heart quickened when she saw Lee. Where was Miss Weston? Hadn't she come after all?

Then she spotted her on the floor with Annie and Pearl. She couldn't help smiling.

She edged up to Lee. "She came."

He nodded. "Would you do me a favor and tell my mother about her? She doesn't know anything."

"I just told her. Don't worry. She's excited to meet her."

Julia reached down and squeezed Miss Weston's shoulder. "Welcome. We're so glad you're here."

Miss Weston's joyful face looked up. "Thank you." She tried to stand.

"No, don't get up. You're having too much fun, and I have things to do."

"Can I help?"

"No, we've plenty of help. Just enjoy yourself."

She hurried back to the kitchen and announced, "She's here."

Aunt Lillian yanked off her apron and threw it over the chair. She dashed out.

Julia remembered being on the Ontario Beach Park pier with Lee and wanting a front row seat when the sparks flew. Well, the sparks were flying now, and if she didn't get out there, she might miss it.

As she joined them in the parlor, Grace stood next to Lee and conversed with Uncle Charles.

Aunt Lillian approached with her arms extended.

Before Lee could finish, "Mother, I'd like you to meet Grace Weston," Aunt Lillian had Grace wrapped in a hug.

Julia's eyes met Lee's. He shrugged as a slow smile spread across his face.

⇢━◉ ◉━⇠

"We're ready," Mrs. Bradshaw announced. "Everyone find a seat."

As they crowded around, David Easterly understood why his dining room had impressed Julia.

With two leaves, this table sat ten. Another smaller table extended into the parlor so all fourteen could fit.

At his house they could have fit around one table and not been crowded.

There was something to be said about being crowded, though. He was so close to Julia that their arms almost touched. Annie sat on the other side, her hand nestled in his. He felt like family.

When everyone was seated, Julia's father said, "Shall we pray?"

They held hands. Little Annie's felt wiggly and sticky, but Julia's? Ah...Julia's. It felt soft and smooth and precious. Tingles shot up his arm.

Mr. Bradshaw's prayer was like none he'd heard, as if God were present and cared about them personally.

What would it be like to know God like that?

This family all seemed to know Him. He had never met people like them, so real and accepting and loving. He wished he never had to leave.

⇢━◉ ◉━⇠

"Just look at them," Julia said to Grace as they watched out the kitchen window over the sink.

As Julia and Grace washed and dried the dishes, two snow forts had been built by the men and children in the back yard. Now snowballs whizzed back and forth.

"I have never seen Mr. Easterly like this," Grace said.

Mr. Easterly whipped a snowball at Richard and whooped when it connected with his chest.

"I wanted him to have a happy Christmas," Julia said.

"You succeeded, that's for sure. I daresay this has been the best day of his life. Mine too."

"I'm so glad Lee invited you."

"Me too. Your family is amazing. To be welcomed and accepted..." Her voice broke. "It means so much. I was dreading this day alone."

Julia's eyes teared. "You've been a blessing to us too."

They hung up the damp dish towels as Jenny returned the dishes to the cupboards.

"Mama, could we make hot cocoa for everyone? They'll be cold when they come in," Julia said.

Mama picked the last of the turkey off the carcass as Aunt Lillian found containers for the leftovers.

"All right," Mama said.

Julia measured the cocoa and sugar and water into a big kettle. She turned up the heat and waited for it to boil.

"Maybe we could set out some cookies too," Julia said.

"Who could possibly eat another bite?" Aunt Lillian said.

"But the men and children may have worked up an appetite again."

"Go ahead," Mama said.

Julia and Grace arranged gingerbread men and cut-outs on a platter. When the chocolate mixture was boiling, Julia added the cold milk.

"It's ready," she said. "I'll let them know."

She opened the back door and stepped onto the porch.

"Would anyone like hot cocoa and cookies?" she called.

Whomp! A snowball hit her squarely in the face. She screamed.

It felt icy and wet. She couldn't see a thing. She clawed the snow away.

"Julia, I'm so sorry." It was Mr. Easterly's voice. "That snowball was meant for me."

His handkerchief gently wiped the snow away. It felt like a caress.

Maybe having a snowball in the face wasn't so bad after all.

->═ ═<-

She stood like a marble statue as David wiped off the snow. He took his time.

With her eyes closed, he studied every contour of her face. Her eyelashes were long against her rosy cheek. Her dimples were adorable, her mouth perfect. If they'd been alone, he may have tried to kiss her.

"You all right, Julia? Richard bounded up the stairs. "Sorry about that snowball."

He wished Richard would go away.

She opened her eyes and looked into his, only inches away. He could drown in their depths.

"I'm fine," she whispered.

The little ones clamored up the steps and hugged her legs.

"Are you hurt?" Mary asked.

He wanted to pick Julia up and carry her away. Some place private. Just the two of them.

"I'm not hurt. Who wants hot chocolate and cookies?"

"Me!" everyone shouted.

The spell was broken.

->═ ═<-

David should have left hours ago with Lee's family and Grace, but the thought of returning to an empty house kept him anchored by the fireplace. Julia was beside him on the sofa, her hand close enough to touch if he'd dared.

It had been quite a day.

He had been surprised when Grace Weston showed up, but pleased, for her sake. He was happy to share this family with her.

Mrs. Bradshaw's turkey and ham dinner with mashed potatoes, gravy, stuffing, sweet potatoes, cranberry sauce, canned corn, homemade bread, pumpkin, apple, and mincemeat pies had filled him to bursting.

The snowball fight left him more invigorated than he'd felt in a long time.

The highlight had been those moments on the back porch with Julia.

They had warmed up with hot cocoa by the fire followed by singing Christmas carols around the piano, with Julia accompanying. He had only mouthed the words to hide his terrible voice, but he had thoroughly enjoyed listening to everyone else, especially the children. When they sang "Away in a Manger," he wished he could play it on his gramophone again and again. It was the sweetest music in the world.

"Time for bed," Mr. Bradshaw said.

"No!" chorused Peter and Annie.

It was his cue. "I must go too."

Peter held onto his legs. "Don't go."

Annie crawled into his lap, wrapped her arms around his neck, and kissed his cheek with the sweetest kiss ever. He hugged and kissed her back.

"Don't go," Peter repeated.

"I have an idea," he said. "How would you all like to come to my house for dinner?"

The children jumped up and down.

"Can we, Papa?" Mary asked.

"That's really not necessary," Mr. Bradshaw said.

"It's the least I can do to repay you for the best Christmas ever. How about this Sunday afternoon?

"Why don't you come to church with us first?" Julia said.

Yesterday he would have refused. Not today. "All right. Let me pick you up in my Packard."

Peter's eyes grew round. "In a motor car?"

He ruffled his hair. "Yes, would you like that?"

Peter vigorously nodded.

"It's settled then. I'll see you day after tomorrow."

The children gave hugs all around once more before following their mother up the stairs.

David headed for the door. "Thanks for an amazing day."

Mr. Bradshaw shook his hand. "It was a pleasure having you here. Come again anytime."

He hoped he meant it. He wanted to return soon. "Thank you, I will."

"Julia, why don't you find his coat?"

Julia retrieved his greatcoat from the closet as Papa returned to the parlor.

He looked down into her lovely face, desperately wanting to kiss her. "Thank you for inviting me today. It was wonderful."

"You're welcome. You made our Christmas extra special. The children loved you."

What he really wanted to know was how *she* felt about him.

"I'm looking forward to seeing your family around my dining room table, just like you imagined."

"I'm afraid they won't know how to behave in such a grand house."

"Don't worry. The servants are off until later in the afternoon. It will be just us, so they can do whatever they want. Speaking of servants...

would you tell Richard not to tell the other staff that I was here today? I don't socialize with my help."

A shadow crossed her face. He wondered if he had offended her.

"Yes, I'll tell him."

"Thanks. Well, I guess I'll say good-night." He stepped onto the porch carrying his Bible. "Thanks again. Merry Christmas."

"Merry Christmas."

As the door closed behind him, never had he felt so alone.

The warmth, the love, the family were gone. Time to go home to an empty house.

He groaned when he saw his car parked in the driveway.

He had forgotten about it. He didn't want to struggle backing it up tonight. He would walk home and send Hopkins for it.

He didn't want to spoil this perfect day.

⊸⊫◉ ◉⊰⊱

Julia nestled between the cold sheets.

Because of Mr. Easterly, it was the best Christmas ever. She loved watching his interaction with the children, like a child himself.

But what made her heart pound was the way he looked at *her*. Tenderly. Watching her every move. She almost thought he was going to kiss her tonight at the door.

And she wanted him to.

But she couldn't let him. He wasn't a Christian.

And he didn't socialize with his staff. He had ignored Richard most of the day except when bombarding him with snowballs outside the kitchen window.

Once he found out she'd been his laundress, he might want nothing to do with her either.

"I think he's sweet on you," Jenny said from the other side of the bed.

Julia was instantly warm. "Why do you say that?"

"The way he looked at you."

Oh, goodness. Had others noticed too? "Well, I'm not interested in him."

"Are you crazy? He's the best catch in Rochester."

"It doesn't matter. He's not a Christian. I won't even consider him."

"But you could live in that mansion."

"You know what the Bible teaches. We are not to be unequally yoked together with unbelievers... no matter how much money they have."

Julia remembered what Papa had taught her many years ago. An unequally yoked team of oxen couldn't work in harmony together. That is what it would be like if she married someone who wasn't a Christian. Their core values would be too different. They would never truly work as one.

She was tempted, though. Not because of the money and the house, but because she really liked Mr. Easterly.

"Maybe he'll become a Christian," Jenny said. "After all, he *is* coming to church. If Mr. Easterly became a Christian, then would you marry him?"

Julia turned over. "Stop it, Jenny. I want to sleep."

"Who do you like better, Mr. Pratt or Mr. Easterly?"

Silly question. Not even worthy of an answer.

Chapter 16

Saturday, December 26, 1908

DAVID EASTERLY DRANK his coffee and finished his toast while perusing the newspaper at the round table in the conservatory.

It was dreadfully quiet. Ordinarily ladies from the neighborhood joined him for Saturday brunch, but they were occupied with Christmas guests this weekend.

He wanted noise and laughter and children hugging him and crawling on his back.

He couldn't wait for tomorrow.

The porte-cochère door opened and closed. Footsteps clicked across the marble. Miss Donovan placed the mail beside him.

"Miss Donovan, I have a special request."

Her lips pinched.

"I have invited eight guests for dinner tomorrow at noon."

Her mouth opened and closed like a fish. "But that's our morning off."

"I realize that. Perhaps the table could be set tonight, and Ellen could prepare some things I could just pop in the oven. I'll do the serving myself."

"That is highly improper, Mr. Easterly."

"Not for this crowd it isn't."

"Who is coming, sir?"

He didn't want to divulge that half the crowd would be children.

"No one you need worry about. I'll take care of everything. Please send Ellen in."

A few minutes later, Ellen lumbered out. "You wanted to see me, sir?"

"Yes, did Miss Donovan tell you I'm having dinner guests tomorrow?"

She nodded, looking disgruntled.

"Could you help me prepare dinner? I was thinking of a pot roast that could simmer for several hours while I'm at church. I can fix the mashed potatoes and biscuits. This afternoon I'll make a lemon meringue pie."

"Who's coming, if I might ask?"

"Just a family of close friends."

He didn't want them to know it was Richard's family.

"I'll take care of it," she said.

"Thanks, Ellen. I'll be in later to make that pie."

He retreated to the library where a coal fire burned. On the desk was the Bible Julia had given him. He picked it up tenderly.

Yesterday it had meant nothing. He felt differently now. This Bible held secrets as to why that family was so special. Peace radiated from their beautiful blue eyes. Or maybe it was joy. Whatever, they had something he didn't have.

He sat in the armchair closest to the fire and turned on the lamp.

The Bible felt soft, like Julia's hands. He opened it. Where was that Christmas story? Luke, he thought. He opened to the book of Luke, hoping he could discover their secret.

⤙⟿◉ ◉⟾⤚

Sunday, December 27, 1908

For church Julia wore a suit of red chiffon broadcloth with a white velvet vest, fashionable enough even for dinner at the Easterly House.

Dinner at the Easterly House. Not at a table in the corridor, but in the beautiful dining room with Mr. Easterly himself. She could hardly believe it.

"Pinch me to see if I'm dreaming," she said to Jenny who pinned her new sapphire brooch on her collar.

Jenny pinched her.

"Ouch, not that hard."

Jenny smirked. "What are you dreaming about anyway?"

"What else? Dinner at the Easterly House."

"What's Mr. Easterly's house like anyway?"

"It's huge and bright and gorgeous. I can't wait to see your reaction."

Jenny shrugged, but Julia knew she wasn't as indifferent as she pretended. Jenny's eyes would absolutely pop.

"I hope the children behave," Julia said.

"Of course they will."

Julia wasn't so certain. They were apt to spill and ruin something, even if it wasn't intentional. And then maybe Mr. Easterly would never invite them back.

Another worry was Miss Donovan. What if Miss Donovan saw her and threw her out again?

She had plenty to pray about today.

Downstairs, Papa hustled the children into their coats and boots and mittens. Julia donned her white cape with the fur-trimmed hood.

"We're riding in Mr. Easterly's car," Peter told her.

"I know, honey."

"Me too?" Annie asked.

"Yes, all of us," Julia said.

The children were as excited as she was.

"Who are we missing?" Papa said as he counted heads. "Your mother. Louise," he called, "are you ready? Mr. Easterly will be here any minute."

"Coming." Mama descended in a brown taffeta dress, dreary as usual.

Mary watched from the parlor window. "He's here," she squealed.

They all spilled onto the porch as Mr. Easterly stepped out of his big green Packard, the engine still running.

"Oh, my," Mama said. "It's so grand."

Mama had no idea what grandeur was yet to come.

Peter and Annie were the first down the steps. Mr. Easterly swooped them into his arms. "Good morning."

"Is this your motor car?" Peter asked.

"It is."

Papa shook his hand. "As you can see, we are bursting with excitement."

"Mr. and Mrs. Bradshaw, Jenny, and Mary, you can sit in the back seat." He helped them in.

"Julia, you can sit in the middle in the front, Richard next, and Annie and Peter on your laps."

Julia scooted in. Peter crawled on her lap, sitting high to look out the window.

Mr. Easterly climbed in on the driver's side.

Oh, my, he was so close their shoulders touched. Julia tried to slide closer to Richard, but couldn't.

She was shocked when Mr. Easterly covered her gloved hand with his and whispered. "Good morning. You look lovely today."

She hoped Mama hadn't heard. "Thank you."

"Everyone ready?" he asked as he shifted. "Tell me where to go."

"Turn left at the corner, and then left again on Brunswick Street," Julia said.

They bounded forward with several jerks.

Peter grasped her hand and snuggled into her lap. Annie looked out the window. The back seat was quiet.

Five minutes later they arrived. Mr. Easterly dropped them off at the front door. "I'll go park," he said.

"I'll wait for you by the door," Julia said.

As she hung up her cape, she saw Lee. "Guess who brought us today. Mr. Easterly."

"Are you serious?"

"And we're all invited to his house for dinner."

Lee looked concerned. "Julia, be careful."

"Why?"

"I don't want to see you hurt. Mr. Easterly doesn't have time for anything but business."

"Maybe he's changing."

"Not likely. He had a wonderful Christmas at your house, but once he's back to work, he'll forget all about your family. I've seen what he's like. He's focused, he's driven."

But Lee didn't know Mr. Easterly like she did.

The last time David had been in church was for his mother's funeral two years ago at St. Paul's, a grand cathedral across the street on East Avenue.

This sanctuary was different. It also had lovely stained glass windows and high beamed ceilings, but it was smaller, more intimate. Perhaps it would be easier to find God here.

Or maybe not. With Annie on his lap, Peter on one side, and Julia on the other, he might not be able to concentrate at all.

Julia couldn't believe Mr. Easterly was here in church. Beside her. Close enough to touch.

She wondered if anyone recognized him. Probably not. He looked so ordinary sitting with her family. No one would suspect.

The pipe organ played softly as more people filled the sanctuary.

Lord, touch his heart today.

Suddenly a shadow loomed over her. She raised her head. Mr. Pratt? Oh, my. She had completely forgotten about him.

He looked eager and hopeful. "Is there room?" he asked.

No! Go away. You'll spoil everything.

She motioned her family to scoot over. He squeezed in beside her.

"How was your Christmas?" he whispered.

"Wonderful. The best ever."

"Who's the man sitting beside you? An uncle?"

An uncle? Did Mr. Easterly look that old? His three-piece expensive suit gave him a distinguished air. But an uncle?

"No, he's a friend of the family."

Mr. Easterly leaned forward to inspect Mr. Pratt. Tension flashed.

"This is Mr. Pratt, a fourth grade teacher at my school," she said to Mr. Easterly. "Mr. Pratt, I'd like you to meet... David."

She couldn't believe she'd called him by his first name. But she didn't want Mr. Pratt knowing he was the famous Mr. Easterly.

The men shook hands, glowering at each other. Julia shriveled between them. This was not the church experience she had wanted for Mr. Easterly today.

⋅→═◉ ◉═←⋅

"May we go in the front entrance?" Julia asked as the Packard pulled into the Easterly House driveway. She wanted her family's first impression to be of the grand staircase.

"Certainly."

They climbed out onto the circular herringbone brick driveway and up three steps to the columned porch. A huge wreath hung over the front door.

"Welcome to my home."

As they stepped into the entrance hall, everyone gasped. Even Julia had not seen it in the sunlight.

The staircase looked as if it were floating on a marble pond with the soaring greenery of the conservatory behind. Everything was light and bright with marble floors, gleaming white walls, and white pillars.

"This is your *house*?" Mary asked.

"Yes, it is, Mary. What do you think?"

"It looks like heaven," she said.

It was an apt description. If Julia could custom-order her mansion in heaven, it would look exactly like this.

Mr. Easterly chuckled. "Let me take your coats. Julia, why don't you show them around while I get dinner ready?"

"Do you need help?" she asked.

"Maybe later." He looked nervous as he disappeared down the hallway toward the kitchen.

She was nervous too, wondering where Miss Donovan lurked.

"My!" Mama gawked at the grandeur. Mama looked like a little brown wren, totally out of place.

Annie darted up the staircase. Peter ran in circles.

"Annie, where are you going?" Julia said. "Peter, stop."

But she couldn't blame them. The wide open spaces invited running.

When Annie reached the landing, she looked confused by the split staircase. She sat and bumped down one step at a time.

Richard rubbed his neck as he looked around. "I've never been in this part of the house."

"Mr. Easterly must be awfully rich," Jenny said.

"This is amazing," Papa said.

"He told me to show you around," Julia said. "So follow me. Annie, take my hand."

They went into the living room first. "Now don't touch anything." They huddled together, as if fearful to venture beyond the doorway.

Across the entrance hall, she took them through the little library to the billiard room.

"Why does he need so many rooms?" Mary asked.

"He doesn't," Mama said. "This is ostentatious."

"What does that mean?" Mary asked.

"He's just trying to show off," Mama said.

"Now, Louise, don't be critical," Papa said. "A man in his position needs a home like this to entertain his clients."

"Are we his clients?" Mary asked.

"No, we're his friends," Julia said. "Come, let me show you the prettiest room of all." She led them through the marble corridor to the conservatory.

With sunlight pouring through the skylights in the two-story ceiling, it was breathtaking, furnished with wicker furniture, palms, ferns, vines, and flowers. Poinsettias partially covered the pipe organ console.

"This feels like a hotel," Mama said.

"It's like a garden," Jenny said.

"Why don't you all sit while I see if Mr. Easterly needs help?" Julia said.

"Shall I come too?" Mama asked.

"No, just relax."

"But Julia, you don't know how to do anything in the kitchen," Jenny said.

Jenny was right, but perhaps she knew more than Mr. Easterly.

"Just wait here, and don't touch anything."

She went through the portière and peeked into Miss Donovan's office. She wasn't there. She sighed in relief.

Where *was* Miss Donovan, though? The thought of her being near raised the hair on her arms.

Lord, keep her away until we're gone.

She hurried through the office and down the hallway to the kitchen.

Mr. Easterly vigorously mashed potatoes. A pot roast rested on the table.

"Something smells good. Need help?" she asked.

He looked relieved to see her. "You can stir the gravy."

As she stirred the slightly lumpy gravy, she said, "I didn't know you could cook."

"I'm not good at it, but I enjoy it. Unfortunately, Ellen doesn't like me invading her domain very often."

"I don't blame her."

"My specialty is lemon meringue pie which turned out pretty well, if I do say so. Oh, the biscuits! I forgot to take them out."

He rushed to the enormous oven and opened the door. "Bring me a pot holder," he said.

After assisting Ellen, she knew where the pot holders were. She opened the drawer and handed him one. He yanked out the pan.

After the pan was safely on the table, he said, "Thanks. Tell me, how did you know where the pot holders were? Lucky guess?"

Her face felt hot. Now would be the perfect time to tell him she had worked here last summer. But not yet. Maybe never.

"Where else would they be? Next to the stove, of course," she said lightheartedly.

She was thankful he had more important things to think about, like putting dinner on the table.

⤙══ ══⤚

Having guests was hard work, David decided. Julia and Jenny had helped carry the food to the table, but still he felt flushed and anxious. He hoped everything tasted all right.

But it wasn't only the food that worried him.

Who was Mr. Pratt? Julia had said he was a fourth grade teacher at her school. So why did he come to church? Why did he sit with her? Rather cozily, no less.

He had competition, no doubt about.

But David thrived on competition. And he usually won.

He had scored the first point by having the Bradshaw family around his dining room table. Mr. Bradshaw was at the opposite end, near his wife, Richard, and Jenny. Julia was down at this end beside him, along with Annie, Peter, and Mary. They weren't crowded.

The table was set with fine china, silver, and a centerpiece of yellow roses.

The children looked afraid to touch anything. Jenny looked awe-struck. Mrs. Bradshaw looked perturbed. Julia looked beautiful.

He hadn't thought of Annie needing a highchair. She was boosted by the fat dictionary from the library.

"Mr. Bradshaw, would you say grace?" he asked.

They all held hands.

It was the first time a prayer had been offered at this table. It added a nice touch.

When the prayer ended, he looked up with an overflowing heart. "I can't tell you how wonderful it is to have you here. There's never been family or children at this table, and it feels just right."

He looked at Julia. She blushed.

"Thank you," Mr. Bradshaw said. "It is an honor to be here."

"I hope you'll feel right at home."

Julia laughed.

"What's so funny?"

"How could we possibly feel at home here? This place is so grand."

He wanted them to feel at home. Especially Julia.

"Please, everyone, pass whatever is nearest you."

He scooped pot roast and mashed potatoes onto Annie's and Peter's plates and cut their meat.

Mary bit into a biscuit. "This is really hard."

He tried biting his. It was like a bullet.

"Sorry about the biscuits," he said. "Don't eat them. I promise my lemon meringue pie will be better."

He helped Peter sip milk. He wished he had put their milk in small glasses instead of goblets.

Peter wiped his mouth on the tablecloth.

"Peter," Julia scolded, "use your napkin."

"Don't worry about it," David said.

"But your poor laundress..."

Peter licked his lips. "Like you, Julia? You were a laundress."

⇢⇥◉ ◉⇤⇠

Julia froze.

A moment passed. No one said anything. She peeked at Mama and Papa at the other end of the table. They were busy eating. Was it possible no one else had heard?

She was afraid to look at Mr. Easterly.

"You were a laundress?" he said.

He *had* heard. Now was the time to tell the truth, but she wasn't ready for this fairytale to end.

She loved being here. She loved David's attention.

She feared she would never see him again if he knew she had been his laundress.

"Oh, yes, I've done laundry before."

He smiled. "You love children, you do laundry. I suppose you cook too."

She sagged in relief. Her secret was still safe. "I'm not a very good cook. Mama and Jenny do most of the cooking."

Later, when he served the lemon meringue pie, Julia said, "That was the best pie ever. Do you share recipes?"

He hesitated. "No one has been able to weasel that recipe out of me, but if you promise not to tell anyone, yes, I'll share my recipe with you."

She felt honored.

"May we help carry these dishes to the kitchen?" she asked.

"No, just leave them. The staff will be on duty soon."

Her heart raced. "How soon?"

"About fifteen minutes."

"Oh, we must go." She felt like Cinderella as the bells tolled midnight.

"Nonsense," Mr. Easterly said. "You've only just come. I hoped you would stay for my Sunday evening concert."

Julia had forgotten he hosted concerts every Sunday night. The servants would be setting up for it. Even more reason to leave immediately.

"The little ones need naps," Mama said.

"Noooo," Peter wailed. "I don't need a nap. I wanna stay here."

Mr. Easterly swooped Peter into his arms. "You heard your mother, young man. But you'll come another time, and we'll have more fun. Is that all right with you?"

Peter nodded.

He was going to invite them back? Why?

To curb his loneliness? Because he enjoyed the children? Or because of her?

She hoped it was because of her.

She heard voices. The servants were back.

"We must go *now*," Julia said. Mr. Easterly might think her abrupt, but better that than being thrown out by Miss Donovan.

Chapter 17

Monday, December 28, 1908

DAVID EASTERLY LOOKED with pride at his six-story Rochester Optical Company building. With a glass and iron front, the inside was equally beautiful with skylights, a marble staircase, and electric lights. He had provided bicycle sheds, lunchrooms, gyms, a retirement program, and life and disability insurance for his employees.

But today it didn't seem so significant.

After that wonderful weekend with the Bradshaw family, he questioned whether he had invested his time and money in the right place.

Better would be a wife and children waiting at the end of the day.

A wife like Julia.

Already he missed her. He wanted to see her again. Soon.

But how soon was too soon?

She had asked for his lemon meringue pie recipe. Perhaps that was the perfect excuse for going over tonight.

People greeted him in the spacious lobby. He shook hands, waved, smiled. These were his people, and he was grateful for them, but he could do without all the delay. He just wanted to be in his quiet office.

He ran for the elevator. It was full. "Is there room?" he asked.

"Of course, Mr. Easterly." One man stepped off and gave him his place.

David squeezed in next to Lee Bradshaw. After the hours spent with him this weekend, Lee felt like a friend. Or family.

"Good morning, Mr. Bradshaw." He was aware that every ear in that elevator strained to hear him.

"Good morning, sir."

The elevator emptied at each floor. When they exited on the sixth floor, only he and Lee were left, and they could finally talk.

"I had a wonderful time with your family this weekend," he said.

"We enjoyed having you there."

"You all have something very special. I can't quite put my finger on it."

Lee smiled. "You're probably referring to our personal relationship with Jesus Christ."

He'd been reading about Jesus in the New Testament, but Jesus had been dead a long time. How could they have a personal relationship with Him?

"I'm intrigued. Tell me more. How about over lunch?"

Lee looked surprised. "It would be my pleasure."

"Meet in my office at noon."

Maybe by understanding more about Jesus, he would understand more about Julia. Or vice versa.

-->≡◎ ◎≡<--

Before the clock struck noon, the secretaries had dropped pens and picked up lunches. "Coming Mr. Bradshaw?"

"Later."

He shouldn't have lied. He wasn't joining them. He was eating with Miss Weston. And Mr. Easterly, of course.

His heart had danced all morning. What would she think when he showed up? Would she be glad? He thought she would.

He kept reminding himself that he was going to converse with Mr.
Easterly about spiritual things. He prayed she wouldn't distract him too
much.

He waited until almost everyone had left, even though it made him
a few minutes late. He didn't want them knowing he was hobnobbing
with the boss.

Before he knocked on the door, he looked both ways and sent up a
prayer for guidance.

"Come in." It was her voice.

Mr. Easterly and Miss Weston sat at a round dining table in the paneled room. Steam rose from china serving bowls.

"Sorry I'm late."

Mr. Easterly rose to shake his hand. "Glad you could make it."

Grace Weston's eyes sparkled.

Lee sat in the empty chair, not taking his eyes off her.

"I guess we need to pray over this food, don't we?" Mr. Easterly
said.

Grace looked stunned.

"Don't look so shocked, my dear. I'm learning." He reached for
their hands. "Lee, would you do the honors?"

As Grace's dainty hand slid into his, he rejoiced that Mr. Easterly
didn't realize holding hands was just a Bradshaw tradition, not how all
Christians prayed. He gave her hand a little squeeze and was overjoyed
when she squeezed back.

David Easterly listened as Lee prayed, "Our dear heavenly Father, thank
You so much for the joy of Your presence and for the blessings of today.
Thanks for this food and for this fellowship. In Jesus' name, Amen."

It was different from Mr. Bradshaw's prayers. Shorter, but still nice. It might be easier to say a short prayer.

As they released hands, Grace passed him the chicken pot pie.

"Tell me," he said. "How do you know what to pray? Do you have a book of prayers?" He scooped the creamy chicken onto his plate.

"No, we just speak what's on our heart, as we would to a friend."

A friend? He wasn't good at making friends. Learning to talk to God might be harder than he thought.

"It seems presumptuous to consider God a friend," he said.

"Not at all. Athough He is a holy, mighty, sovereign God, the Bible refers to Him as being closer than a brother. He goes with me wherever I go. Jesus is my best friend."

Was this what made them different?

He had much to learn.

--->===⊙ ⊙===<---

Julia loved being home for Christmas vacation. Today she helped Mama with the laundry, went downtown to replace Papa's Bible, and still had time to read.

After the supper dishes were done, they gathered in the parlor near a crackling fire. Papa transferred notes from his old Bible to his new. Mama darned socks. Jenny read on the sofa. Richard was up in his room. Peter and Annie arranged the Noah's Ark animals on the floor. Mary played with her dolls under the Christmas tree.

Julia worked on lessons. Next week her class would make a twelve-page Book of the Year. Each month had a different picture to color, cut out, and paste. She had already traced the banner for January and the hearts for February. Now she worked on the windmills for March.

But she wasn't thinking about windmills. She was thinking of piercing blue eyes that looked into her soul. Of a gentle stroke on her snowy face. Of shoulders touching in the front seat. Of his chagrin over the hard biscuits.

It had been the most magical weekend, and now all she had left were memories.

She wondered if she would ever see him again. As Lee pointed out, Mr. Easterly was obsessed with work. He had likely forgotten about her now.

Perhaps it was a good thing. She should not be thinking about a man who didn't know the Lord.

Footsteps stomped on the front porch followed by a knock.

"Who could that be?" Mama asked.

Julia's pulse raced. It couldn't be him, could it?

"I'll get it," she said.

She flicked on the porch light as she swung the door open.

It *was* Mr. Easterly, bundled in his greatcoat.

"Mr. Easterly, what are you doing here?" What a stupid thing to say. She should have welcomed him right in.

"I brought you the recipe for the lemon meringue pie."

She had forgotten all about it.

"Thank you. Won't you come in?"

As he stepped inside, his eyes never left her face.

"I've missed you," he said.

"But I just saw you yesterday." Instantly she regretted her words. She was glad, glad, glad he was here.

"You're right. But after a day at the office, yesterday seems like forever ago."

"Did you have a good day?"

He nodded. "Lee ate lunch with us. I admire that man. He reminds me of you."

Did that mean he admired her too?

"Who's there, Julia?" Papa called.

"It's Mr. Easterly."

The children yelped and spilled into the foyer. Mr. Easterly knelt, opened his arms and hugged all three at once.

Julia wished they had stayed in the parlor. She wanted him all to herself.

"Come see my Noah's Ark," Peter said.

"I really shouldn't intrude." He looked to Julia for permission.

Papa stepped in and shook his hand. "Come on in, Mr. Easterly."

Peter tugged him to the floor. In the glow of the dancing flames, Mr. Easterly made one giraffe talk to the other in a giraffe-sounding voice.

Peter and Annie giggled.

Soon all three talked in animal voices.

Julia forgot all about The Book of the Year.

Later, Mr. Easterly looked over Papa's shoulder at the notes he had written in his new Bible.

"I didn't know it was proper to write in a Bible," he said.

"Oh, yes," Papa said. "I've made notes about verses that have meant so much to me. This is my treasure."

Then Mr. Easterly sat beside Julia and watched her trace pictures.

"That looks like fun," he said. "Need help?"

"Sure. You can trace the birds for April or the flowers for May."

"I'll do the flowers. Flowers are my passion."

"Really? Lee thinks work is your passion."

"I am a man of many passions." He wiggled his eyebrows suggestively.

She liked his playful mood. "Let me see. Work, flowers, reading, hunting, fishing, baking lemon meringue pies. Have I forgotten anything?"

"Only one. The most important."

He covered her hand with his.

His meaning was clear. *She* was his most important passion.

Goodness gracious!

When Mama announced it was time for bed, he stood.

Julia didn't want him to go.

The children kissed him good-night and reluctantly followed Mama upstairs.

Julia and Mr. Easterly were once again alone in the foyer.

"I almost forgot." He reached into his pocket. "The recipe."

She took it. "Thanks so much. That was the best pie."

"I hope you'll try it."

Oh, dear. She had never made a pie before.

"Thanks for coming tonight. It was wonderful having you here," she said.

"I can't seem to get enough of you."

Her face flamed. She couldn't believe he'd said that.

But that was exactly how she felt about him.

"Come whenever you want."

He grinned and wrapped his arms around her. She wasn't sure, but she thought she felt a kiss on her hair.

After she closed the door, she heard whistling all the way to the street.

Could Lee possibly be wrong? Instead of being obsessed with work, was Mr. Easterly obsessed with *her*?

⇥⇤

"Please, Mama, can't you help me?" Julia asked the next day.

"You can't make a lemon pie until you have a pie crust."

"He didn't give me a recipe for pie crust."

"You can use mine."

"Making pie crust is hard," Jenny said.

"I don't care. I have to learn."

"Why?" Jenny asked. "If you marry him, you'll never have to cook again."

Mama's eyes flashed. "Julia will not marry that man."

Julia was surprised at her vehemence.

"Why not? I think he's sweet on her," Jenny said.

"I'm not going to marry Mr. Easterly," Julia said. "He's not a Christian." Now if she could only convince her heart.

"He'll become one," Jenny said. "Did you see how interested he was in Papa's Bible notes?"

"Julia will never marry that man." Mama's teeth were clenched.

"Why? What do you have against Mr. Easterly?" Jenny said. "I like him."

"He is a worldly man. We have nothing in common with him. Admit it, Julia. You could never live in that house with all those servants."

"You're right," Julia said.

She would love to live in that house with Mr. Easterly, but not with Miss Donovan. No, never with Miss Donovan.

--->==◎ ◎==<---

The next morning David had the newspaper open while sipping breakfast coffee, but his mind wasn't on the news.

He was thinking of the bottomless depths of Julia's eyes and the laughing, sparkling eyes of Annie, Peter, and Mary as they crawled over him. He wanted to return, not go to work.

When could he next see them? Julia had said to come whenever he wanted. He didn't suppose he would be welcome every night.

Miss Donovan's footsteps click-clacked across the marble floor. She deposited the mail on the table.

"Thank you," he said without looking up.

"Mr. Easterly, we need to discuss your plans for New Year's Eve," she said. "It's only two days away."

Often he had hosted a New Year's Eve party for the city's elite. This year the Christmas Eve party had preempted it.

"There will be no party this year."

"How about New Year's day? Are you expecting guests?"

He wanted no one but the Bradshaws. He'd rather be in their cozy home, but he could hardly invite himself.

"No guests this year. You may give the staff the day off."

"Thank you, sir." Miss Donovan strode from the room. The others would be delighted with the plan.

If only he had a delightful plan of his own.

Chapter 18

Thursday, December 31, 1908

DAVID HAD DISMISSED everyone from work several hours early on New Year's Eve, knowing many had party plans.

Not him. He would be welcoming in the New Year alone. Perhaps he should invite Miss Weston. She would be good company, even if she wasn't Julia.

"You can go home now," he told her as her fingers flew across the typewriter keys.

"I know. I just want to finish this."

"Would you like to come over tonight to welcome in the New Year?"

"Oh, I'm sorry, I have other plans." She didn't miss a beat in her typing.

Even she had plans? He felt sulky.

It was none of his business, but he asked anyway. "What are you doing?"

"Lee invited me to the New Year's Eve service at his church."

A New Year's Eve service? He'd never heard of such a thing. No doubt the Bradshaws would be there too. He wondered if he could show up uninvited.

"What time is the service?"

"It starts at nine with games and refreshments downstairs. Would you like to come?"

"I'll think about it." But his mind was already made up. He would be there.

⊷▭◉ ◉▭↢

Lee was oblivious to the cold wind as he approached Miss Weston's apartment. He walked on clouds, not icy streets.

He couldn't believe she'd said yes.

He had eaten lunch with Mr. Easterly and Miss Weston every day this week. Because Mr. Easterly had showed such interest in the Bible, Lee had been studying the book of John with him. Daily he had seen his understanding grow. When they reached chapter three where it talked about being born again, Lee explained that to have a personal relationship with Jesus, he had to believe that Jesus died for him, ask Him to forgive his sins, and invite Him to live within him. He prayed that soon Mr. Easterly would submit to Christ. That wouldn't be easy for a man who liked to be in control of his own life.

Today as Mr. Easterly took a phone call, Lee had leaned close enough to see the gold flecks in Miss Weston's brown eyes. "If you don't have other plans, would you like to come to our New Year's Eve service tonight?"

"I'd love to." No hesitation.

"Great. I'll pick you up at eight forty-five. Dress warmly. We'll be walking."

How he wished he owned a car so he could escort her in style.

The light was on in her upstairs apartment.

He knocked. Footsteps skipped down the stairs.

She swung open the door, beaming. "Hello."

She was so beautiful.

"Ready?" he offered his arm.

"What a lovely evening," she said.

"You think so? It's quite windy and cold."

"I hadn't noticed. I guess I was distracted by the tall, handsome man at my side."

Was she flirting with him?

"Thanks for joining me at my church tonight. Do you have something going on at yours?"

"No, we're too small for that."

"Tell me about your church."

"It's a little mission church for the poor families down by the river on Front Street. We have more women and children than men."

"Is it safe? Those are bad neighborhoods."

"The Lord protects me."

"Now I'll worry about you every Sunday."

"You could always come with me."

"Maybe I will," he said.

"Your church seems to have made quite an impression on David Easterly. He told me that Julia gave him a Bible for Christmas, and he's been reading it every night."

"I suspect it's Julia who's made the impression."

She laughed. "You've got a point there. She's perfect for him."

"Really? Everyone thinks you'd be perfect for him."

"No, we're too much alike. We'd grow tired of each other. Besides, he's not a believer."

"What if he became a Christian?"

"I still wouldn't be interested."

"Doesn't his money entice you?"

"Not really. What good is money without happiness?"

"Could you be content in a small cottage?"

"Absolutely, as long as love dwelt there."

"Oh, it would."

She squeezed his arm.

He no longer noticed the wind and the cold either.

-»≡◎ ◎≡‹-

Julia positioned her lemon meringue pie on the table next to a chocolate layer cake. Three long tables were covered with luscious desserts.

The church basement buzzed with good cheer as friends clustered in small groups. It was a large, cheery room with a cement floor and six white poles supporting the ceiling.

Her mother sat with some ladies beneath the high windows. Papa was in a circle of men. Children raced around the poles.

Julia looked for someone to talk to. She didn't see Lee yet, although his parents and Pearl were here. Just as she was about to join some young women, she spotted him at the door.

Next to him was a woman. Was that Miss Weston? Her cheeks were rosy and her nose red. But her eyes shone. She looked like a radiant, half-frozen bride.

Had he finally summoned the courage to ask her out? Good for him.

Lee stood tall with his shoulders back. A grin escaped as his eyes met hers.

She hurried to greet them. Grace looked relieved to see a familiar face.

"I'm so glad you're here. Welcome. Come in and warm up," Julia said.

"Thank you. I'm thrilled to be here."

Lee's mother stepped forward. "Come, dear, I have some people who can't wait to meet you." Lee followed closely. Julia doubted Grace would be out of his sight all night.

How wonderful to have someone special to welcome in the New Year with. If only Mr. Easterly...

"Julia." The male voice behind her sounded familiar.

She whirled around.

It was Mr. Pratt. He quirked an eyebrow and smiled.

The night suddenly felt bleak.

"Surprised?" he asked.

"Y-yes." She could think of better adjectives. Dismayed. Disappointed.

"I heard the New Year's Eve service announced on Sunday. It sounded like fun."

He deserved to be treated civilly no matter how she felt.

"Well, come on in. Let me introduce you around." She headed toward Papa's circle of friends.

"Papa, look who's here." Her voice held no enthusiasm. "Mr. Pratt from school."

Papa's eyes sought hers. He understood.

"Welcome, Mr. Pratt." Papa shook his hand and introduced him to the others. They peppered him with questions about his work and family.

Mr. Pratt looked relaxed and happy. It was good for him to meet these Christian men. He needed to see that faith wasn't just for women and children.

She breathed a sigh of relief and stepped away, glad to be alone if only for a moment.

"Miss Bradshaw?" A voice spoke from behind.

She recognized that voice too. Could it be? She spun around.

Mr. Easterly's blue eyes bore into hers. He captured both her hands. His felt cold.

She wanted to twirl and shout. Instead she steadied herself and said, "It's so good to see you. I never expected you. I assumed you'd have your own party."

He shook his head. "I hope you don't mind that I'm here. Grace told me about the service tonight."

"Of course I don't mind. I'm thrilled. Come in."

She wondered if he'd seen Mr. Pratt. Probably not, for he hadn't taken his eyes off her.

But what would he do when he realized Mr. Pratt was here too?

Would he think she had invited him? Would he think she preferred Mr. Pratt's company? Oh, how could she communicate that she was not interested in Mr. Pratt at all?

But wait. She had no business encouraging Mr. Easterly either, for he wasn't a Christian. She would need to keep her distance, as hard as that would be.

"Look at all those desserts," he said.

"Our church has the best cooks in Rochester."

"Which one did you bring?"

"Your lemon meringue pie."

"Really?" He looked pleased.

The pastor clapped for everyone's attention. "Thanks for braving the cold and wind tonight to welcome in the New Year with the Lord. Let's ask the blessing on the food, and then we can dig in."

After the prayer, a line formed. Julia swallowed hard as Mr. Pratt weaved through the crowd to her side.

"There you are," he said.

Then he noticed Mr. Easterly. He looked from him to her.

Mr. Easterly stepped closer to her.

"Mr. Pratt, look who showed up, Mr. ... David."

Mr. Pratt's eyes hardened as Mr. Easterly shook his hand.

Ignoring the thick tension, Julia lightheartedly said, "How will we ever choose from all these desserts?"

"Which one did you bring?" Mr. Pratt asked.

"The lemon meringue pie."

"Then that's what I'll take."

"Me too," said Mr. Easterly.

Oh, dear. She imagined them competing for her attention all evening. This had to stop. It was time to do what she should have done long ago.

The men each cut a slice of her pie and filled their plates with other desserts as well. They found chairs in a quiet corner facing each other, just the three of them.

She lifted a bite. "I'm afraid to taste this."

"Why? It looks wonderful," Mr. Easterly said.

The lemon flavor exploded in her mouth. She puckered.

"It's not as good as yours," she said.

Mr. Easterly thoughtfully chewed and swallowed. "It *is* more tart."

Mr. Pratt's eyes questioned.

"I served lemon meringue pie when she came for dinner," Mr. Easterly said. "I shared my recipe with her."

Mr. Pratt's ears reddened.

"My whole family went for dinner," Julia said.

"Where did you two meet?" Mr. Pratt asked.

"At a party," Julia said.

"How long have you known each other?"

"A week," Mr. Easterly said. "We met at my Christmas Eve party, and my life hasn't been the same since."

Mr. Pratt drooped. She had to say it now before this became more unbearable.

"Gentlemen, let me clarify something. My first love is Jesus Christ. I owe Him everything, and I cannot consider a close relationship with someone who has not surrendered his life to Christ."

Mr. Easterly's swinging foot stilled. Mr. Pratt twitched his mustache.

"I've been reading my Bible," Mr. Easterly said. "Every day."

"I've been coming to church," Mr. Pratt said.

"I know. Those are all good things, but it's not the same as commitment to Christ."

They both looked determined.

Oh, dear.

⇥⟭ ⟬⇤

David Easterly was accustomed to winning. But competition in business was different than competition for the heart. He was in uncharted territory. He didn't like feeling helpless.

He wished he could snap his fingers and have his board of directors make Mr. Pratt disappear.

He had thought Julia reciprocated his feelings. Now he was unsure. How long had she known Mr. Pratt? Probably longer than one week.

The pastor clapped his hands. "Attention, everyone. Time for some games before we head upstairs for our service. Everyone under the age of twenty line up at the far end for a three-legged race."

Chairs were pushed back and the floor cleared.

"This looks like fun," Mr. Pratt said.

David couldn't remember when he had last seen a three-legged race. Probably in grade school. He hated to agree with Mr. Pratt, but it did look like fun.

Mary partnered with her cousin Pearl. Peter wiggled between them.

"Oh, dear. Peter is too young for this," Julia said as she rose. "He'll get hurt."

"I'll fetch him," David said.

As he stood, people smiled at him, but no one rushed forward to shake his hand.

They don't know who I am. It was a nice reprieve from the fawning attention he usually received.

He crossed behind the excited teams tying cloths around their ankles. Reaching around Pearl and Mary, he scooped up a squirming Peter.

"Come here, you little rascal." He tickled him.

Peter protested until he looked up into David's face. "It's you!" His arms circled David's neck.

Love rushed over him as he returned the hug. Could anything be more precious than the love of a child? He looked over at Julia conversing with Mr. Pratt. Actually, yes. The love of that sweet, gorgeous woman with the dark hair, radiant blue eyes, and dimples.

He was determined to win her.

"Come sit with me, Peter." He returned to his chair and bounced Peter on his knee.

Julia held out her arms to Peter. "Want to sit on my lap?"

Peter shook his head and clung to David.

Her eyes locked with his. She approved. A point for him.

A whistle blew and the race was off. The cheers were deafening. Some tripped. Some bumped into each other. Mary and Pearl ran a crooked path. A team of teenage boys quickly won.

"Now," the pastor said, "Couples over twenty."

"That's us." Mr. Pratt stood and grabbed Julia's hand.

She looked at David expectantly. What did she want him to do? Volunteer too? This was out of his realm. He did concerts and dinners, not childish games.

Perhaps for once he should discard his pride.

He was too late. Mr. Pratt led her to the starting line. He tied a cloth around their ankles.

Beside them were Lee and Miss Weston. Grace looked uncertain as Lee tied their ankles together. She probably had never been in a three-legged race either.

David felt left out.

He ground his teeth as Mr. Pratt wrapped his arm around Julia's waist. Julia awkwardly reached behind him.

David bounced Peter harder than he intended. Peter giggled.

It wasn't funny.

The whistle blew.

They were off. Mr. Pratt stepped with the wrong leg first, and they faltered. Julia showed him how to step with the inner legs first. Then the outer. They rushed forward, their heads down, watching their steps. They apparently didn't see the white pole until Mr. Pratt's head cracked against it. His arms flailed as his feet flew up, pulling Julia down with him. They landed hard on the floor.

"Julia!" David dropped Peter as he rushed to her side. He lifted her to her feet. "Are you hurt?"

Her face was inches away. She looked up at him and whispered, "I'm fine."

His arms wrapped around her. She snuggled.

Mr. Pratt struggled to his feet. His face was scarlet. "I'm so sorry, Miss Bradshaw. Are you all right?"

She pulled away. "I'm fine."

With his arm around her waist, David led her back to their chairs.

He may not have run the race, but he'd won anyway.

⇢▷◉ ◉◁⇠

David Easterly had never welcomed in the New Year like this. After the games and food, they went upstairs for singing and a short sermon. Now it was five minutes before midnight.

"Use this time in meditation before the Lord," Pastor said. "Reflect on the past year. Has your life brought glory to God? Commit this next year to Him."

The auditorium was silent. The children had fallen asleep long ago.

David bowed his head. He knew his life had not brought glory to God. His goals were self-seeking. God had never been a consideration.

But now He was.

God, I haven't talked much with You, but I would like to get to know You this year.

He didn't know what else to say, but at least he'd made contact. He hoped.

Julia bowed her head, her hands clenched.

What would this next year look like? It could be quite different considering the men on either side.

Had God chosen one of them for her?

Lord, please speak to their hearts. Open David's eyes. Give him a burning desire to know You as his personal Savior. Use me in any way You can.

And, Lord, I guess I should pray the same for Mr. Pratt. He needs You too. Give him understanding. Help him commit his life to You.

Make me willing to submit to Your will and Your choice.

Did she really mean that? What if God had chosen Mr. Pratt for her?

Then He would have to change her heart.

"Maybe some of you need to do serious business with God," the pastor said. "Come, kneel at the front. Start the New Year with a clean slate. Surrender to God."

Julia was startled by movement on her right. She peeked. Mr. Pratt stood and walked to the front.

Pastor shook his hand and knelt with him, his arm around his shoulders. They prayed together.

Oh, my! God had answered her prayer so quickly.

Just not the way she'd hoped.

Chapter 19

Sunday, January 3, 1909

WITH HER ARMS wrapped around her knees, Julia was mesmerized by the glowing embers as the warmth of the fire enveloped her.

Mama and Papa had taken the little ones up to bed. Finally she had a moment to herself.

Things were happening too fast. Yes, Mr. Pratt really had accepted the Lord. He told her this morning in church. The glow in his eyes was unmistakable.

Afterwards Mr. Easterly had whisked them all home in his Packard. Mr. Pratt was left on the sidewalk looking after them in heart-wrenching agony. Julia had been tempted to invite him for dinner too.

Mr. Easterly spent the afternoon at their house. The children had monopolized him, but she hadn't minded. Their eyes connecting over a game or a song was enough for now.

She heard footsteps. Papa eased himself next to her on the floor. So much for time alone. But time alone with Papa was even better.

"A penny for your thoughts, princess."

She shook her head. "My thoughts are whirling. I'm so confused."

"About...?"

"Men."

He chuckled. "I figured."

"I was praying that God would show me His will, and then Mr. Pratt accepted the Lord. Does that mean he is God's choice for me?"

"Not necessarily. God is working on Mr. Easterly's heart too. This afternoon while you were doing dishes, we had a nice chat. He asked lots of questions. He's understanding more and more about the Bible. I believe it won't be long until he turns his life over to Christ."

"Oh, I hope so. Then everything would be perfect."

"You like him, don't you?"

"It's that obvious?"

He nodded. "Just be careful, dear. His life is very different from yours."

"I know."

"He has great wealth and powerful friends."

"And you're saying I wouldn't fit in?"

"Would you?"

"I think I could. After all, I've been to college."

"There's more to it than that. They see things from a secular perspective. You would be bombarded with challenges."

"But couldn't I be a witness to them?"

"Or would they suck you into their way of thinking?"

Certainly she was strong enough to stand up for her beliefs. Or was she?

"Perhaps you should attend his concert next Sunday when we go for dinner again. See what his world is like. See what his friends are like."

The thought of mingling with his uppity friends caused her pulse to race. Maybe she wasn't as ready to be part of his world as she thought.

"He's much older than you."

"I know."

"Do you know how old he is?"

"Not exactly. In his thirties, I think."

"Upper thirties, probably. And you're only twenty-three."

"I'll be twenty-four in a few months."

"That's still a big age difference."

"It doesn't seem so when I'm with him."

"How does he feel about your being his laundress last summer?"

"He doesn't know."

"He doesn't? Julia, you need to tell him. That might be an issue for him."

"I will. Someday."

"The longer you wait, the harder it will be. He will think you've been deceptive."

Oh, dear. She didn't want that.

"And how do you feel about Mr. Pratt?" he asked.

"I like him as a friend."

"He likes you far more than that."

"I know. That's the problem. And now he's received the Lord and Mr. Easterly hasn't."

He patted her hand. "Just keep praying and trusting. God will direct you."

But would she be willing to accept it when He did?

Tomorrow school started again. She would see Mr. Pratt every day.

Oh, dear.

⇥▣ ▣⇤

Monday, January 4, 1909

Lee threw down his pencil and stared at the cubbyholes in his desk. Who wanted to think about numbers when he could think about Grace?

Taking her to the New Year's Eve service had started something. Something wonderful. Something he wanted to never end.

Yesterday they had taken the streetcar to her mission downtown by the river. The children swarmed her. It made no difference that their fingers were sticky, their faces filthy. She had opened her arms and loved them. He sat in her class and was impressed with how she made God's Word simple enough for a child to understand.

She had pressed money into one woman's chapped hand. He suspected much of her income went toward food and clothing for those families.

He had thought to persuade her to attend his church. Not anymore. She was needed there. Maybe he was too.

He felt a hand on his shoulder and a breath at his ear. "Lee, can you come? Mr. Easterly needs you."

It was her. He turned and gazed into her warm brown eyes which were mere inches away. She looked excited.

"Of course." He pushed back his chair, careful not to snag her skirt, and followed. Every female in the aisle watched them.

"Is something wrong?"

"Nothing's wrong. He's been asking spiritual questions all morning. I believe he's under conviction. I thought you should be the one to talk to him, not me."

"Why? You're probably better at sharing your faith than I am."

"No, I wanted you to do it."

He hoped he could handle it. What if Mr. Easterly asked a question he didn't know the answer for? *Lord, give me wisdom.*

--›══◉ ◉══‹--

David Easterly was terrified. Most of the weekend he'd been in his library reading the Bible when he'd found a devastating story.

He paced around the table, the blood pounding in his ears. At this rate, he'd have a heart attack before Lee arrived.

And if he died, his soul would go straight to hell.

Lee walked in.

"You're here. Thank God."

"What's wrong?"

David rapped his finger on the open page. "Explain this to me."

Lee skimmed it. "It's the story of the rich young ruler."

"Does that mean that just because I'm rich, I'll never enter heaven? Look, it says it's easier for a camel to go through the eye of a needle than for a rich man to enter the kingdom of God."

"No, it doesn't mean you can't go to heaven."

David's pounding heart stilled. "What does it mean then?"

"What's at stake is your attitude toward your wealth. God wants to be first in your life, more important than your money."

"So I have to give it all away like it says here?"

"No, Jesus was just testing the rich young ruler to see where his heart was. Unfortunately, he was not willing to put God first." Lee paused. "Are you?"

David had struggled with that question for days. He liked being in control. Could he relinquish that? Could he surrender his life to God?

But even more he wanted the peace and joy and love the Bradshaw family oozed. He yearned for a relationship with God like they had. "Yes, I want to put God first. Tell me what to do."

Lee flipped to the sixteenth chapter of Acts. "It says here, 'Believe on the Lord Jesus Christ, and thou shalt be saved.' Do you believe that Jesus died on the cross for your sins and rose again?"

"I do."

"Then repent of your sins and invite Him into your life."

"Let's do it. I'm ready."

⇥➡ ⬅⇤

After a day at school, Julia felt as if she had never been on vacation.

The children were subdued, even Joey. She remembered to bring bread and jelly for his breakfast, and bread, cheese, an apple, and Christmas cookies for his lunch. He hadn't been a problem all day.

She watched out the frosty window. Children still romped in the snow, their happy voices echoing. She wished she had their energy.

"Knock knock," came a voice at the door.

Mr. Pratt. She had been expecting him.

She turned, forcing a smile. "How was your first day back?"

"The kids were good."

"Mine too. They seemed half asleep."

"Julia." He stepped closer.

Her pulse raced. His face was too serious. She looked away.

"Julia, I wanted you to know that my decision to accept Christ was genuine. I wanted to be right with God. I didn't do it just for you."

"I'm so glad."

"Are you? You haven't acted glad. In fact, you seem to be avoiding me." His face was anguished. "It's David, isn't it? You've known him a week, right?"

"A week and three days."

He grimaced. "You're counting the days."

Her gaze darted to the floor.

"I've been patiently waiting for over a year, and this guy sweeps you off your feet in a week and three days. Who is he, anyway? What does he have that I don't?"

Magnetism, charm, kindness, vulnerability, a love for children, a love of her family, wealth, a beautiful home. Poor Mr. Pratt could never measure up.

"Actually, you're wrong. There's nothing between us. He's friends with my family."

"I'm not blind, Julia. I've seen how you look at him."

Oh, dear.

"Well, there can't be anything between us. He's not a believer," she said.

"Then I won't give up." He spun toward the door and left.

That's what she was afraid of.

→⟫⊚ ⊚⟪←

Saturday, January 9. 1909

David Easterly waited in the conservatory as his butler, Solomon Merrick, answered the porte-cochère door. He heard women's voices.

It had been two weeks since his last Saturday brunch with the neighborhood ladies. He'd been so busy with new friends that he'd hardly missed them.

Catherine Townsend was the first through the portière. He greeted her with a kiss on her cheek. Catherine kept him up-to-date on the latest fashions, wearing something new every week. She was pretty and perky. Her husband was a banker and they lived in an impressive stone mansion down the street.

"David, darling, how are you?"

"Never been better." That was the truth. He was literally a new person with his sins forgiven and a place reserved for him in heaven. He still could hardly believe it.

Only Lee and Grace knew. He wanted the Bradshaws to be next. He planned to announce it at dinner tomorrow.

In bustled nervous Miriam Branson, tall, homely Nancy Jones, and short, round-faced Elizabeth Schuyler.

"Look at him, ladies. Doesn't he look marvelous?"

They all kissed his cheek.

"Is that a smile I see?" Miriam asked.

"You actually look happy," Nancy said. "What happened?"

He hadn't realized it showed.

"I'll tell you later. Come and sit. Our meal is ready."

The footman brought in plates of broiled sugared grapefruit.

The ladies placed the cloth napkins on their laps, keeping up a constant dialogue as they ate.

He wondered if he should interrupt and pray over the meal. But he had never prayed out loud, and he didn't want to practice on these ladies. Perhaps he would try tomorrow when the Bradshaws were here.

They chattered about their holidays, their gifts, their guests, and their extravagant meals. But nothing equaled his holiday around the cozy fire in the Bradshaw parlor.

"David, you're so quiet. Tell us about your holidays," Catherine said.

"I met someone special."

"Let me guess," Elizabeth said. "The President of the United States."

"Thomas Edison," Miriam said. "What's your guess, Nancy?"

"The dancer, Isadora Duncan."

"Are we close?" Catherine asked.

Now he regretted mentioning it. Julia's memory was too precious to be scrutinized by them.

Catherine touched his sleeve. "We didn't mean to tease, David. Please tell us."

"I met a woman."

"Oooo..." Her eyes danced.

"It's about time," Nancy said.

Round-faced Elizabeth leaned closer. "Tell us. Tell us."

"Her name is Julia Bradshaw."

"I love her name," Miriam said. "Very aristocratic. Where did you meet her?"

"At my Christmas Eve party."

"This is getting better and better," Catherine said. "What does she look like?"

"She has the most striking blue eyes, dark hair, and dimples. She's beautiful and fun to be with."

"So that's why there's a smile on your face," Catherine said. "I'm dreadfully excited. Tell us more. Where's she from?"

"She actually lives down the street on Barrington. She teaches kindergarten at the Francis Parker School."

They were quiet.

Catherine broke the silence. "A teacher? How quaint."

"She loves children. In fact, she has little brothers and sisters that I have fallen in love with."

"Really, David? You and children?"

"I've become a new man in more ways than one."

"She sounds... extraordinary. When can we meet her?"

He suddenly wanted them to see how wonderful she was.

"I'll invite her next Saturday morning."

He hoped they would fall in love with her too.

⋆⊷⊷ ⊶⊶⋆

Sunday, January 10, 1909

Julia studied the table. Orchids in little vases were above each plate as well as in the extravagant floral centerpiece. Instead of a dictionary, Annie sat on a wooden highchair. Replacing Peter and Annie's stemmed crystal goblets were squattier glasses. Mr. Easterly had thought of every detail.

Her eyes rose to his. He had been watching her. She smiled back.

Something was different about him. She had noticed it when he picked them up for church. His eyes looked softer, more peaceful, expectant.

"Have a seat, everyone," he said. He pushed in her chair and then Jenny's. Papa pushed in Mama's.

Mr. Easterly reached out his hands. "Shall we pray?"

His fingers wrapped around hers. Goose bumps shot up her arm.

She waited for Papa's voice. Instead Mr. Easterly prayed. "God, thank You for this dear family and for this food. Amen."

He'd prayed? It was simple and heartfelt, but he'd done it himself. Yes, something definitely was different today. Dare she hope?

He squeezed her hand before releasing it.

"Before we eat, I have an announcement to make." He immediately had everyone's attention.

Lord, let it be what I think it is.

"Monday I asked God to forgive my sins and come into my life."

Her breath caught. She couldn't believe it. Yes, she could. It was what she had prayed for and longed for. The wonder of it rolled over her.

Papa was first out of his chair. They met in a bear hug. "Welcome to the family of God, son."

She suddenly couldn't get out of her chair fast enough. He waited for her with outstretched arms, his eyes gentle.

As his arms enfolded her, her heart overflowed. Now she had God's permission to love him. And she did. With all her heart.

She had a million questions. She wished they were alone.

He released her and faced the family. "Thank you, all of you, for showing me what Jesus was like."

"But what made you finally decide to do it?" she asked.

"It was the story of the rich young ruler. Lee explained it to me."

She couldn't wait for more details from Lee.

She was hardly aware of eating. Her happy heart had filled her up.

His blue eyes crinkled as he laughed at something little Peter said. He felt her gaze. Their eyes locked. She drowned in their warmth.

"Mary, eat your chicken," Mama said.

"Perhaps she doesn't like it," Mr. Easterly said. "Ellen put some unusual seasonings on it."

Julia watched Peter shovel it in. "Peter likes it, don't you, honey?"

Peter nodded, his mouth full.

"I don't feel good," Mary said.

Her face was flushed, her eyes glassy.

"What's wrong?" Mama said.

"My stomach hurts."

"Feel her forehead," Mama told Richard who sat beside her.

He did. "She feels hot."

"Would you like to lie down?" Mr. Easterly asked her.

Mary nodded.

"We need to go home," Mama said.

"Wait until we finish eating," Papa said.

They brought a bench from the hall for Mary. Mr. Easterly tucked a blanket around her.

The rest of the meal felt rushed. When the last crumbs of caramel cake were finished, Mama said, "We must go now."

Julia didn't want to go. She needed time with Mr. Easterly.

As Papa gathered up Mary, Mr. Easterly touched Julia's arm. "Can you stay?"

He looked as desperate to talk as she. She nodded.

"I'll call the chauffeur and have him drive your family home."

By the time they were bundled into their coats, Edgar Hopkins had the Packard waiting at the porte-cochère entrance.

"Julia, you need to come too," Mama said.

"Now, Louise, it won't hurt her to stay," Papa said.

"I'll take good care of her. I promise," Mr. Easterly said.

Mama's lips tightened as she flung Julia a dark look.

One of these days Mama would have to accept that just maybe Mr. Easterly was the one God had chosen for her.

-→■◎ ◎■←-

Mr. Easterly added another log to the fire before joining her on the plush burgundy tufted sofa in the billiard room.

"Warm enough?" he asked.

The room felt chilly. Or maybe it was nerves from being alone with him. She nodded anyway.

"I'm glad you stayed," he said. "I have so much to tell you."

"And there's so much I want to know. Tell me more about your accepting Christ. How did it happen? Tell me everything." She leaned against the upholstered arm so she could face him.

He looked vulnerable, not like the mighty Mr. Easterly the world knew. Her heart melted.

"I wanted what I saw in your family, so I started reading the Bible. Through things I gleaned at church, and through your father, Lee, and you, God helped me understand."

Her eyes blurred with tears.

"But the story of the rich young ruler is what did it. I feared my riches excluded me from heaven. Lee explained that I needed to make Christ first in my life, not my money. And I desperately wanted to do that."

This was real. Tears dripped down her cheeks.

He pulled a handkerchief from his pocket and wiped her face. "Happy tears, I hope?"

She nodded, not trusting herself to speak.

"Thanks for sharing your life and your family with me. And thanks again for the Bible. I must admit I wasn't thrilled when I first opened it, but it has become my best gift ever."

"I'm so glad."

He captured her hands in his. "Julia, I feel drawn to you, now more than ever. I desperately want to know you better. I'd spend every waking minute with you if I could. May I...?"

What was he trying to say? Her eyes urged him on.

"Perhaps I should have asked your father's permission first, but may I court you?"

Suddenly she felt light-headed. This was what she wanted, right? She had trusted God to direct her path, and now that Mr. Easterly was a believer, God's leading seemed clear, didn't it?

She looked at the well-appointed room. The square-paneled light wood walls. The carved fireplace with wall sconces on either side and a lovely portrait above. The richly patterned Oriental rug. The velvet burgundy drapes. Everything reflected luxury.

How different from Mama's cluttered parlor and well-worn horse-hair sofa.

Could she ever feel comfortable here? Would it ever feel like home?

How ironic that all her life she had thought of herself too highly. Now she felt unworthy. She didn't know how to dress for his crowd. Or talk. Or act. She didn't know how to run a large household or manage servants.

"I won't fit in with your world. I'll embarrass you," she said.

"No, you won't. I can teach you. So can the ladies from the neighborhood who brunch here on Saturday mornings. They want to meet you."

"You told them about me?"

He shrugged sheepishly. "I couldn't help it. Would you come next Saturday to meet them? Please?"

She nodded. She had to eventually, ready or not.

"And would you stay for the concert tonight?"

She nodded again.

"Excellent. And by the way, it's time you called me David instead of Mr. Easterly."

That would take practice.

The telephone rang.

His forehead furrowed. "Sorry." He answered it.

"Hello?" Pause. "Actually this isn't a good time, Stanley. Can you call me tomorrow at the office?" Pause. "All right. Hold on a minute."

He turned to her. "Sorry, I need to take this. Business. Would you mind waiting in the hall?"

She nodded as she stood and exited through the portière into the library. She would rather linger in one of the cozy wing chairs, but no, he said to wait in the hall. She pushed through another portière to the entrance hall.

She felt exposed in the wide-open space. If Miss Donovan or another servant came along, they would spot her instantly.

On the other side of the staircase was an upholstered bench with curved ends, visible only if coming from the living room. It was a perfect hiding place.

She collapsed onto the bench and leaned her head against the polished cream-colored wall beneath the staircase. Straight ahead she looked through the living room door. To the left, the potted plants of the conservatory formed a shield. To the right a grandfather clock stood near the front door.

She felt safe for now. She hoped Mr. Easterly... David wouldn't be too long.

She closed her eyes. My, had David Easterly asked to court her? Unbelievable.

Out of all the women in the world, he had chosen *her.*

Had she given him an answer? She couldn't remember. She felt dazed.

Imagine! This mansion would be hers. It would be her children running down the stairs and through the hallways.

Lord, help me to make it a true home for him, a refuge.

Her heart stilled. But wait. She had never told him about being his laundress. Would he still want her?

Of course he would. He loved her, didn't he?

Perhaps he didn't have to know.

Oh, yes, he did. If she didn't tell him, a servant would.

The servants. She would be in charge of them. Would they respect her or forever treat her like a servant?

And how about Miss Donovan? Miss Donovan would never let her be in charge. Miss Donovan would have to go, no doubt about it. She hoped David felt the same way. She could not live in the same house with that woman.

She brought a shaky hand to her forehead. She needed to tell him about being his laundress. Now. As soon as he finished his call. Before she gave her answer.

The grandfather clock chimed the quarter hour.

The servants would be on duty soon.

Wasn't David done yet? Perhaps he had looked and couldn't find her hidden back here.

She would check.

Looking all ways, she tiptoed into the library and listened. He was still on the phone and sounded upset.

Must she return to that bench? The chairs here looked so inviting.

But she didn't want to eavesdrop.

She sighed as she pushed aside the portière.

Too late, she heard the click-clack of footsteps in the marble foyer.

Miss Donovan appeared, dressed in white. She stopped and stared at Julia. Her eyes protruded.

The hair lifted on Julia's arms.

A vein pulsed in Miss Donovan's forehead. "You?" Her lips curled. "What are you doing here?"

"I-I-I'm visiting Mr. Easterly."

"You are not. You are trespassing. How did you get in here?"

"I was invited for dinner."

"You liar!"

Miss Donovan grabbed her by the ear and dragged her to the front door. She unlocked it and thrust her out onto the snowy porch. "And don't you ever come back."

The door slammed and locked.

Chapter 20

JULIA STARED AT the door, too stunned to move.

She had been thrown out by the ear. Just like Alan Pierce.

Waves of shame engulfed her.

Fortunately no one had witnessed it. She hoped. If she could get back inside, no one would ever know.

But dare she? What would Miss Donovan do if she caught her again? Her teeth chattered. She had to try. And fast. It was bitterly cold, well below freezing. Not good when she had no coat or gloves.

She tried the door. Yes, it was locked. She peered through the decorative filigree on the glass. She saw no one inside to rescue her.

The porte-cochère entrance would be open, but that was by Miss Donovan's desk. She couldn't risk it.

Perhaps the French doors in the living room were unlocked.

She followed the shoveled brick sidewalk around the corner to the covered porch where massive pillars framed the Vista, the snowy side lawn that stretched from East Avenue to University Avenue.

The terra cotta tiles underfoot were slippery. She stepped gingerly as she tried both French doors. They were locked. She should have known.

At the end of the porch, the gravel paths that crisscrossed the formal garden were not shoveled. Her ankles would freeze if she tried to wade through that snow. Besides, the doors to the conservatory and loggia were surely locked too.

She returned to the front porch, hugging her arms. She felt like an icicle. She had to get inside soon. Her toes were numbing.

Perhaps she could attract David's attention from the window. But then she would have to explain why she was locked out.

What would she tell him?

Oh, Lord, I am so ashamed. Please give him understanding.

She must tell him before Miss Donovan did. Certainly he would be sympathetic to her and not Miss Donovan.

She followed the brick walkway to the billiard room window. She stepped up to her knees in snow. Leaning into a snowy bush, she pressed her nose against the window.

David was still on the phone, facing her. She waved. He didn't see her.

"Mr. Easterly," she yelled.

He didn't hear.

She knocked on the glass, her fists like bricks of ice.

He still didn't hear.

God, please let him see me.

She knocked again and waved her arms.

He looked up. His mouth formed an O. He slammed down the phone and hurried out.

She was stuck in the bush. She didn't have the strength to move.

The front door opened. "Julia, what are you doing?"

"Help." Her voice was frozen too.

When he reached her, he lifted her to the sidewalk. "What are you doing out here? What happened?"

"I was locked out."

"How did that happen?"

"I'll explain inside. I'm frozen solid."

He helped her to the door.

"How long have you been out here?"

"I don't know. Too long."

In the entrance hall, he brushed off the snow and removed her snow-filled shoes. She couldn't speak through her chattering teeth.

He looked alarmed. "You're freezing," he said. "We must warm you up."

He put his arm around her and gently led her back to the billiard room. Her legs buckled in front of the fire.

"You poor thing. Sit there and warm up. I'll get you a blanket." He left.

She held out her hands and soaked in the warmth. She watched a little tendril catch fire and burn off a log. The embers looked like chunks of gold. She wished she could crawl in.

David was so kind and compassionate. Would that change when she told him about what happened with Miss Donovan? Surely not. David would understand, wouldn't he?

She couldn't stop trembling. Yes, she was cold, but she was fearful too. What if he was not sympathetic?

"Here we are," he said. He wrapped the blanket around her, massaging her wet feet. "Now tell me what happened."

The moment of truth was here. *Lord, help me.*

"Miss Donovan locked me out. She thought I was an intruder."

He scowled. "This is inexcusable. I'm so sorry."

It would be easy to leave all the blame on Miss Donovan, but she had to tell him.

"David, I need to confess something."

"Hey, you called me David." His eyes softened. "I like it."

"I have a long story to tell you. I hope you'll understand."

"Yes?"

"In June, my father fell off a bridge at work. His broke both legs and was in the hospital for two months."

"Really? I would never have known."

"Because of the hospital bills, Richard and I needed summer jobs. Richard was hired as your gardener and heard you needed a temporary laundress when Sally broke her arm. Miss Donovan hired me."

He blanched. "You were my laundress?"

"Only for two weeks."

A shadow passed over his eyes.

"Until Miss Donovan dismissed me."

His eyes snapped to her face. This sounded bad even to her ears. She plowed ahead, eager for him to know the truth.

"We didn't hit it off from the beginning. She thought I was uppity because of my college education, and she looked for an excuse to get rid of me. My downfall was my obsession with your house. When it was being built, I walked by every night, wondering what the inside looked like. Then when I worked here, Miss Donovan wouldn't let me see a thing. One day the curtain was open, and I couldn't help peeking. Miss Donovan dismissed me on the spot."

He closed his eyes and massaged his forehead. She wished he would say something.

"Today was the first I'd seen her since then. She didn't believe I was your guest. She threw me out again."

He stared into the fire, a muscle in his jaw contracting.

"I'm so sorry," she said.

"I am too." He turned to look at her, the warmth gone. "Why didn't you tell me sooner?"

"I was afraid to. I knew you didn't socialize with servants."

"So you purposefully deceived me?"

She turned her gaze to the burning embers. "I was going to tell you. The time never seemed right. I'm so sorry."

Minutes passed. The silence was broken only by the ticking of a clock as they both stared into the flames.

Say something, she begged. This was not going well. She had expected him to be more forgiving.

She snuck a peek. He looked like stone. She shuddered.

Finally he said, "This isn't going to work."

She bit her lip. "What isn't going to work?"

"Us. I've made it a firm policy not to socialize with my staff, not to show favoritism, not to demean myself. I can't bend my rules."

"But I only worked for you for two weeks. It barely counts." Desperation colored her voice.

"It does count. If word escaped that I'd married my former laundress, I would be a laughingstock. And you can't hide something like that, not with my whole staff knowing."

"So what are you saying?"

"You have to leave. Now."

No! She never dreamed it would end like this. "Will I ever see you again?"

"Probably not."

"What about church?"

"There are other churches right here on East Avenue."

"But ... " He might not grow in his faith in those churches.

"Go, Julia, now. I'll call Hopkins to bring the car around."

She didn't want anyone else to witness her humiliation. "No need. I'll walk."

"You can't walk. You're still cold."

She threw off the blanket and scrambled to her feet. "I'll walk."

He followed as she marched into the hall and slid into her wet shoes.

"Bring my cape, please."

"I didn't realize you were so stubborn."

"It's not stubbornness. It's pride. In case you didn't know, it's one of my weaknesses."

As he helped with her cape, Alan Pierce descended the stairs, carrying folding chairs for the evening concert. He paused when he saw her, then winked and waved.

David witnessed it all.

She wished she could melt away like the snow in her shoes.

Her humiliation was complete.

—⟶▆ ▆⟵—

David watched her stumble down the porch steps. Her feet probably hadn't fully thawed yet. He should insist she ride home.

But he didn't have the energy to go after her. He felt hollow, alone, hurt, betrayed. Why hadn't she told him sooner, before he'd fallen in love with her?

Alan's wave hadn't gone unnoticed.

As Alan crossed the marble foyer with the chairs, David said, "Do you know her?"

"Julia Bradshaw? Yeah, I know her."

"How well do you know her?"

He smirked. "The laundry was right across from the carpenter's shop."

That said it all.

Julia was not the woman he thought she was.

He strode back to the billiard room, picked up her damp blanket, and hurled it across the room.

—⟶▆ ▆⟵—

It was a mistake to walk home. Julia couldn't feel her feet. Her tear-streaked cheeks were frozen. Icicles dangled beneath her nose.

What had happened? How had she gone from daydreaming about a home with David Easterly to having him kick her out?

Surely he would change his mind about never seeing her again.

And if he didn't, how could she bear it?

The sobs erupted once more. She clutched her cape around her and ran down the icy sidewalks, not caring if she fell.

How could he suddenly change his mind just because she was his laundress? He was so disgustingly proud and arrogant and lofty. Worse than she.

But that's who he was. The mighty Mr. Easterly. He would never change.

As she ran past Miss Weston's apartment, she felt disgraced. What would Miss Weston think? And Lee?

And how would she tell her family? They would be devastated, except for Mama. Mama would likely say, "I told you so."

Mama was right. Julia had been a fool to think she could enter Mr. Easterly's world. Mama had tried to shelter her from this.

Past the school she ran. Perhaps God's plan was Mr. Pratt after all. She cried harder.

When she reached home, her feet felt like cement blocks. She could barely climb the steps. Her hands were too frozen to turn the knob. She banged her head against the door. Papa came.

His face registered shock. "Julia, what happened?" He pulled her inside.

"Oh, Papa." She snuggled into his warm arms and cried.

He patted her back. "What happened, princess?"

"Mr. Easterly threw me out." She quivered.

"That doesn't sound right. Here, get out of those snowy clothes, come in by the fire, and tell me all about it."

Mama dozed in her chair. Richard thumbed through a magazine. Jenny read on the sofa. Mary slept under a blanket on the couch, her cheeks flushed. Peter and Annie napped upstairs.

Julia collapsed by the fire.

"What's wrong with *you*?" Jenny said.

"Mr. Easterly threw me out." Her voice was ragged.

"I don't believe it. Why would he do that?" Jenny said.

"While he was on the phone, Miss Donovan locked me outside. When Mr. Easterly let me in, I told him about being his laundress this summer. He couldn't handle it. He said his reputation would be ruined."

Mama squinted. "I knew you weren't good enough for that man. Good riddance."

Papa sighed. "I don't know what to think. I had such high hopes for him, especially since he seemed so sincere in his faith."

"Now I wonder if it was real at all," Julia said.

"I believe it was," Papa said. "You just took him by surprise. If you had told him under other circumstances, he might have reacted differently."

"So what do we do now?" she asked.

"We pray for him," Papa said. "Let's do it right now." He gingerly lowered himself beside her, one arm around her shoulder. "Our dear heavenly Father, our precious brother is probably hurting as much as Julia. Help him see this from Your perspective and not his own. Turn his heart toward You and Your Word. I pray that You would lead them into Your perfect will. In Jesus' name, Amen."

"Thanks." Julia sniffled. "You've given me hope."

"Princess, where God is concerned, there's always hope."

->▬◉ ◉▬<-

"You called, Mr. Easterly?" Miss Donovan said.

"Yes, come in. I have a few questions. What can you tell me about Julia Bradshaw?"

Her eyes hardened. "Somehow she sneaked in today. I should have her arrested for trespassing. Fortunately, I caught her before she stole anything else."

"Anything else? What do you mean?"

"When she was a laundress here last summer, I dismissed her for stealing your mother's silver urn."

It was worse than he thought. Julia hadn't shared that.

"What kind of worker was she?"

"I didn't trust her from the beginning, the way she put on airs."

"How did she get along with the staff?"

"She held herself aloof. Nobody liked her."

He had been completely duped. Julia had charmed him into believing she was someone she was not.

Miss Donovan had been a faithful servant and friend. He had no reason to doubt her word.

"Thank you. You may go now. Please send Rose in."

Rose entered a few minutes later. "Yes, Mr. Easterly?"

"I understand you know Julia Bradshaw."

"Yes, sir. She was a laundress here last summer."

"What kind of worker was she?"

"She got the job done."

"What was she like?"

"She was a flirt. The men couldn't leave her alone."

David winced. He wasn't sure he wanted to hear more.

"How did she get along with the female staff?"

"She was nice enough. We all liked her."

That was interesting. Miss Donovan said no one liked her.

"How did she get along with Miss Donovan?"

"She didn't. She stayed out of Miss Donovan's way."

"Why was she dismissed?"

"Miss Donovan said she stole something."

"Do you know what?"

"A vase."

"Thank you. You've been most helpful. You may go."

David groaned and leaned his forehead into his hands. It was worse than he imagined. She was insubordinate, a flirt, and a thief. Could it be any worse? And this was the woman he had almost married. She was nothing more than an illusion.

God, thank You for sparing me.

God? Maybe God was an illusion too.

⇢▬◎ ◎▬⇠

David hosted his Sunday evening concert in a daze. After everyone left, he retreated to his bedroom, his heart in shambles.

God, why?

Julia had seemed so kind and sincere. Was it all a ruse to be the mistress of his home?

The Bible she had given him was on his bedside table. With a guttural roar, he hurled it across the room. It hit a black marble column on the fireplace, landing close to the flames.

Better to be burned than be a constant reminder of her betrayal.

He tore across the room, but stopped short of kicking it into the fire when he saw his reflection in the mantel mirror.

Was that him? His face was flushed, his eyes so wide the whites showed. His nostrils flared, his neck was corded. He looked like a madman.

He was no longer dignified, orderly, or in control.

He crumpled to the floor and scooped up the Bible. *God, what have I done? I don't want to be like this.*

He wanted the peace he had experienced last week.

God, help me. Forgive me. His forehead touched the ground. *Take away my anger.*

He would not give up on God too.

But what should he do about Julia? Already he missed the dream of her being there when he returned home, of having the dinner table filled with adoring little faces. Empty, lonely years stretched before him.

He would have to fill his life with other things. Take more trips. Host more concerts and parties. Find someone to take Julia's place.

Chapter 21

Monday, January 11, 1909

DAVID HARDLY SLEPT. When Solomon woke him at seven-fifteen the next morning, he didn't have the energy to say his usual, "Good morning, what's the temperature today?"

He frankly didn't care what the temperature was. He didn't care about anything.

Were it not for pressing matters at work, he would have stayed in bed. But forty-five minutes later he was down to breakfast, dressed as immaculately as always. The organ music was a balm to his headache, as were the fresh lilies on the table.

As he read the newspaper, footsteps tiptoed across the floor. Curly-haired Katie, the second-floor maid who kept his quarters spotless, stood before him.

"Mr. Easterly, might I have a word with you?" Her eyes darted around the room before resting on him again.

"What is it?"

She twisted her hands. "I've been wrestling all night about whether to tell you this."

"Yes?"

"I heard Miss Donovan and Rose whispering yesterday, and whatever they told you wasn't the truth."

"Go on." His head throbbed.

"Julia Bradshaw did not steal a vase. She was dismissed simply for looking beyond the portière."

That was exactly what Julia had told him.

"Why would Miss Donovan and Rose lie about it?"

"Because they're jealous of her."

That made sense. Julia was a beautiful woman.

"What did *you* think of Julia?"

Katie fidgeted. "At first she didn't know anything about laundry. But I showed her how, and she caught on quickly. She was a hard worker, one of the best laundresses we've had. I was sad to see her go. She was a wonderful person."

"What was her relationship to Alan Pierce?"

Katie's eyes fluttered. "Alan? She didn't have a relationship with him except for staying out of his way."

Now he didn't know what to think.

⇥ ⇤

When David entered his office, Miss Weston looked up. "Good morning." Her smiled faded. "What's wrong? You look ghastly."

"I barely slept, and I have a raging headache. Don't bother me."

"Why didn't you stay home?"

"I need to handle an urgent matter for Stanley from Chicago."

The phone call after which everything had changed.

"So that's what gave you the headache?"

"Not really."

"Is something else bothering you?"

This woman knew him too well.

"If you must know, I'm not going to see Julia Bradshaw ever again."

Her chin dropped. "Are you crazy? She's perfect for you."

"I found out she was my laundress last summer."

"Really?" Her eyes had a faraway look. "So that's where I saw her... the morning I came for breakfast. I remember now. Here I thought she was a teacher."

"She's both. She was my laundress for two weeks. I can't marry someone who was my servant."

She sighed. "You are exasperating, Mr. Easterly. Julia is one of the most wonderful women I've met. I can't believe you'd let that stand in your way."

"There's more. My housekeeper dismissed her for stealing my mother's silver urn."

Again she looked thoughtful. "That's not true."

"How do you know?"

"I was there. I heard Miss Donovan yelling at her when I was inside the ladies' room. She accused Julia of looking beyond the curtain. Nothing more. It seemed rather harsh to me."

David felt a glimmer of hope. So Miss Donovan and Rose *had* lied. It didn't solve anything, though. He still couldn't marry his laundress.

"Have you prayed about it?" she asked.

"I've had a hard time praying about anything since this happened."

"That's your problem. You need to spend time with the Lord. Ask Him what to do."

David had always handled things himself. He didn't need advice from Miss Weston or God.

"I'm too busy." He opened the cabinet and searched for Stan's file.

"I'll be praying for you this morning."

He ignored her as he sat.

Immersing himself in his work proved futile. Swirling were the arguments for and against Julia Bradshaw.

She was so beautiful. He could drown in her sapphire eyes. But it was her heart that had drawn him. No one else made him feel like a person and not just a boss.

The thought of never seeing blond Peter again or having bouncy Annie on his back grieved him almost as much as not seeing her.

Was he willing to forfeit his happiness for lies?

On the other hand, his reputation would be ruined if he married his laundress.

Perhaps marrying Grace Weston would solve the problem.

"Miss Weston?"

"Yes?"

"Now that I'm a Christian, would you consider marrying me?"

"Never."

He winced.

"I would never marry a man who was in love with someone else."

Was he still in love with Julia?

Perhaps he did need to get away and pray.

"Congratulations, Miss Weston, you have done it again."

"Done what?"

"Accomplished exactly what you wanted. Call Hopkins. Tell him to pick me up after lunch. I need to drive around and pray. I won't come back until this is settled."

Her smile was satisfied.

⇢═ ═⇠

The gray skies and dirty snow piled along the sidewalks outside her classroom window were as dismal as Julia's heart.

Her shrouded mind didn't know what she'd taught today.

She felt humbled and ashamed of her behavior toward Mr. Easterly.

Angry too. He was so disgustingly proud and arrogant.

But not so long ago she had also been disgustingly proud and arrogant. Too good to work as a laundress when she had a college education.

It was no wonder God had humbled her.

But the thought of never seeing him again severed her heart.

Why, God, would you allow him to find You and then snatch him away from me?

Perhaps Mr. Easterly never was God's plan for her. Maybe she was only the instrument to point him toward God.

In time, she could accept that. But now the wound was too raw.

"Knock, knock."

Oh, she couldn't face Mr. Pratt today.

His smile faded as he entered. "What's wrong? Hard day?"

Her throat was too clogged to speak. She nodded.

"Joey again?"

She shook her head.

"What then?" He sat on the corner of her desk.

She couldn't tell him. She closed her eyes. A tear seeped out.

"Hey, what's wrong?"

His footsteps neared. Then his arms enfolded her.

She couldn't help it. The tears erupted.

He caressed her back. "Everything will be all right."

She knew it would be. After all, God promised that all things worked together for good. This was part of His plan. If only it didn't hurt so much.

She wondered if His plan included Mr. Pratt now. Perhaps it had all along. He was a good man. He would love her dearly.

But he wasn't Mr. Easterly.

Someone knocked on the door and it swung open. Who now?

She extracted herself from Mr. Pratt's arms.

It was David Easterly in his greatcoat and leather gloves.

Her breath caught.

What was he doing here? She drank in the sight of him. He looked haggard. Under his eyes were dark circles. His hair was rumpled. His eyes were pained.

Mr. Pratt stiffened and circled her waist with his arm.

Mr. Easterly's jaw jutted out. "So sorry to interrupt." The steel in his eyes told her he had seen everything. He turned to leave.

"Wait. Don't go. Why did you come?"

"It's not important now." His parting look was heartrending.

"Wait."

But he was gone.

"What just happened here?" Mr. Pratt said.

"I don't know."

But she suspected she had just lost Mr. Easterly a second time.

⭒⭒⭒

David Easterly hung up his coat and hat on the coat tree in his office.

"I didn't expect you back this afternoon," Miss Weston said.

"Neither did I." He was in no mood to talk. He should have gone home and lamented in private.

"What happened?"

Maybe he *would* feel better talking about it. "Hopkins has been driving me around for the last three hours. I was thinking and praying, and I concluded that Julia was more important to me than what others think."

"Bravo." Miss Weston clapped. "That's exactly what I was praying."

"I couldn't stand the thought of living without her."

"Then why the long face?"

"I stopped by her school, and I found her in Mr. Pratt's arms."

Her face crumbled. "Oh, I'm so sorry. Perhaps it wasn't what it seems."

"It's exactly what it seems. He loves her, and she has chosen him. It didn't take her long to find refuge in his arms."

"She doesn't love him. I've seen how she looks at you."

He shrugged. "It's too late."

"Go see her tonight. Apologize."

"Apologize? She should be apologizing to me for not telling me she was my laundress."

"No, you should apologize to her for thinking the worst about her."

He ground his teeth.

"I take that back," she said. "Don't see her tonight. You need more time to process this."

"It's too late. I've lost her."

"Fight for her. I've never known you to lose, Mr. Easterly."

"There's always a first time."

She huffed as she rolled a sheet of paper into her typewriter.

→═ ═←

Sunday, January 17, 1909

"Why can't we ride with Mr. Easterly?" Peter said as Julia stuffed his hands into mittens. The whole family crowded into the foyer, elbows bumping, as they donned coats and boots.

Peter's question was like a knife twisting in her wound.

"Because Mr. Easterly is not coming with us to church today," she said.

"Why?"

"He's going to another church."

"Why? Doesn't he like me anymore?"

"Of course he does."

"Then why isn't he coming?"

"Because he doesn't like Julia anymore," Jenny said.

"Why?"

"Because I was his laundress," Julia said.

"Doesn't he like clean clothes?"

"That's enough, Peter," Mama said. "We will not be seeing Mr. Easterly again."

Mama didn't have to look so happy about it.

"We'll be late if we don't leave now," Mama said.

"I want to ride," Peter said.

"Me too," said little Annie.

Papa swooped Annie into his arms. "Come on, everyone, it's a beautiful day for a walk. See how the sun is shining."

He opened the front door, stopping abruptly. "Julia, look."

"What?" She pushed in front of Jenny.

The big green Packard was parked out front. Mr. Easterly, in his greatcoat, leather gloves, and black hat, leaned against the side, arms crossed, facing them. His smile was tentative.

Julia's heart leaped to her throat. He was here. Why?

"Mr. Easterly!" Peter ran down the steps.

Mr. Easterly opened his arms and caught him in a bear hug.

Julia wanted to run into his arms too.

"You came," Peter said.

Mr. Easterly ruffled his blond hair. "Wouldn't miss it."

So had he come for church, for her family, or for her?

Julia squeezed beside Mr. Easterly on the front seat. She held herself rigid, leaning into Richard, but it was impossible for their shoulders not to touch.

He said nothing as he turned the key.

Should she be hopeful?

Or not?

⇥〇 〇⇤

Julia's heart plummeted. Instead of sitting next to her, Mr. Easterly, with Peter on his lap, sat on the other end of the pew, as far away as possible.

Her throat clogged. *Lord, don't let me fall apart now. Not here. Not in front of everyone.*

His message was clear. He was not interested in her. He had come for church and her family.

At least he had not given up on God too. She should be thankful.

Mr. Pratt slipped in beside her. "Good morning," he said.

Oh, why did Mr. Pratt have to come? He just made everything worse.

"Hey, what's wrong? Are you crying?"

She shook her head as a tear slipped down her cheek.

"What's wrong?"

She closed her eyes and shook her head again.

His hand covered hers. Another tear slipped out.

The first hymn was announced. They both reached for the hymnal. Their hands touched. She yanked hers back and let him open it.

She glanced down her family's pew. Peter was still snuggled contentedly on Mr. Easterly's lap.

Oh, to be Peter.

->=== ◎===<-

After church, David pulled the Packard close to the curb so the Bradshaws wouldn't step into the slush in front of their house.

"Would you like to join us for dinner?" Mr. Bradshaw asked.

Julia tensed beside him.

"Thanks, but not today." He couldn't bear to be with this family until things were right with Julia.

When she had been stiff and quiet on the ride to church, he had all but given up. Her message was clear. She wanted nothing to do with him. So he kept his distance during the service.

But seeing Mr. Pratt beside her, his hand over hers, was too much. He would not go down without a fight.

As the doors opened and the family spilled out, he touched her arm. "Could I talk with you? Alone."

She blinked rapidly and nodded.

Good. She was giving him a chance.

"Tell Mama I'll be in soon," she said as Richard slid out with Annie. Go on, Peter. Go with Richard."

"I wanna stay here with you." He didn't budge from her lap.

David bent down to his ear. "Come on, sport, I need to talk with your sister. I'll see you soon."

Peter's lower lip pouted as he crawled out. Julia slid across the seat and closed the door behind him.

He wished she had stayed close, although looking at her now was easier. She was pressed into the door, as far away as possible. Her eyes were wary.

He took a deep breath. "I have three questions."

She flinched.

"I've heard rumors about you."

"Like what?"

"That you are a flirt. That all the men like you."

Her cheeks flamed. "Who told you that?"

"Alan Pierce. Rose."

She shriveled. "It's not true. Alan flirted with *me*. I tried to ignore him. And Rose was jealous of how the men looked at me, but believe me, I did nothing to encourage it."

"How about Mr. Pratt?"

"He's liked me for a long time, but I have not encouraged him either."

His heart lifted. That was excellent news.

"I've heard other things about you too."

Her eyes narrowed.

"Miss Donovan said you were dismissed because she caught you stealing my mother's silver urn. Rose confirmed it."

"That's not true. I was dismissed because I disobeyed her command not to look beyond the curtain. Believe me, I have regretted it ever since and begged the Lord's forgiveness."

"Thirdly, why did you deceive me? Why didn't you tell me sooner that you were my laundress?"

Her eyes flooded. "I wanted to, but I was afraid you would reject me. Turns out I was right." She opened the door. "Now if you are done with your interrogation, I'll leave." She stepped down.

"Wait. I'm *not* done."

The door slammed.

He yanked open his door and ran around the car. She was halfway up the stairs.

"Julia, wait."

She spun around, her eyes flashing. "I'm done with your accusations. I'm not perfect, but I never thought you would believe those lies."

He had handled her badly, more like a business client. How did a man convince a woman he loved her?

He stood below, looking up. He reached for her gloved hand. "I believe your every word. In fact, Katie and Miss Weston backed up everything you've said. I just needed to hear it from your lips."

She looked uncertain.

"I struggled all week thinking about you. Were you the greedy flirt or the sweet, compassionate woman who cared enough to look into my heart? I could either believe the lies others told or follow my instinct.

God helped me see the truth. You are an amazing woman, and I desperately want to be with you."

"But I was your laundress. What about that?"

"I've concluded that you are more important than what others think. Please forgive me for reacting so badly."

Her lashes fluttered. "What are you saying?"

"I miss you. I was miserable last week. I couldn't bear the thought of living life without you. Can we start over?"

She didn't answer. Emotions flashed across her face. Guardedness. Suspicion.

Had he wounded her so deeply?

He held his breath. *Please, God, let her say yes.* He needed a second chance.

Her eyes softened.

Finally she nodded. "All right."

He leaped up the steps and held her close. "Oh, thank you." Her arms reached around him.

He could feel the healing as their hearts beat in rhythm.

She looked up with her warm sapphire eyes. "Why don't you stay for dinner, David?"

"Don't mind if I do."

->=◎ ◎=<-

When the little ones went down for their naps, David swallowed hard before addressing Mr. Bradshaw, "Sir, would you take a walk with me? There's something I'd like to ask you."

Mr. Bradshaw's eyes darted to Julia. "Sure."

They donned their coats, hats, and gloves.

David felt more nervous than when standing before his board of directors.

Together they went outside. The sun warmed the chilly air. They walked down the stairs to the shoveled sidewalk, the snow mounded up to their knees on either side.

David didn't bother with small talk. "I would like to ask permission to court your daughter."

Mr. Bradshaw twirled the end of his mustache. "Why?"

He wasn't making this easy.

"Because she is the most amazing woman I've ever met, and I can't imagine my life without her."

"You obviously didn't feel that way last week."

David winced. "I was a fool."

"How do I know you won't reject her again?"

"Because then I was reacting the way I used to. I've spent hours in prayer. I've asked the Lord's forgiveness, I've asked Julia's, and now I ask yours."

"I don't want to see her hurt."

"Believe me, neither do I."

"Julia is not of your social class. She might embarrass you."

"I have humble beginnings myself. I grew up on a farm until my dad died, and then we moved to the city where my mother opened a boarding house."

"Yes, but look at you now. Can Julia fit into your world?"

"Absolutely."

"Of even more concern is your being the spiritual head of the home, leading as a wise Christian example, encouraging Julia and your children in their faith."

Sweat beaded on David's forehead in spite of the cold.

"I am new in my faith, but it is my desire to know God better. I want to create a home and family just like yours."

"Son, I believe you. I also firmly believe God has His hand on your life. Yes, you have my blessing to court her."

The tension in his body released.

They clasped hands and Mr. Bradshaw pulled him into an embrace. It was a remarkable feeling. Not only would he be gaining a wife, but also a father.

Chapter 22

Saturday, January 16, 1909

JULIA'S STOMACH FELT like the inside of a hornet's nest as David helped her from the green Packard and up the steps of the porte-cochère for brunch with the ladies. David had told her to dress up, so she had worn her suit of red chiffon broadcloth with a white velvet vest. She hoped David wouldn't be ashamed of her.

Lord, help me, she had prayed for days. She felt totally inadequate. It was one thing to dream of being David's wife. It was another to step into his world.

David swung the door open. "You'll do fine." He squeezed her hand.

Solomon's hulking frame filled the hallway. He smiled as he helped her with her cape. "Good to see you, Miss Bradshaw."

"Thank you." His friendly countenance bolstered her courage.

She furtively glanced into Miss Donovan's office. It was empty.

What if Miss Donovan threw her out by her ear in front of all these ladies?

David had assured her she wouldn't. He'd talked with her and told her he was courting Julia Bradshaw.

She was glad she hadn't been there. Miss Donovan must have been livid.

David placed his hand on the small of her back as they crossed the short hallway to the open portière. This was one time she had no desire to go beyond the curtain.

She heard women's chatter as they stepped into the light-filled conservatory.

Four well-dressed women sat in green wicker chairs at a round table covered with a lace tablecloth. The china was white, rimmed in gold. The goblets sparkled. The centerpiece was red roses and maidenhair ferns.

The voices stopped. Four faces turned toward them. The ladies stood.

Julia feared her smile looked more like a grimace.

A handsome woman in her forties wearing a luxurious gown of pink satin approached with open arms and a bounce to her step. "Look who's here."

She grasped Julia's cold hands. "Aren't you the prettiest thing? David has told us so many wonderful things about you."

Julia liked her immediately.

"Julia, this is Catherine Townsend."

"Pleased to meet you," Julia said.

Next he introduced Miriam Branson, a thin woman with a clammy handshake and a nervous laugh. Nancy Jones towered above her. It was hard to see her eyes through the glare of her glasses. Elizabeth Schuyler was shorter and rounder and younger than the others. Her greeting was wary.

"Sit down, ladies," David said.

He re-seated them one by one, starting with Julia.

When Solomon brought in the fruit cup, David said, "I know we've never done this before, but I would like to ask God's blessing on our food. Shall we hold hands and pray?"

Shock colored their faces. They reluctantly held hands. Julia felt proud of him as she nestled her hand in his.

"Dear God," he began, "thank You for this food and for these ladies. In Jesus' name, Amen."

"Short and sweet, just the way I like it," Miriam said.

"Now, David, what precipitated this?" Catherine asked. "Since when are you a religious man?"

"It happened recently as a result of being around Julia's family and going to her church and reading the Bible. I've accepted Christ as my Savior. I'm a Christian now."

Nancy fidgeted with her glasses. "Well, I never expected that."

Catherine looked at Julia, "Oh, the power of a woman. Good for you."

Julia felt embarrassed. It wasn't her. It was God.

"Now, Julia, we want to know all about you," Catherine said. "David says you're a kindergarten teacher."

"Yes, I'm in my second year, and I love it."

"And what do you do in your spare time?"

"Spare time? I don't have much because I'm so busy preparing lessons. But I love to read."

"You two have something in common then. Have you seen David's library?"

She nodded.

"He has enough books to keep you going forever. Are you in any clubs?"

"Clubs?" Julia's face colored.

"You know... a garden club, literary club?"

"No." Maybe she would have time for that after she married, although she would rather invest her free time serving in the church.

"Do you like music?"

"I think so." Now she felt like a ninny. She liked the music in church, but she had never been to a secular concert.

The ladies looked at each other. Elizabeth rolled her eyes.

Julia wanted to go home.

"David, you have your work cut out for you," Miriam said.

"I was hoping you ladies could help," David said.

"How?" Miriam asked.

"With fashion, etiquette, how to manage servants, and anything else you can think of."

Catherine's eyes sparkled. "What a fun project. Of course we'll help."

Julia wasn't sure she liked being a project.

"There's one more thing you should know about Julia," he said.

They looked expectantly at her.

"This summer she was my laundress."

Looks of horror ringed the table.

Julia's face flamed. She wished he hadn't told. Things were bad enough before.

"Her father had an accident and broke both legs, so she needed to supplement the family's income. That was when Sally, my laundress, broke her arm. I never met Julia then, not until she was escorted by her cousin to my Christmas Eve party."

The room felt icy.

"Ladies, I need your support here. I'm not going to advertize it, but I wanted you to know in case of rumors. We'll just treat it matter-of-factly and not make an issue of it. Agreed?"

The food on their plates suddenly demanded their attention. No one would look at her. She feared she would never be welcome now.

"I will admit it was an obstacle for me too," David said. "In fact, I almost walked away from this lovely lady last week. But I realized she was more important to me than what other people thought."

Catherine's eyes darted to his face. "That was a lovely thing to say. If she's that important to you, yes, of course we'll support you, won't we, ladies?"

The others looked noncommittal.

"What should be our plan of attack?" Catherine said. "I know. I'll host a ball where you can introduce her. A Valentine's ball."

A ball? My goodness, Mama would disown her. They didn't dance.

"That gives us about a month to plan and get ready," Catherine said.

"That's not enough time to order gowns from Paris," Elizabeth said.

"Oh, I don't need a gown from Paris," Julia said. "I'll just buy one at Sibley's."

Again those same looks of horror. What had she said now?

"Don't worry about the cost, Julia. I'll pay for everything," David said. "You do what these ladies say."

She wasn't thinking about the cost. She just hadn't realized department stores weren't the only places to shop. She did have a lot to learn.

She was a project after all.

-→-►=◎ ◎=◄-←-

Solomon helped the ladies with their coats.

"Now, Julia, I'll expect you at two o'clock," Catherine Townsend said. "We've no time to waste in finding your gown."

Julia nodded.

The ladies hugged and kissed each other before emerging into the cold where Edgar stood by the Packard.

"Wait here," David told her. "I'll see them off."

Julia watched from the open doorway. She was glad that was over.

Over? Hardly. It had only begun.

All she wanted was David. Instead, she had to embrace a whole new lifestyle. She would be poked and prodded and fashioned to meet their approval. She was happy with how she was, thank you very much.

But she didn't want David to be ashamed of her. She would submit for his sake.

She heard the click-clack of high heels on marble.

No! Not Miss Donovan now. *Please don't throw me out in front of these ladies.*

Miss Donovan grabbed her arm and spun her around. Her eyes were fiery. "What are you doing here?"

Julia quaked. "I was invited for brunch. Mr. Easterly told you I was coming, didn't he?"

Solomon looked concerned. Surely he would protect her.

Miss Donovan dragged her into the office and shoved her against a wall. She waved her index finger in Julia's face. "You will not marry Mr. Easterly, do you hear?"

Julia felt faint.

Solomon stepped in and pried Miss Donovan away. "Come, Miss Donovan, let's see if Ellen has a nice hot cup of tea for you."

His eyes motioned for Julia to return to the hall.

David bustled in as she did.

"Why, Julia, what's wrong? You're as white as a sheet."

To her dismay, she burst into tears.

"What's wrong?" He drew her close.

"Miss Donovan..." Her chest heaved.

"Come, let's go into the billiard room. We'll talk."

He helped her to a sofa in front of the fire. He put on another log before sitting beside her and caressing her hands. "Now tell me what has upset you. Miss Donovan? The ladies?"

Sobs welled up. How could she explain? It was Miss Donovan, the ladies, everything. She shouldn't even try to fit in.

"Don't let the ladies upset you. They may seem critical, but they told me how much they like you. You've nothing to fear."

"Why did you tell them I was your laundress? That made it worse."

"I was proving to myself it didn't matter."

"But it does matter."

"Not as much."

"At least you could have told them I graduated from the University of Rochester."

"It didn't seem important."

"Not important? I worked hard for that degree. I'm the first person in my family besides Lee who has been to college. It's a huge accomplishment, and I'm proud of it."

"As you should be, but none of those ladies has been to college. Julia, *I* have not been to college."

Julia felt disoriented. How could that be? Look at this place. Look at all he had achieved.

"My father died when I was six, and we left the farm and moved to the city. We had no income, so my mother took in boarders. I dropped out of school when I was thirteen so I could work and support my mother. Julia, I never even finished high school."

She felt humbled. Here she thought her college degree made her superior. How wrong she was.

"I educated myself with all those books in my library."

He was smarter than she was, even without an education.

"But how did you become so successful?"

"It was a long process of ups and downs. A man who lived at my mother's boarding house told me of a job opening at the Rochester Savings Bank. They hired me as a clerk. Then I was promoted to assistant bookkeeper when I was twenty. I made good money which gave me the freedom to expand my interests. I'd always been fascinated by photography, so I invented a dry plate-coating machine which I had patented. I was still working at the bank while I was making it on a small scale. Then a partner supplied me with the funds to expand, and it just exploded from there."

"I'm amazed."

He stroked her hand. "Enough about me. Tell me what's bothering you regarding Miss Donovan."

She sighed. "She just pulled me into her office, stuck her finger in my face, and told me that I could not marry you. I'm afraid of her. I will never feel comfortable with her in this house."

"She's just a stubborn old woman, nothing to be afraid of."

"You didn't see the look in her eye. She hates me. I can't live in the same house with her. She needs to go."

"I'm sorry but that's not possible. She's been a friend of the family since before I was born."

She was a friend of the family? He couldn't get rid of her?

"What do you mean?"

"She was my mother's best friend growing up. When her husband died and she was penniless, we hired her as our housekeeper, and she has done an outstanding job. I promised my mother I would care for her the rest of her life. I could no more get rid of her than my own mother."

She felt faint. This changed everything.

"Julia, you need to learn to get along."

"I can't. Not with her."

"Come on, you're a Christian. Aren't you supposed to love everyone?"

Her chest heaved.

"Let me call her. We'll work this out."

"Now?"

"We can't have this drag on."

"Wait." She wasn't ready. She needed to pray about it. She needed time to change her heart.

He stood and pressed the bell beside the fireplace.

Lord, help!

⋯⊷⊚ ⊚⊶⋯

David paced around the billiard table while waiting for Miss Donovan.

He was accustomed to peace, quiet, and orderliness. Julia had been in his house for two hours, and already things felt chaotic. Was this how married life would be?

If so, he might have to re-think this.

Julia watched him from the sofa. He had the distinct impression she wasn't too happy with him right now.

Well, he wasn't too happy with her either. This feud between the two women was ridiculous. Julia was being unreasonable. He was shocked she had even suggested getting rid of Miss Donovan.

"What am I supposed to say to her?" Julia said.

"I don't know. Just... apologize."

He heard footsteps. Miss Donovan appeared through the portière.

She didn't see him behind the table as her eyes snagged Julia. Her face was vicious. She raised her arm. "You again? Get out!" He had never heard such venom in her voice.

Perhaps Julia hadn't exaggerated.

David stepped into the light. "Miss Donovan."

Her mouth slackened. She blinked rapidly. "Oh, Mr. Easterly, I didn't know you were there."

He wrapped his arm around Julia's waist. "We'd like to talk with you."

Her eyes became slits.

"I want to ask your forgiveness," Julia said. "I never should have looked beyond the curtain after you told me not to. I was insubordinate. Please forgive me."

Miss Donovan glared, spun around with a swish of her white skirts, and left.

"Wait," David said.

She did not stop.

They looked at each other.

"What now?" Julia said. "I tried."

He glanced at the mantel clock. "It's almost two o'clock. Catherine is expecting you. While you're gone, I'll find out what's wrong."

And what would he do about it then?

Oh, the challenge of keeping two females happy.

It had better be worth it.

⇀⟫═◉ ◉═⟪↽

After David tucked Julia into the Packard, he strode into Miss Donovan's office.

She was not there. His words of rebuke fizzled.

Where was she?

He marched down the hall to the kitchen. Ellen sat at the table writing in her account book. A kitchen maid stirred batter in a yellow bowl.

"Ellen, have you seen Miss Donovan?"

She looked up. "Oh, hello, Mr. Easterly. No, not in a bit."

"Any idea where she is?"

She shook her head.

Perhaps she had gone to her room.

He took the elevator up to her third-floor suite and knocked. "Miss Donovan, are you in there?"

He listened against the door. All was quiet. "If you're in there, open up. I need to speak with you."

Nothing.

Where could she be? Would he have to search every room? He peeked into his play room on the third floor. Empty. Down the stairs on the second floor, he looked into his bedroom.

Nothing.

"Miss Donovan," he called.

Was that a whimper?

"Miss Donovan, where are you?"

In the upstairs hall, he heard sniffling. She was near.

He stepped into his mother's suite.

There she was in an overstuffed floral chair by the fireplace.

Gone was the fire-breathing dragon. She looked feeble and aged. Tears streaked her wrinkled face.

"Miss Donovan?" he whispered.

She didn't acknowledge him.

He knelt in front of her. "Miss Donovan, what's wrong?"

She blinked and looked into his eyes. "I promised her," she said.

"What did you promise?"

"I promised your mother to look after you."

"And you've done a wonderful job."

"*She* will take you away from me. *I* must look after you."

"No, no, no, that is still your job."

She shook her head vehemently. "She must not come. I am in charge."

Her eyes looked vacant.

What was wrong with her? He had never seen her like this.

"Come, Miss Donovan, let's go up to your room. You need to rest."

He pulled her up. She tottered as if she had no strength.

Should he call a doctor?

"That's a good girl." He clutched her arm and helped her walk. When they reached the nearest twin bed, she flopped onto the white coverlet and closed her eyes. It was the bed his mother had died in.

No matter. Let her sleep here. It wouldn't do any harm.

And perhaps it would do some good.

Chapter 23

EDGAR STOPPED THE Packard in front of Catherine Townsend's mansion. He opened the door for Julia.

"Thank you, Edgar."

"You're welcome. Good luck." He winked.

It appeared she had an ally in Edgar.

It was an imposing gray stone house with a three-story round tower, peaked gables, and many chimneys. Climbing a flight of stone steps to a small porch with granite pillars, she knocked on the heavy oak double doors.

A butler in a black tuxedo answered.

"I've come to see Mrs. Townsend."

He motioned her in. "Do you have a calling card, ma'am?"

A calling card? No, she had never had calling cards or time to visit. Perhaps someday she would. *Mrs. David Easterly* the card would say. She would decorate it with orchids, David's favorite flower.

"No, I don't. Just tell her Julia Bradshaw is here. She's expecting me at two o'clock."

"Please have a seat." The butler indicated a wooden chair in the entrance hall before disappearing.

With abundant dark mahogany woodwork, the house had a heavy, closed-in feeling, unlike the brightness and airiness of the Easterly House.

She faced the open doorway of the drawing room, paneled in mahogany. At the far end was a great fireplace with a heavily carved mantel. Above it, a mirror rose to the ceiling. The carpet, upholstery, and curtains were crimson.

She shivered. She liked David's home so much better.

Mrs. Townsend glided down the white marble staircase, her hand on the wrought-iron railing. "Sorry to keep you waiting. Come on up. I can hardly wait to begin."

She followed, passing a red satin Chinese wall hanging embroidered in gold. At the turn of the stairs was a niche with a large vase filled with fresh flowers.

"I thought we would start in my gown room to see what styles and colors look good on you. Then we'll look through some fashion magazines and choose something just for you. I've already arranged for the dressmaker to come next Saturday."

So this was how the rich did it. This might be fun.

Catherine's room was pink and turquoise with French imports and crystal chandeliers. It was extravagant and feminine. Julia tried not to gape.

Through a dressing room with two wardrobes and a chiffonier, they passed into the gown room where an electric light automatically turned on as they opened the door. The floor, walls, and ceiling were highly polished hardwood. A delicate scent of lavender lingered.

Rods hanging on all sides were heavy with well-spaced skirts and gowns of every color imaginable.

This time Julia did gawk. It looked like a store, not one woman's closet.

She wondered if she would ever have this many clothes. It seemed excessive.

Catherine yanked a peach satin gown off a hanger. "Try this one on. I'm only slightly larger than you. It should fit well enough."

Did Catherine expect her to disrobe in front of her?

"Let me call Amelia to help." She pressed a button.

"Who's Amelia?" She didn't want an audience.

"My lady's maid."

A petite, doe-eyed young woman in a black dress and white apron appeared in the doorway.

"Assist Miss Bradshaw in undressing."

"Really, I can do it myself." Julia removed her red jacket and unbuttoned the white velvet vest. As she unhooked her skirt, she hoped her undergarments were clean and without holes or ripped lace. She hadn't anticipated others seeing them today.

When she was down to her petticoats and chemise, Catherine said, "No corset? My dear, you must wear a corset."

She didn't want a corset. Her hips and stomach were slim enough.

Catherine pawed through a wardrobe in the next room and returned with a boned and ribboned contraption.

Catherine slipped it around her and Amelia laced it up. It protruded her torso into an S shape. Julia felt caged.

She raised her arms as Amelia slipped the peach satin over her head. The gown was too big. It hung off her shoulders. It dipped too low in front.

"Come into my room and look in the mirror," Catherine said.

A floor-length cheval mirror stood in one corner of the pink and turquoise room. Julia looked ridiculous, like a little girl playing dress-up.

"No, the color is all wrong. It makes you look washed-out. Amelia, find something blue or red. That should complement her dark hair and blue eyes."

Julia could have told her that.

"Could you find something not so low in front?" Julia asked.

"My dear, you have the figure of a goddess. You might as well show it off. We'll have every man in the room drooling over you."

She didn't want every man drooling over her. "I prefer to be more modest," Julia said.

"See what you can find," Catherine told Amelia.

The door inched open. A young woman peeked in. "There you are, Mother." She stared at Julia as she stepped into the room. "Who's she?"

"Come in, dear, I have someone I want you to meet."

The daughter looked to be sixteen or seventeen. She was enchanting. Her blond hair was styled in a careless pompadour that framed a doll face with enormous brown eyes and a pouty mouth.

"Sophie, this is Julia Bradshaw, a very special friend of David Easterly's. I am hosting a Valentine's ball for her, and we're just deciding on a gown. Julia, this is my daughter, Sophie."

"Pleased to meet you," Julia said.

Sophie scrutinized Julia's ill-fitting peach gown. "You have exquisite taste." She smirked, reminding Julia of Jenny.

Julia crossed her arms over the low bodice. "This wasn't my choice. We are searching for something else." She felt humiliated again, by an adolescent, no less.

"I might have some hand-me-downs you can wear."

"Sophie!" Catherine said. "She's not wearing hand-me-downs. We're just trying colors and styles. A dressmaker is coming next week."

"I want a new dress for the ball too," Sophie said.

Somehow Julia knew Sophie's dress would outshine hers.

"Of course, darling. Now why don't you leave us alone so we can get back to work?"

Julia was relieved when Sophie left without another word.

This was harder than she thought. Would she be forever scorned by this crowd? How could Sophie sense that she wasn't one of them? Did she look that different?

Her head didn't have that nose-in-the-air tilt like Sophie's. Her eyes were softer without that critical glint. She wouldn't go so far as to call herself sweet, but she was nicer than Sophie.

But was acceptance that important? She was pleasing to God and David Easterly. No one else mattered.

After two hours of trying on and another of looking through a catalog of the newest Paris fashions, they decided on a blue dress with a scooped neck, shirred long sleeves, a narrow skirt, and a train. Even Mama would be pleased with how modest it was.

But Mama would not understand why the blue dress she had sewn wasn't good enough.

"David will have to buy you diamonds or sapphires to wear around your neck and in your hair," Catherine said.

"Oh, that's not necessary."

"It most certainly is. You must look the part, my dear."

She might look like one of them, but she would never *be* one of them.

->▪=◉ ◉=▪<-

"Where have you been all day?" Mama's sharp voice greeted Julia as she walked through the front door.

The family was seated around the supper table.

"You were gone all day," Jenny said. "I had to bake the pies myself."

"Sorry. It's been quite a day." She hung up her cape and joined them.

"You look tired," Papa said.

"Have you been with Mr. Easterly all this time?" Jenny asked.

"No." Julia helped herself to a pork chop. "I had brunch this morning with Mr. Easterly and his four neighbor ladies, and this afternoon I went to Catherine Townsend's home on East Avenue. She is hosting a Valentine's ball for us. I had to pick out a dress."

Mama's lips tightened. "You're not going to a ball."

"It's expected of me. Don't worry. I'll maintain my Christian testimony."

At least she hoped so. It was too easy to go along with whatever Catherine Townsend demanded.

"You're not going," Mama said. "We'll talk later."

Julia was too tired to argue.

After the supper dishes were done and the children bathed and tucked into bed, Mama motioned Julia into her room.

Julia didn't venture into Mama and Papa's room often. She perched on the quilt atop the massive carved walnut bed and looked around. The flowered wallpaper was gloomy. The lights were dim. The furniture was dark. The room reflected Mama more than Papa.

She glimpsed herself in the mirror on the marble-topped dresser. She looked worried.

Relax, she told herself. How bad could it be?

Mama paced in front of the fireplace.

Julia swallowed hard and waited.

"You are not marrying Mr. Easterly," Mama said.

It was worse than she thought. Apparently Catherine Townsend wasn't the only issue. She must tread lightly.

"Why, Mama?"

"He will destroy you."

Her chin dropped. "He will not. He's kind and protective and nice."

"And wealthy. His wealth will destroy you."

"Why would you say such a thing?"

"Because wealth almost destroyed me."

Her mind raced. "What do you mean?"

"I've never told you about my life before I married your father. It's time you knew. I don't want the same thing to happen to you."

Julia raised her eyebrows.

"I grew up in a mansion in New York City. My parents were both independently wealthy from inherited money."

Julia gasped. Nothing about Mama indicated wealth. She was frumpy and plain and practical. This couldn't be.

"My parents didn't need to work. My father went to his club to read the paper and socialize. My mother visited, entertained, and went for rides in the park. My brother Martin and I were raised by a nanny who took us for walks and served us the same lunch every day."

Julia was stunned. "So I have family? Grandparents? An uncle? Why haven't I heard of them before?"

Mama held up her hand. "Let me finish. After Martin went off to boarding school, I was alone much of the time. I had no one to play with and no one to talk to but my governess. I was shy and miserable and bored.

"The only bright spot was going to our summer home in the Adirondacks. My soul came alive as I dipped my toes in the mountain lake and inhaled the fresh, clean air. I sprawled on the grassy lawn and imagined pictures in the clouds. I fashioned necklaces out of wildflowers. But the Bradshaws were the best part. Mr. Bradshaw was our caretaker. His wife mothered me like one of her own. She was the one who taught me to sew and helped me accept Christ as my Savior when I was ten. But it was their son Alver who stole my heart. I fell in love with his curly black hair, his bright blue eyes, his enthusiasm, his chatter. We romped through the woods, looking at every wildflower and bird. Our friendship deepened every summer.

"When I was eighteen, my parents arranged a marriage for me with the bland, boring son of a friend. That summer when I told Alver, he grabbed my hand and said, 'No, marry me instead.'

"I knew my parents would never consent, so we eloped. As a result, they disowned me, but I didn't care. I had Alver. We followed his brother Charles to Rochester where Charles was already working for the railroad. He arranged for Alver to be hired too. We struggled to make ends meet, but I had never been happier.

"Father Bradshaw lost his job as caretaker as a result of our marriage, so they also moved to Rochester. We were all happy here."

Julia had faint recollections of Grandma's smothery hugs and Grandpa's belly laughs. They both died when she was younger than Mary.

"Then when my mother's uncle died, I received a small inheritance, and we bought this house. We've never had much, but it was enough. I owe your father everything for rescuing me from a life of wealth and boredom."

"And your parents and brother? Where are they now?"

Mama's lips tightened. "I don't know, and I don't care. That life is in the past. Your father's family was more family to me than mine ever was."

"So why tell me this now? What does this have to do with Mr. Easterly?"

"It's a warning not to marry a wealthy man, or you will be bored and miserable like my mother with nothing more important to do than calling and socializing."

Julia thought of the orchid calling cards she intended to order. Maybe Mama was right.

"I don't want your children growing up neglected and forgotten."

"Mama, I would never do that. You know how I love children."

"You might not have a choice. Certain responsibilities will rob you of time with them. Mr. Easterly is an important man. Duties will call him, too. *You* may feel neglected and forgotten. You would be much happier married to an ordinary man like Mr. Pratt."

"But I don't love Mr. Pratt. Doesn't love matter?"

Mama shrugged. "Other things matter too."

"What matters most is what God wants for me."

"And do you know what that is?"

"God is leading my heart toward Mr. Easterly."

"You're making a big mistake."

"I'm sorry you feel that way." Julia stood and gave Mama's bony shoulders a hug. "I hope you'll change your mind."

"Don't hold your breath."

-->==⊙ ⊙==<--

Sunday, January 17, 1909

Lee had never ridden in Mr. Easterly's Packard before. He could get used to this.

He watched Edgar Hopkins escort Julia down the steps of her home. A blast of cold swirled inside as the door opened. Julia scooted in beside him.

"Lee, how good to see you. I've missed you."

He had gone with Grace to her mission church again this morning. He hadn't seen Julia since New Year's Eve.

"So we've both been invited to David's concert tonight," she said. "Are you as nervous as I am?"

"Probably not. I'll just be there as Grace's escort. I won't be the star attraction like you."

"I hope I'm not the star attraction. No one is supposed to know David is courting me until Mrs. Townsend's Valentine's ball."

"So it's official. Your father gave him permission?"

Even in the dim light, her face glowed as she nodded.

"I'm happy for you. Mr. Easterly is a wonderful man."

"Are you still meeting for Bible study?"

"The three of us have lunch, Bible study, and prayer every noon. It's the highlight of my day. Mr. Easterly is always talking about you, you know."

"Really? What does he say?"

"He sings your praises. And he asks lots of questions."

"Like what?"

"Oh, your favorite color and your favorite meal, things I don't have answers for."

"I don't even know."

"He definitely has a bounce in his step and a smile on his face these days. How are you doing?"

"Fine, I guess, but I'm having problems with Miss Donovan and Mama."

"How so?"

"Miss Donovan is still hostile. She claims I will never marry Mr. Easterly. I tried to apologize yesterday for what I did last summer, but she ran off. I'm on pins and needles with her in the house. I can't wait until she's gone. I will not marry him until she leaves."

"What is David doing about it?"

"He talked with her yesterday. I haven't heard how it went."

"And what about your mother?"

"She doesn't want me to marry him either. She's afraid his wealth will make my life miserable."

He chuckled. "I find that hard to believe."

The Packard pulled up in front of Grace's apartment. All thoughts of Julia's problems fled as he bounded out to greet her.

⇥▭⊚ ⊚▭⇤

Julia and Grace climbed the porte-cochère hall steps to the second floor. They had arrived early so Grace could hostess for David.

"It won't be too many more weeks until you're doing this," Grace said.

After the Valentine's ball, Julia would be by his side.

"I will be scrutinizing everything you do tonight," Julia said.

"It's not hard. Just smile and shake hands and be friendly."

"What if I don't know names?"

"I don't know everyone's name either. We have a rotating list of about fifteen hundred, some from work, the university, the neighborhood, and some civic leaders. About a hundred will be here tonight. You'll gradually learn some names."

They reached the upstairs hall. Julia looked down into the conservatory. Even on a cold night, it felt like a tropical garden.

They continued to the coat room where Katie was stationed.

"Julia, what are you doing here?" Katie said.

Julia embraced her. "I'm here for the concert. It's so good to see you again. How are you?"

Miss Weston handed Katie her coat "I'll let you two get caught up. I need to be at my post."

After she left, Katie said, "Tell me what's going on with you and Mr. Easterly."

"Can you believe it? He asked my father for permission to court me."

"Oh, Julia!" Katie clapped her hands. "I wondered. I heard you had been here for brunch."

"Does anyone else know?"

"Rumors are flying. Everyone is wondering."

"Don't tell anyone yet. In fact, I probably shouldn't even have told you. We're announcing it on Valentine's Day. Tell me, how is Miss Donovan taking it?"

"She's acting strange lately. Sometimes I wonder if she's in her right mind."

But she was still here. Mr. Easterly apparently hadn't kicked her out yet.

She heard a step at the door. Rose walked in.

"What are you doing here?" Rose's eyes were frosty.

"I've come for the concert."

"Moving up in the world, are we?" Her voice was brittle.

"Rose, don't be offended. I wish we could be friends again."

"Parlor maids aren't friends with the ladies."

"I'm no lady yet."

"Nor will you ever be." She flounced away.

She hoped Rose wasn't right.

-»╾● ●╼«-

Julia descended the carpeted staircase into the marble foyer. Mr. Easterly, Miss Weston, and Lee stood on the expansive Oriental rug looking up at her.

David stepped forward and reached for her hand. "How beautiful you look."

She smiled.

"I love seeing you in my home, right where you belong."

"Is anyone else here?" she asked.

"Not yet. We still have a few minutes."

"I didn't get a chance to ask you this morning how your talk with Miss Donovan went yesterday."

David led her to a bench. "It was very strange. I found her weeping in my mother's room. She apparently had promised my mother that she would look after me. She sees you as a threat to fulfilling that promise."

A promise? To his mother? That was... concerning. Surely David wouldn't let that stand in his way. "What did you say?"

"I assured her it was still her job to look after me."

Her finger nails dug into her palms. "She's staying?"

"Of course. She's my mother's dear friend."

"But I told you I can't live in the same house with her."

"Julia, you must learn to get along."

"What if I can't?"

"You must."

"What if I made you choose between her and me?"

He stroked her hand. "Of course I would choose you. But don't make me choose, Julia. Please learn to get along."

"I've tried. I asked her to forgive me, and she won't. What more can I do?"

"Just be nice. Let her feel in charge."

Miss Donovan would always be in charge. And Julia would always cower. It wasn't how she wanted to live.

Julia and Lee leaned against a white marble pillar in the hallway and watched David and Grace greet the guests.

Grace was gracious and kind, a perfect hostess. Julia's stomach clenched as she pictured herself there. Now she wasn't sure she wanted to be.

It was rather sickening how the visitors fawned and bowed, almost as if David were royalty. He wasn't. He was far from perfect. Disappointing, in fact.

She had expected him to stand up for her, and he hadn't. Was she acting like a spoiled brat? She didn't think so. Miss Donovan was a genuine problem, and David wasn't doing anything about it.

David's smile was forced. He looked tired, stressed. She felt a twinge of guilt. Her reaction to Miss Donovan had probably contributed to it.

Footsteps click-clacked down the long hallway. Miss Donavan carried a heavy tray of dinner plates. Fortunately, she turned in the opposite direction toward the dining room. She didn't see Julia behind the pillar.

"She looks too old to be carrying that load," Lee said.

"Don't let looks deceive you. She's wiry and strong."

"How did David's talk go with Miss Donovan?"

"Not so well. Apparently she made a promise to his mother to look after him, so he won't get rid of her. He told me to learn to get along."

"Good advice."

"Not you too. Isn't anyone on my side? How can I possibly get along with her? We can't even have a civil conversation. I asked her to forgive me yesterday and she marched out of the room."

"Maybe *you* need to forgive *her.*"

"Are you serious? She was mean and told lies about me. She's not sorry at all."

"Jesus doesn't tell us to forgive if they're sorry. He just says to forgive."

She felt as if Lee had punched her in the stomach.

She didn't want to forgive her.

"Have you prayed for her?" Lee asked. "When you pray for someone, your heart softens toward them."

"I've prayed that she would leave, but I haven't prayed *for* her."

"Try it."

Suddenly the tray flew out of Miss Donovan's hands. Plates crashed to the floor as she tottered and fell.

"Miss Donovan!" Julia raced down the hall, Lee beside her.

Miss Donovan was sprawled limply on top of the broken china.

Julia squatted. "Are you all right?"

Miss Donovan moaned. She tried to get up and couldn't. Julia gripped one arm and Lee the other. Together they lifted her and helped her to a bench. Blood trickled down her forehead. Both hands were cut.

Julia squatted before her. "What happened?"

Miss Donovan looked dazed. Her eyes fluttered as she tried to focus.

Julia picked her glasses off the floor. She gently perched them on Miss Donovan's nose.

Now Miss Donovan recognized her. "You!" Her voice was fragile.

"What happened, Miss Donovan? Are you all right?"

"Dizzy. Lost my balance."

Footsteps came running. Rose and Katie gasped. "What happened?"

"She was dizzy and fell," Julia said. "Can you help pick up this broken china?"

Fortunately it was not David's expensive china but what the servants used.

As Rose, Katie, and Lee piled the broken pieces onto the tray, Julia went to the kitchen in search of something to bind her wounds.

Ellen lifted a pie from the oven.

"Ellen, Miss Donovan fell and hurt herself. Do you have an old towel I can use to stop the bleeding."

"Oh, dear." Ellen reached in a drawer for towels. She dampened one. "Let me help. I have some clean rags we can wrap her with."

Relieved, Julia led her back to the hallway.

As Ellen cleaned the cuts in her hands, Julia worked gently on her forehead. Miss Donovan winced, closed her eyes, and leaned against the wall. She looked like a frail old woman.

Lord, help her be all right.

Lee was right. It did help to pray for her. She was softening already.

-->====() ()====<--

Julia sat in a canvas chair in the front row of the living room. A stringed quartet obscured the cherub-decorated marble fireplace as they tuned their instruments. Behind her, the guests quietly conversed.

They had tucked Miss Donovan in bed, her head and hands bandaged. She seemed to be all right.

Surprisingly, Julia found herself still praying for her.

Now she had to switch her focus to the concert. She scanned the printed program in her lap. It was all classical music, a combination of stringed instruments and piano. She would receive a musical education tonight, another step in transforming her into a woman of culture.

She hoped she liked it.

David stood and waited for the crowd to quiet. He looked handsome in a dark gray suit and gray striped tie with a great iridescent black pearl tie pin. The two gold candelabra sconces above the fireplace cast a glow behind him.

She found herself praying for him too.

"Welcome." He looked directly at her. "I'm so glad you're here. Tonight we'll be hearing the Herman Dossenbach Quintette." With a hand flourish, he said, "Let the music begin."

He sat on the opposite end, not near her. They had agreed not to be seen together until after the Valentine's ball.

The music crashed, startling Julia with its intensity. In amazement, she watched the bows saw and the fingers fly.

The next song was quieter, more contemplative. It reminded her of a spring day with birds chirping and bees buzzing.

The third song had discordant notes she didn't like.

By the fifth song, her mind wandered to what she still had to finish for tomorrow's lessons. After an hour, she was ready for it to be done.

She had disappointed herself. She had expected to love it, but she'd rather listen to church music any day.

Maybe she wasn't suited to this life. Imagine having to do this every Sunday afternoon.

She was glad when the musicians finally stood for a bow. She clapped as vigorously as anyone.

They withdrew to the dining room where long, bare wooden tables had been set up. It looked more like a church supper than a formal dinner.

She sat next to Lee with Grace on his other side. David was at the head of the table. Pitchers of milk took the place of floral centerpieces. There were no orchids at each place setting. The dishes were cheap, the silverware cheaper.

This wasn't David's usual style. She had known him to be meticulous and generous and impressive. What must these people think of him? Why was he doing this? She didn't understand. She felt embarrassed for him.

Solomon brought in bowls of corned beef hash. Next were some perfectly cooked green beans and homemade bread, a meal so ordinary Mama could have served it at her table.

Everything was delicious, though, especially the apple pie.

After dinner, as they retired to the conservatory for another hour of organ music, an elderly woman wrapped in furs and feathers, held out her hand to Julia. "I don't believe I've seen you here before. My name is Mrs. Clarena Chambers."

Julia smelled rose perfume as she shook her hand. "Pleased to meet you. I'm Julia Bradshaw."

"And how do you know Mr. Easterly?"

"I met him at a work party."

"Oh." The woman turned away.

She felt snubbed.

When this woman next saw her on David's arm, she would have more respect for her. She hoped. Or would she be forever snubbed? Snubbed by society. Snubbed by servants. Not fitting in anywhere.

→✦═○ ○═✦←

"How did you enjoy your evening?" Grace asked as they nestled into the back seat of the Packard. Julia noticed Lee and Grace holding hands. Good.

"It wasn't what I expected."

"Oh?"

"I thought I would enjoy the music more, and I was surprised at the dinner. No tablecloths, no centerpieces, ordinary food."

"It wasn't always like that, but after people stole his monogrammed silverware, he scaled way back."

"Who would do that? Those people have plenty of money."

Grace shrugged. "Perhaps they wanted a souvenir. It's quite an honor to be invited. These Sunday evening concerts have become a tradition."

Oh, dear. Would she have to attend them forevermore?

Maybe at least she could improve the meal.

→✦═○ ○═✦←

"Mr. Easterly?" Ellen appeared as the last guest exited.

"Yes, Ellen?"

"Did anyone tell you what happened tonight with Miss Donovan?"

He frowned. "No, what?" All he needed was another confrontation between Julia and Miss Donovan. He felt a headache returning.

"Miss Donovan had an accident. She fell while carrying a large tray of dinner plates. Banged herself up something good."

He blew his cheeks out. "Why didn't someone tell me? How is she? What happened?"

"Apparently she felt dizzy and fell. The dishes crashed... don't worry, they were the cheap ones... as she fell on top of them. She cut her hands and her forehead and has some nasty bumps and bruises. We patched her up, but she seemed disoriented. I'm wondering if a doctor should take a look at her."

"Well, of course. I wish someone had told me sooner. I would have had him come immediately."

"You were busy with your guests, and Julia and I had it under control."

Julia had helped? His pounding head stilled. That was a good sign.

"She's resting in bed now. It's probably not wise to disturb her," Ellen said.

"Don't worry. I'll have a doctor here first thing in the morning."

David berated himself as he headed upstairs. He should have done something sooner. Her unreasonable anger towards Julia, her weakness and confusion in his mother's bedroom, and now this dizziness and disorientation were signs of something wrong. Or was this a natural part of the aging process?

He would find out.

He undressed, washed up and slid between the clean, smooth sheets. He adjusted the pillow behind his back before reaching for his Bible on the nightstand.

More than Miss Donovan was on his mind.

The evening had not been satisfying. His house had been filled with people he didn't care about. Empty chatter. People trying to impress. People criticizing his food.

He only cared about one person, and his brief talk with her hadn't gone well. He wished Julia understood his position. He had a responsibility for Miss Donovan. He would not relinquish it merely for a silly quarrel between two women. Julia simply had to learn to get along.

He had stolen glances at her throughout the evening, wondering if she was enjoying herself. At the concert, she had looked awestruck and glassy-eyed. At the dinner she had seemed confused.

He wanted to talk to her right now.

Instead, he would settle for talking with God.

Chapter 24

Saturday, January 23, 1909

"Let me tell you how plans are progressing for the Valentine's ball," Catherine said as they ate their Eggs Benedict in the conservatory the next Saturday.

"Catherine, let us eat in peace," round-faced Elizabeth said. "I don't want to think about business."

"This isn't business. It's fun, isn't it, Julia?"

Julia shrugged and smiled. Honestly, it wasn't much fun. She did not want to be on display.

Like Mama, she wished David was just an ordinary office worker.

"The invitations went out yesterday," Catherine said.

"So soon?" Nancy scooted up her glasses.

"It's only three weeks from today. It's barely time enough. We have Julia's dress picked out. Today the dressmaker is coming at one o'clock to fit her. Cross your fingers that she'll get it done in time."

"I appreciate all you're doing," David said.

"Only the best for you. This is a momentous occasion. Do you realize how long people have waited for you to find someone? This is going to make headlines." She turned to Julia. "You will be famous."

She didn't want to be famous. What would the people at church or school think?

And how about Mr. Pratt? The poor man continued to stop by every day after school. She sensed an urgency in him, as if he knew he had a short time to win her. Would it be kinder to tell him in person or have him read it in the paper?

Yet she wasn't supposed to tell anyone until after the ball.

After the announcement, her principal, Miss Whiton would wonder if she was returning next year. Was she? She had no idea. It all depended on when David proposed and how soon the wedding was. Maybe she could squeeze in another year of teaching.

The conversation turned to the college Nancy's son was applying to. Julia's mind wandered.

She watched David's fine, long fingers cut another bite of the English muffin, egg, and Canadian bacon smothered in sauce. She hadn't seen him since the concert last Sunday night. They were both so busy.

Since, her attitude had changed. She had prayed for Miss Donovan every day, and God had worked on her heart. She had forgiven her. It was not easy, especially when bitter thoughts continued to spring up. But yes, she had forgiven her.

She desperately wanted to tell David and ask his forgiveness too.

Tonight. Tonight he was taking her downtown for dinner. She couldn't wait to be alone with him.

After the meal, David ushered the ladies out to the car. As Julia waited by the door, she felt someone watching her. She looked into Miss Donovan's office. The woman was sitting at her dining table, glaring daggers at her.

"Oh, hello, Miss Donovan." She moved into the office. "How nice to see you up again. How are you feeling?"

The bandage was gone from her forehead. The cut was healing, but her left eye had blackened. Her nose was slightly swollen.

Miss Donovan said nothing, but continued to stare, her hands wrapped around an empty tea cup.

"I'm glad you weren't more seriously injured. That was quite a fall you took."

Still she said nothing.

This was so hard, but she was determined to be nice.

"You've finished your tea. Would you like me to refill it for you?"

Still she said nothing.

She reached for the teacup.

Miss Donovan pounced, grabbing her wrist and digging her sharp fingernails into Julia's tender flesh.

She winced and tried to extract her hand. Miss Donovan's grip tightened. Julia didn't look, but she was sure blood was flowing.

"It was all your fault," Miss Donovan said.

"What was my fault?"

"The fall."

"No, it wasn't. Remember, you said you were dizzy?"

"You made me dizzy."

This woman was impossible.

Love her. Forgive her.

This was so hard.

She touched Miss Donovan's shoulder. "I am so sorry for upsetting you."

Miss Donovan released the hold on Julia's wrist as she slapped away her hand from her shoulder.

Free, Julia quickly stepped back. "I hope you'll feel better soon."

She fled to the conservatory and collapsed into a green wicker chair. She looked at her wrist. Four deep gouges oozed blood. Miss Donovan had never hurt her physically before.

What should she do about it? Tattle to David?

No, he didn't need more to worry about. She wanted to handle this God's way. She would continue to forgive her. And stay out of her way.

⸻ ⚫═⚫ ⸻

Edgar Hopkins steered the Packard down Clinton Street and onto Cortland where he stopped under the porte-cochère of the Seneca Hotel.

David was reluctant to leave the back seat. With Julia cuddled under his arm, even the elegant Crystal Dining Room didn't entice. He just wanted to be alone with her. The food didn't matter.

He rarely ate out. He'd only been here once since it opened last year, but he remembered it as a place special enough to bring her.

Edgar swung the door open and she stepped out. David slid out after her.

"Thanks, Edgar. Be back at ten."

He led her into the lobby. He heard her quick intake of breath.

"Like it?"

"It's so grand."

With wainscoting of marble, greenish brown wall panels, ivory columns with caps of gold, and a two-story ceiling that looked like old leather, it was open and spacious with carefully placed leather sofas and chairs.

They passed into the Crystal Dining Room where linen-draped square tables crowded a room divided by massive pillars. Two rows of crystal chandeliers sparkled.

"I have dinner reservations for David Smith," he told the maitre-d.

Julia raised her eyebrows.

"I'm incognito tonight," he whispered.

"Right this way." The tuxedoed man grabbed two menus and led them to a secluded corner.

Once seated and alone, they opened their menus. It was overwhelming even for him. He noticed her confusion. "Would you like me to order for both of us?" he asked.

She closed the menu, her relief evident. "Please do."

When the waiter returned, he ordered turtle soup, whitefish, Lobster Newburg, young guinea hens with currant jelly, potatoes in cream, tips of asparagus, and raspberry pie.

When the waiter left, she leaned toward him, "I can't eat all that."

He loved giving her a glimpse into his world, even if she didn't always seem impressed.

Sometimes he wasn't either. Nothing could surpass a dinner around the cozy Bradshaw table.

"No matter," he said. "I just want you to sample them. Ever have turtle soup before?"

She shook her head.

"It's really quite special, but not as special as being here with you." He reached for her hand across the table. "I've missed you."

"I've missed you too."

"You're ruining my concentration at work."

Her eyes twinkled. "Sorry."

"How did it go with the dressmaker today?"

"The measuring, pampering, looking at the beautiful fabric samples... I felt like a princess. I'm not used to having all the attention on me."

He smiled. "Get used to you. It will be my pleasure showering you with attention. So tell me what you thought of the concert last Sunday night? We haven't had a chance to talk yet."

She glanced down at the rose in the bud vase. She looked guarded.

"It was a new experience. I'd never been to a classical concert. I expected to love it."

"But you didn't?"

"I hate to say this, but I was a little bored by the end."

He twitched his mustache. "Can I let you in on a secret? I was a little bored too."

"Really? I assumed you loved it."

"Music soothes my soul and helps me think more clearly, but I don't necessarily love all of it."

"But if you don't love the music, why do you have so many concerts?"

He let go of her hand and leaned back in his chair. "That's what I love about you. You get right to the point. You challenge me. You want to know what I'm thinking. You care. No one else does."

Her dimples deepened.

"Why *do* I have so many concerts? The obvious answer is that I want to share my music and my home with the community. The real reason? I think it's to surround myself with people so I don't feel so lonely in that big empty house."

"Do you still feel lonely?"

Now *he* contemplated the rose in the center of the table.

"My life has changed since I met you. I feel as if I belong to someone now, and you have given me a family to love. No, I don't feel lonely anymore."

"That wasn't the answer I was hoping for."

It wasn't? What more could she want?

"I hoped you would say that you don't feel lonely because of the Lord's presence in you."

Of course. That *is* what he'd been feeling. He just hadn't recognized it. "You're right. The Lord has filled that empty place in my life."

Her smile was warm.

He continued, "You know, after the last concert I felt dissatisfied. Even though my house was filled with people, I wasn't enjoying them. It felt more like a chore than a blessing. Perhaps it's time to make changes."

"Like what?"

"Maybe I should invite different people, people I know and like."

"Such as?"

"Your family and the people from church."

Her smile widened. "That would be wonderful."

"Perhaps we could play some sacred music too."

"They would love that."

"That settles it. Right after the Valentine's ball, we'll have our first concert."

Meanwhile, he would cancel the other scheduled concerts. They had lost their appeal.

→═◉ ◉═←

Thank You, Lord, Julia prayed. Now she would enjoy those concerts so much more.

The turtle soup arrived. Heavy and brown, it looked like gravy. Nasty.

He held her hand and prayed over the meal before he put the napkin in his lap and lifted his spoon.

He sipped it. He didn't die. He didn't grimace.

She took the littlest slurp. She gagged.

"You all right?" he asked.

She didn't want to spit it out in front of him, so she closed her eyes and swallowed. It wasn't as bad as she expected. The flavor was a cross between chicken and beef.

"I wasn't sure I could eat it."

"I'm proud of you for trying."

The next spoonful had some meat. It tasted like really chewy chicken. She almost gagged again, but she swallowed it.

The next mouthful went down easier. By the end, she was almost enjoying it.

"So how are the plans coming for the ball?" he asked.

"Catherine has it under control. The dressmaker assures us my dress will be ready in time."

"And how do you feel about the ball?"

It was time to be honest again. "Nervous. Afraid of the implications."

He looked confused. "What do you mean?"

"Afraid of losing my quiet life. Afraid of being famous."

"Hopefully it won't be so very different for you."

She almost laughed. Not different? Just living in that huge house with servants would be immeasurably different.

"There is something else you need to know about me that affects the ball," she said.

He looked worried.

"I've never danced before."

His face relaxed. "Well, that is good news because I don't dance either. I hired a dancing teacher awhile back, and I was a hopeless case. I just can't feel the beat. I'm too clumsy. So if you don't want to dance, that's fine with me."

"What will we do instead?"

"Circulate among the guests and receive their congratulations."

That she could do. "I'm so relieved."

"Don't ever be afraid to tell me things," he said. "I want to know what's on your heart."

Her eyes fluttered. "Well, then, I'll tell you something else. I've been working on my attitude toward Miss Donovan. Lee suggested I pray for her. So I have been. Every day. She hasn't changed, but I have. I have forgiven her, and my attitude toward her is softening."

He reached for her hands across the table. "You are incredible. Thank you."

No, she wasn't incredible. She was sinful and weak and struggling. She still wanted Miss Donovan gone.

Suddenly he noticed the red gouges in her wrist. "Julia, what happened?"

The ladies had asked this afternoon too, and she had laughed it off saying, "It looks like I was in a cat fight, doesn't it?" She couldn't do that to David. She needed to be truthful.

"Miss Donovan did it."

His mouth dropped. "When? Why?"

"When you were saying good-bye to the ladies, I went into her office to greet her. I went too close, I guess. She blames me for her fall. She said I made her dizzy."

His brow wrinkled as he reached for his coffee.

Oh, dear. She had added to his burden, exactly what she didn't want to do. But perhaps God would use this to get rid of Miss Donovan.

"I'm in a quandary," he said. "I had a doctor come last Monday morning to check her out."

"And?"

"He believes she had a slight attack of apoplexy that caused her to fall."

"Is that serious?"

"Not terribly, but she is at high risk for it happening again. And there's more. She is also in the early stages of dementia."

"Can she still carry out her duties?"

"I suggested she might like to retreat to some lovely facility in the country. She flatly refused. She said she needed to take care of me."

"You told her that wasn't necessary, didn't you? I'll take care of you from now on."

"That's the problem. She won't relinquish me. Especially to you."

"So what are you going to do?"

"I'm going to let her stay on, but I've asked the others to keep an eye on her, to take on her unfinished duties, to report to me if they see further decline. Eventually she will have to go, but not just yet."

Her shoulders drooped. That wasn't what she wanted to hear.

-→⟩═▷ ◁═⟨←-

Sunday, January 24, 1909

Julia placed the trivet on the marble-topped work table as David slid the baked ham from the oven.

"I love cooking with you," she said.

"We make a good team."

Their eyes connected. His gaze was intense.

"Come here," he said.

His arms drew her close. She nestled close to his heart, her arms stealing around him.

Who cared if dinner was delayed? She hoped her family waiting in the conservatory didn't pop in right now.

He felt strong and secure and precious. He smelled like ham.

Footsteps click-clacked down the hall. Oh, no. Not Miss Donovan now.

David was oblivious as he buried his face in her hair.

Julia pulled away, but not in time.

"What is going on here?" Miss Donovan's voice was brittle.

Julia took a step back.

White, wavy tendrils had pulled loose from Miss Donovan's usually tidy bun. She looked as if she had slept on it.

"Did you need something, Miss Donovan?" David asked.

"Just a cup of tea."

"Help yourself. The tea is hot."

Miss Donovan's hands quivered as she reached for a cup and saucer. Julia feared she might drop them.

"Here, let me help you with the teapot."

"I don't need your help." She pushed Julia out of the way and poured it herself.

David looked exasperated.

The cup wobbled in Miss Donovan's hand. The tea sloshed onto the saucer.

"I would be happy to carry that for you," Julia said.

To her surprise, Miss Donovan handed it to her.

"Where were you going?" she asked.

"To my office."

Julia went down the long, tiled servants' hallway to the office, wishing David had followed. She didn't feel safe alone with Miss Donovan.

She placed the cup on the round table in the corner.

"Look, the sun is beaming right on your chair. That will warm you up on this cold winter day."

She stepped aside to make room for Miss Donovan. But Miss Donovan moved closer until her face was inches from Julia's. Her eyes were rheumy. She did not look well. She smelled old.

She waggled her finger. "David is blinded. He doesn't know what you're really like. But I will show him. I will make certain you don't come."

Her threat hung in the air.

Should she report this to David? Should she take her seriously, or was this the ranting of a senile old woman who wouldn't remember it later?

She didn't want to be vindictive. She would keep her eyes open like everyone else for signs of further decline.

Chapter 25

Friday, February 12, 1909

JULIA PRESSED HER nose against the cold windowpane over the kitchen sink as she finished the supper dishes. Another five inches of snow had fallen since her walk home from school. She hoped it didn't hamper the Valentine's ball tomorrow night.

Her stomach fluttered. Tomorrow night her world would change forever. She wasn't ready. She wanted to be the oldest Bradshaw girl, her papa's princess, an obscure kindergarten teacher. After tomorrow night, she would be criticized, admired, and scrutinized wherever she went.

She should be grateful. Not many lived such a fairy tale.

Lord, help me. Help me bring honor and glory to You.

Her gown hung in Catherine Thompson's closet. She would arrive in the late afternoon to be transformed into a real princess.

"Hurry up." Jenny snapped the dish towel in her face. "Stop daydreaming and wash a little faster."

"You'd be daydreaming too if you were going to a ball with David Easterly."

"Jenny won't ever be going to a ball," Mama said as she stirred a coffee cake for breakfast. "She knows better."

"I've prayed that I would bring glory to God even there," Julia said.

"You'd bring more glory to God by not going."

"I have to go. It's David's world."

"His world will not make you happy."

"No, but he will."

Mama harrumphed.

Someone knocked on the front door. Mama and Jenny looked at each other.

"Who can that be at this hour?" Julia swished the sudsy dish cloth against the dinner plate.

"Maybe you should go see, Julia." Jenny's voice teased.

"Papa will answer it," Julia said.

"I'd get it if I were you," Jenny said.

"Julia," her father called from the other room, "you have a guest."

She hoped it wasn't Mr. Pratt. She had refused every invitation this week.

It must be David, although he rarely stopped by on week nights.

She wiped her hands on her apron and stepped into the foyer.

It *was* David with rosy cheeks, a fur hat, and his greatcoat.

"What a surprise." She snuggled in his arms. His coat smelled like cold and snow and the outdoors. "I didn't think I would see you until the ball tomorrow night."

"I couldn't wait that long. Grab your cape, your boots, and dress warmly. I'm kidnapping you for the evening."

As she happily untied her apron, Peter and Annie tumbled down the stairs shrieking, "Mr. Easterly."

He held out his arms to them.

When they saw Julia's cape, Peter asked, "Where're you going?"

"I'm taking your sister for a ride," David said.

"I'm going too," Annie said.

"Not this time. This is a special evening just for Julia."

They were disappointed, but she wasn't.

"Ready? You'd better bring a scarf. It's cold."

He lovingly pulled up her fur-trimmed hood and wrapped a wool scarf around her neck. His breath tickled her cheek. She yearned to feel his lips on hers.

"Good-bye, everyone," she said as David hustled her outside.

Instead of the green Packard, a two-seater black sleigh waited behind a mahogany horse pawing the ground.

"A sleigh ride? Oh, David, what fun."

"I hoped you would like it."

He helped her onto the velvet seat before jumping next to her and tucking a bearskin rug around them. She felt cozy and safe.

He flicked the reins. "Giddy-up."

The horse bobbed its head, the bells on the harness jangling as the runners skimmed over the new-fallen snow. More snow swirled in her face and powdered the rug.

"Where are we going?" she asked.

"Not far." He held the reins with one hand and slipped an arm around her. "Happy?"

"So happy. Thank you." She nestled closer.

"I wanted to make this evening very special for you."

"You have."

"The best is yet to come."

"Oh?"

At the corner, he turned right. At the next corner, he turned right again.

They had the neighborhood to themselves. It was quiet and still as the snow sifted down.

"It's like a postcard," she said.

"Cold?"

"Not yet."

"We won't be out long."

They turned right onto East Avenue. His home was on the left. He turned into the driveway.

"What are we doing?" she asked.

His smile was mysterious. "You'll see."

They skimmed around the circular driveway to the front door. The house was lit from top to bottom. What was going on? It looked like a party, but no other vehicles were here.

A stable boy waited at the curb. David handed him the reins before lifting Julia down.

They walked up the steps to the porch. He surprised her by not stopping at the door but continuing down the shoveled path to the living room's side porch.

"Careful, these tiles are slippery," he said. She clutched his arm.

Because she was watching her feet, she didn't see the garden until they reached the end of the porch. She gasped in delight.

It was a snowy wonderland with twinkling white lights wrapped around the balustrades on the patio, the stone urns flanking the pond, and the pergola pillars. More snow softly fell on the shoveled walks.

"Come." He led her down two steps and across the herringbone brick patio to the pergola.

The glory almost hurt her eyes. Lights sparkled from the cross-beams above and were wrapped around each of the eight pillars on either side of the long corridor. At the far end was a stone bench with a fire blazing in a pot.

She felt as if she were in a dream as he led her toward the bench.

"Have a seat." He sat her close to the fire. "Are you warm enough?"

She nodded. She honestly didn't feel anything.

He sat beside her. He reached inside his coat and pulled out a slim box. He seemed nervous.

"Catherine told me you needed sapphires or diamonds to wear to-morrow night, so I bought both." He handed her the package.

With trembling hands, she slipped off her gloves so she could untie the ribbon. She lifted the lid. Her breath caught. Inside was a dazzling sapphire necklace, eight oval blue stones surrounded by diamonds set in lacy sterling silver. Beside it was a jeweled comb for her hair.

"I'm speechless."

"Will it match your dress?"

No one would notice the dress now.

"It's perfect. Thank you so much." She threw her arms around his neck. He held her like a treasure.

When he released her, he said, "There's more."

"Please no more. I'm overwhelmed."

He took a smaller, square box from his pocket and dropped to one knee. He snapped open the lid to reveal an enormous diamond ring.

Her heart raced.

"Julia, I love you with all my heart. Would you do me the honor of becoming my wife?"

She looked into his yearning blue eyes, loving him more than ever. "Yes," she whispered.

He slipped the ring onto her finger. It fit perfectly.

He pulled her up and tipped her chin. He looked at her mouth.

Gently his lips captured hers.

Her heart soared. This was her man, the man she loved, the man she would spend the rest of her life with. She returned his kiss passionately, committing herself to him.

Finally they broke apart.

"Well," he said, "that was worth waiting for."

She snuggled into him, embarrassed. "I love you."

"And I love you, sweetheart. I can't wait to make you my wife."

"I wasn't expecting a proposal so soon."

"I thought it best to announce you as my future wife tomorrow night instead of my intended."

It would be a surprise for everyone, including Catherine Townsend.

"How soon can you be ready for a wedding?" he asked.

"I need to finish the school year."

"Then how about the end of June? I don't want to wait a moment longer than I have to."

"I guess so." That was only four months away.

"Come, I have another surprise."

More? She couldn't handle any more surprises.

He led her down the steps, around the pond, and up three more steps to the door of the Palm House.

Inside it was steamy and warm.

"Let me take your coat." He tenderly unwound her scarf and threw back her hood, kissing her again before he unbuttoned her cape. He draped it across a bench and removed his own coat and hat.

Then he clasped the sapphire and diamond necklace around her neck.

"Beautiful," he said. "The exact color of your eyes."

"I wish I had worn something other than this old shirtwaist."

"You look beautiful in anything. Now are you ready?"

"Ready? For what?"

"For this." He opened the door into the loggia and flicked on the lights.

"Surprise!" echoed down the corridor.

Lined up on each side were about twenty of the servants.

She was stunned. They'd all known about this?

They started down the line, shaking hands and receiving congratulations from everyone. She could hardly believe it. They all seemed happy for her, as if they actually welcomed her as their mistress.

She shook hands with Solomon, the butler, and Edgar Hopkins, the chauffeur. The gardeners and dairymen had dressed up for the occasion. Alan Pierce tried to kiss her. She couldn't believe his audacity with David there.

Richard stood next to Katie, looking embarrassed.

"It's all right if *you* kiss me." She laughed as she hugged him and kissed his cheek.

Katie's hug was especially dear. "You're going to make him the best wife," Katie said.

"I feel so inadequate."

"We'll all be here to help you."

That was an amazing promise.

"I hope you'll let me make your wedding cake," Ellen said.

"Of course."

"And the whole wedding supper," David said.

"Just give me plenty of notice," Ellen said.

"How about the end of June?" he said.

Ellen looked panicked.

David chuckled. "I have complete confidence in you."

Rose's hug was brief.

Missing was Miss Donovan. Julia was relieved. "Where is Miss Donovan?" she asked David.

"Let's just say I strongly suggested she stay in her room this evening."

She was grateful but couldn't believe Miss Donovan had actually obeyed.

When the dining room door opened, she was met with more "Congratulations!"

There were Papa, Mama, Richard, Jenny, Mary, Peter, Annie, Lee, Aunt Lillian, Uncle Charles, Pearl, and Miss Weston.

How had David arranged all this? Was she the only one who hadn't known?

Everyone hugged her and wanted to see her ring. It was almost too heavy to lift. She was embarrassed at its size.

Mama's lips tightened as she examined it, but thankfully, she didn't express her opinion.

"Congratulations," Grace Weston told her. "You're perfect for him."

"I always thought you'd make him the perfect wife."

Miss Weston chuckled. "Oh, my, no. I've found my perfect match." She walked away hand-in-hand with Lee, both smiling.

On the table was a three-tiered cake with punch and coffee.

David pulled her behind the table. "We're going to serve our guests. Is that all right?"

She nodded. A servant to the servants again. Perfect.

"I'm going to ask my future father-in-law to say the blessing."

"Gladly," Papa said. "Shall we pray?" He bowed his head. "Our dear heavenly Father, we stand in awe at how You have brought David and Julia together. We ask that You bless their upcoming marriage. May all the honor and glory belong to You. In Jesus' name, Amen."

It was a happy time. Afterwards, the dirty dishes miraculously disappeared into the kitchen as one-by-one the servants returned to their posts.

As her family donned their coats at the porte-cochère entrance, David helped Julia with her cape. "You've made me the happiest man alive," he said.

Julia couldn't believe it when he kissed her in front of the family. Her cheeks heated, and she avoided looking at Mama.

He turned to her parents. "Mr. and Mrs. Bradshaw, thank you so much for welcoming me into your family and for raising such a wonderful daughter. I will cherish her forever."

"We know you will," Papa said, "and we love you like a son. We would be honored if you would consider us your parents now."

David's eyes misted. "You have no idea how much that means. I haven't had a father in a long time." He embraced Papa.

Then David turned to Mama. Julia held her breath. Mama's eyes darted.

"May I call you Mama?"

Mama's eyes fluttered. Two red spots bloomed on her cheeks. She looked at Julia before looking back at David and nodding.

As David enveloped her in his arms, Julia was stunned at the dazzling smile on Mama's face.

When the children clamored for hugs too, Julia said, "I want to run back to the kitchen and thank everyone one last time. I'll be right back."

She passed through Miss Donovan's empty office, grateful she wasn't there. Her absence had made the evening much more enjoyable.

In the white-tiled servants' hall, she stopped suddenly. Miss Donovan marched toward her. She had come after all.

Miss Donovan stared at her with malevolence. Julia could almost see smoke billowing from her ears.

Julia backed up, her heart pounding.

Surely she wasn't in danger. The maids were only steps away in the kitchen.

Miss Donovan's eyes twitched. She swayed and reached for the wall.

"Are you all right?" Julia asked.

Miss Donovan pressed on. "Don't think you've won. You will never marry David Easterly."

"I will, Miss Donovan. Tonight he asked me to marry him. Would you like to see my ring?" She held it up. Prisms bounced off the shiny tile walls.

Miss Donovan's step faltered. She covered her eyes. "No!" She stumbled on.

"Please, can't we be friends?"

The veins stood out on Miss Donovan's forehead. Her eyes were bloodshot and bleary.

She suddenly lunged. Her fingers hooked around Julia's throat.

"Help," Julia feebly uttered before her air flow was constricted. She couldn't believe this was happening. Miss Donovan was an old woman. Surely she could fight her off.

She tried to pry her hands off, but Miss Donovan's grip was like iron. Black spots danced before her eyes. She couldn't breathe. Would she die right here in the hallway?

Lord, help!

Then she was falling with Miss Donovan on top of her. Her head hit hard on the tile floor. The grip on her throat relaxed.

She heard running footsteps.

She tried to catch a breath, but Miss Donovan was dead weight on top of her. She gasped for air.

"Are you all right?" It was Rose's voice.

"Help," she whimpered.

"Get that woman off her." It was Ellen's voice.

They rolled Miss Donovan off.

Julia gulped air.

Miss Donovan lay still.

"What happened?" Rose asked.

Julia sat up. Her head throbbed. "I think she tried to kill me."

"I'll go get Mr. Easterly," Rose said.

Miss Donovan still didn't move. Was she dead? Would they think *she* had killed *her?*

Ellen shook Miss Donovan, calling her name. She didn't respond.

Julia leaned against the wall, still struggling to breathe. Her throat felt raw and sore.

More running footsteps.

David knelt beside her. "Oh, my dear, I'm so sorry." His arms wrapped around her.

She sobbed into his shoulder. Safe at last.

Her family hung back, gawking at Miss Donovan.

"What's wrong with her? She's not moving," Mary said.

David's attention turned to the prostrate form. "Ellen, is she...?"

Ellen's finger was on the pulse of the wrinkled wrist. "She's still alive."

"Rose, call the doctor," David said.

As Rose rushed away, her family clustered around her.

"Look at her neck," Richard said. "It's all red."

"You can see where her fingers were," Jenny said.

"I feel responsible," David said. "I had no idea she would do something like this. I never would have intentionally put Julia at risk. I'm so sorry." He stood. "I will take care of this. Julia will not be in danger again, I promise."

Finally.

Chapter 26

Saturday, February 13, 1909

"Julia, darling, come in." Catherine Townsend greeted her at the door.

Julia wondered how long before she noticed the ring on her left hand.

The mansion was abuzz with activity. Servants hurried in and out of the drawing room with bouquets of flowers.

A tall, handsome gentleman dressed in casual clothes stood in the doorway watching.

"You haven't met my husband yet, have you? Clinton, come here. I want you to meet the guest of honor, Julia Bradshaw."

He assessed her from head to toe with appreciation. "Pleased to meet you." He kissed her left hand.

It was then that Catherine saw the ring. "A ring? Julia?"

Julia held it up. "David proposed last night. We're getting married at the end of June."

Catherine squealed as she flung her arms around her. "What wonderful news. This will make tonight even more special. Let me see it. That is quite some ring."

It was even larger than Catherine's. Julia felt embarrassed.

"Come, we've no time to lose." Catherine took her hand and led her up the stairs. "Clinton, you should dress too."

"In due time," he said.

Amelia was waiting for them. She helped her remove her clothes and wrapped her in a soft floral robe. She plunked her on a chair in front of a dressing table cluttered with silver-topped jars, small embroidered boxes, tortoise-shell combs, and perfumes. Amelia removed the pins from her hair and brushed.

"What happened to your neck?" Amelia asked.

"I had a little incident last night."

Catherine stepped closer. "It's all mottled. What happened?"

The redness had faded somewhat, and Julia had hoped no one would notice. "We had trouble with David's housekeeper last night. She had a fit of apoplexy and is in the hospital."

"What a shame. Will she be all right?"

"The doctor doesn't give much hope of a complete recovery. It affected her left side. Her face droops. She's disoriented. She can't talk or walk."

"I'm so sorry. I can help David find a new housekeeper."

"Actually, I have some ideas," Julia said.

Catherine looked surprised. "Well, all right then. But tell me what happened to your neck."

"Nothing serious."

Catherine rolled her eyes. "You're not going to tell us, are you? Amelia, see if you can find some makeup to cover it up."

"David gave me a necklace to wear with my gown," Julia said.

"Good man. I was hoping he would. Where is it?"

"In my bag there."

"Do you mind if I look?"

"Go ahead."

Catherine gasped when she opened the slim box. "Oh, my. David went overboard again."

Julia detected a hint of envy.

"That man must really love you," Catherine said.

He did, but it wasn't the jewels that communicated his love. It was his tenderness, the look in his eye, his joy around her family.

She wondered how much Catherine's husband loved her. She certainly wouldn't want David looking at another woman the way Mr. Townsend had looked at her.

She hoped Amelia hurried. She didn't want to be here when he came up to dress.

Amelia took her time. Julia felt nervous.

"What time will Mr. Townsend be up?"

"Who knows?"

"Will we be out of here before then?"

"He doesn't come in here, silly girl. He has his own room and his own valet."

"I don't understand."

"What don't you understand?"

"Why don't you share the same room? My parents do."

"That's not how it's done here. He has his suite and I have mine. I wouldn't want it any other way."

Julia hoped David didn't expect them to have separate rooms. She wanted her husband beside her. Besides, David's room was huge, plenty big for both of them.

Amelia worked wonders with her hair. Rolled back at each side, loose braids coiled at the back of her head, held in place by a glittering comb of sapphires and diamonds.

Catherine handed her a mirror to view the back.

It was gorgeous. It made her look elegant and sophisticated, just as the wife of David Easterly should.

"Thank you. It's perfect. I couldn't have done it without you, Amelia."

"Speaking of which," Catherine said. "Who's going to be your lady's maid?"

She couldn't imagine herself with a lady's maid. She would rather do things herself. Although looking at herself in the mirror, she admitted she did need help.

"What does a lady's maid do?"

"She is your personal attendant, at your beck and call twenty-four hours a day. She must understand hair-dressing, washing and dressing you, mending, and taking care of your clothes. If you travel, she goes with you. If you have guests who do not bring a lady's maid, she will assist them too."

Perhaps having someone take care of her would be nice.

She could imagine the tight set of Mama's lips already. Mama wouldn't think she needed a lady's maid.

"I can help you find someone. Only the best for David's wife," Catherine said.

Actually, dear Katie would be perfect. Katie was an expert at caring for clothes. Who better to spend all that time with than a friend?

"I do have someone in mind. I'll talk to David about her."

Katie would love the job. It was a giant step up from being a housemaid.

She could hardly wait to tell her.

→⊷═◁ ◐═▷◅←

Standing below the marble staircase, David shivered each time the butler opened the door. A groom in livery out by the curb assisted guests down from carriages or cars.

The Valentine's ball had begun. He didn't care about mingling. He just wanted Julia.

He paced beside the staircase. How was it possible to miss someone so much in less than twenty-four hours?

Last night had been a dream. His plan had gone like clockwork. Her expressions had been priceless. The moment she said yes and he held her in his arms was the pinnacle of his life. No power or prestige could compare.

Unfortunately, the evening had ended abysmally with Miss Donovan. He blamed himself for not providing proper care sooner for the old woman, now shrunken and helpless in her hospital bed.

At least Julia was all right. In bed last night, thinking of what might have happened, he had been half paralyzed with fear as he tossed and turned. Finally he realized he could trust God to protect her.

Major changes were coming. A new housekeeper. A new wife. He had never liked change. This time it would be good. He couldn't wait.

"Mr. Easterly, how nice to see you here."

David hadn't noticed when Catherine's daughter had sidled up to him.

"Hello, Sophie. Don't you look lovely tonight."

She wore a high-waisted gown of red chiffon with a cross-over bodice that dipped lower than he thought appropriate for a girl her age. She looked up at him with her large baby-doll eyes.

"Will you save a dance for me?" she asked.

Had she actually batted her eyelashes? My goodness, this girl was flirting with him. He was practically old enough to be her father.

"Sorry, but I won't be leaving the side of my fiancée tonight."

Her eyes widened. "You're engaged?"

"Yes, to the loveliest woman in the world, Julia Bradshaw."

Her mouth twisted. "Her?"

"Have you met her?"

"You could say so."

Catherine approached. "It's time. I've sent a maid for Julia." She winked at him. "Are you ready?"

His mouth felt dry.

"Sophie, wait until you see her ring. It's magnificent," Catherine said.

"Later," Sophie said as she disappeared into the drawing room.

David looked up the staircase.

And then there she was. She looked terrified.

As her eyes locked with his, she seemed to gain confidence. He smiled, and she smiled back. With a hand on the wrought iron railing, she descended, her eyes never leaving his.

Her beauty was astonishing. She held her head regally. Her gown was a Capri-blue satin with a flared skirt and long train. His sapphire and diamond necklace fit perfectly in the scoop of the neck. The sleeves were long and shirred. A scarf of silver netting draped over one shoulder. Soft, matching slippers peeked out under the hem. The diamond on her hand flashed between the folds of the skirt.

He could hardly believe this woman was his. He had never expected to marry, never saw a need. But now he couldn't imagine life without her. He felt rich far beyond his wealth. *Thank you, God, for this gift.*

At the bottom, she took his hand.

"You look exquisite," he said. "I will be the envy of every man in the room."

Her hand trembled in his. "Thank you."

"So, David," Catherine said, "what do you think? Isn't she perfection?"

David kissed Catherine's cheek. "Beautiful. Thanks so much."

But Julia had looked just as beautiful in her school shirtwaist last night. He wouldn't burst Catherine's bubble.

"Are you ready to go in?" Catherine asked.

Julia looked panicked again.

"Can you give us a minute?" he said.

Catherine frowned but nodded as he led her to a secluded spot behind the staircase. He took both her hands and looked into her eyes. "I think we should pray before we go in. What do you think?"

Relief filled her eyes. "Oh, yes. Thank you."

He bowed his head. "Lord, this is a special night to announce the wonder of what You've done for us. Please calm Julia's spirit. May somehow these people see Christ in us. In Jesus' name, Amen."

She looked up. "Thank you. I'll be all right, really I will."

She had never felt so precious. He leaned down and kissed her.

Her eyes sparkled. "That helped."

He longed to kiss her again, but he didn't want to keep Catherine and Clinton waiting.

They emerged, their hands entwined. "We're ready."

"Excellent. Come."

Together they walked into the enormous drawing room filled with velvet, satin, and silk gowns shimmering in the rosy light from the pink silken lamp shades. The hardwood floors gleamed where the carpets had been rolled up. Diamonds flashed on fingers, in hair, around necks, on gowns.

Hickory logs crackled and blazed on gilded fire-irons in the huge fireplace. The mantel was laden with red roses. He could barely hear the small orchestra above the buzz.

"Welcome to our Valentine's Ball," Clinton boomed. The crowd gradually quieted, and he repeated himself.

When it was silent, Catherine said, "We have the most exciting news. We would like to announce the engagement of our wonderful friend and neighbor, David Easterly, to this lovely lady, Julia Bradshaw."

The gasps were audible, the surprise on their faces genuine. Spontaneously, they burst into applause.

He had never felt so proud. No other accomplishment could compare to her.

-->==◉ ◉==<--

Monday, February 15, 1909

Julia didn't know what to expect when she entered the school building Monday morning.

She decided to meet the gossip head-on by giving the principal, Miss Whiton, the facts.

She walked into the outer office. The secretary gasped and stood. "Miss Bradshaw, you're here. I had no idea you and Mr. Easterly..." She stared at the ring on her finger.

Julia held out her hand so she could see it better. "Is Miss Whiton in?"

She nodded and motioned her through the door, still staring unabashedly.

Miss Whiton stood and extended her hand. "Julia, I saw the picture in the paper. Congratulations."

The picture of them standing hand-in-hand in the ballroom, she in her satin gown with her enormous ring and he in his tuxedo, had made the front page. She suspected everyone in the city knew by now.

It had caused quite a stir in church when people realized that the nondescript man among them was the richest man in the city.

Mr. Pratt had been noticeably absent.

"Frankly, I was astounded," Miss Whiton said. "For goodness' sake, girl, how did you ever meet David Easterly?"

"At an employee Christmas Eve party in his home. I was the guest of my cousin Lee."

"Well, good for you. I'm assuming this means I'm losing a kindergarten teacher."

Julia nodded. "I have my letter of resignation here. We're getting married right after school is out."

"We'll miss you. You've been a wonderful teacher."

"Thank you. I've loved it here. I appreciate all you've done to give me such a positive experience."

As Julia returned to the hall, she almost ran into Mr. Pratt. His face was ashen.

"Why didn't you tell me?"

"I wasn't supposed to tell anyone until after the Valentine's ball."

"You let me make a fool of myself."

"You didn't make a fool of yourself, Mr. Pratt. I enjoyed talking with you every day. Thank you for your friendship."

"I knew I didn't have a chance, but I had no idea I was competing with..."

"I know. I'm sorry. I didn't want people to know who he was."

"I won't be stopping by anymore."

"I understand, but please don't stop coming to church."

He nodded. "I'll be there next week."

"You never know. You just might meet someone else there."

He nodded sadly.

"And this time she'll be perfect for you."

Epilogue

Saturday, June 26, 1909

"THANK YOU, KATIE," Julia said as Katie pinned the flowing bridal veil over her low pompadour.

She sat at the dressing table in David's mother's floral bedroom.

"You look beautiful," Katie said.

"Let me see." Little Annie pushed her way to the mirror. "Aw... pretty."

"If you don't need anything else," Katie said, "I'll go down and take my seat."

"Please do, and thanks for everything."

Julia was thrilled when Katie agreed to be her lady's maid. It was a role they would both have to adjust to, but Julia had no doubt it would work.

Julia swiveled toward her mother and sisters. "You all look beautiful."

Jenny and Mary wore bridesmaids dresses of white-and-purple-flowered chiffon holding bouquets of white roses with orchids and lilies of the valley.

Annie's dress was white with a lavender sash. She had a crown of lilies of the valley tucked into her mop of dark curls. She twirled away.

"Calm down, Annie, or you're going to knock those flowers out of your hair," Jenny said.

"Surely it must be time to go down." Mama looked uncomfortable in her violet silk suit.

"Rose will tell us when," Julia said. Rose was at the top of the stairs with Papa. It was Julia's suggestion to make her the head housekeeper. Rose had assumed her responsibilities gratefully and seriously, coordinating the wedding as well.

The reception would be in the Terrace Garden with tables in the pergola where David had proposed, now shady with hanging purple wisteria and grapevines. More tables were in the loggia where the removable glass wall had been taken down to open it to the garden.

David and Ellen had planned the meal of Escalloped Crab Flakes in their own shells, Breast of Squab, Guinea Hen Sauté, Chicken and Lobster Salads, individual creams, fancy iced cakes, and bon-bons, and of course, the three-tiered wedding cake.

Mama had protested, of course. She thought cake and punch sufficient.

The ceremony would be in the marble entrance hall. The gardeners had worked all morning turning it into a bower of white roses and purple orchids.

Julia would come down the grand staircase to Pastor and David standing in front of the double front doors. Chairs for the guests had been set on either side of the staircase, extending into the columned marble hallway adjacent to the conservatory.

The organist had been playing in the conservatory for half an hour already.

"Girls, go wait in the hall with your father. I want a minute alone with Julia," Mama said.

Julia braced herself as the girls left.

Mama surveyed her from head to toe. "I never dreamed I would have a daughter so beautiful."

Julia's eyes filled with tears. "Don't make me cry now."

Mama took both her hands. "Are you sure this is what you want? Marrying Mr. Easterly? Living here?"

"I love him, Mama. Yes."

"Then I must admit I was wrong. It wasn't fair of me to discourage you just because I was unhappy with my past. David is a wonderful man. I will pray every day for your happiness and that God would be glorified in your marriage."

"Thank you."

Mama kissed her forehead. "God bless you, dear. You will make David a wonderful wife."

After she left, Julia needed a moment to herself. She looked down at the Terrace Garden where the formal, symmetrical garden was criss crossed with brick pathways around the sunken oval lily pond. Low boxwood hedges bordered the perennial gardens bursting with color.

Mama had never been so tender. Maybe now they could be friends.

Her heart was full. *God, thank You for giving David to me. Help me to be the wife he needs. Help us to be a light for You in our world. Help our children to love You all the days of their lives.*

She was interrupted by a booming chord of the wedding march. It was time.

Only one thing was left.

Propped up in one of the twin beds, Miss Donovan watched her every move. Miss Donovan could not speak. She could barely move.

At Julia's suggestion, David had brought her home from the hospital to his mother's room with the best view of the gardens. A full-time nurse attended her.

Julia squeezed her frail hand. "I'm sorry you can't come down to the wedding," she said. "At least you can hear the music."

Miss Donovan grunted. The good side of her face smiled.

send up food from the reception. Perhaps the nurse can ~u to the window so you can watch." David's mother's wheel-
c.   ~ad been put to good use.

Miss Donovan's eyes brightened.

Julia squeezed her hand again and kissed her forehead.

Praying for Miss Donovan had worked.

→━◉ ◉━←

David waited by the front door, hands behind his back, next to Pastor, Lee, Richard, and little Peter. Jenny was on the other side with Mary. Tired of standing, Annie had plopped on the marble floor, her white dress spread around her like flower petals.

He faced the audience, trying not to look impatient as he waited for that first glimpse of the bride.

Grace Weston, in the front row next to Mrs. Bradshaw, kept her eyes on Lee. Lee had proposed a month ago. David would be their best man in October. He was overjoyed for them. What they didn't know was that he was in the process of purchasing the house next-door as a wedding gift for them. Actually, having them so close would be more a gift for himself.

On one side of the staircase were friends from church, looking surprisingly at ease in his mansion after having attended many Sunday afternoon concerts. Behind them sat the servants.

On the other side were David's closest friends from the neighborhood, including Catherine, Clinton, and Sophie Townsend and his other brunch ladies. Many of his former Sunday concert crowd were probably offended because they hadn't received invitations. So be it. He had invited the people he cared most about.

"Where's Julia?" Annie's squeaky voice rose above the organ music.

The audience laughed.

Jenny bent over and clapped her hand over her mouth.

And then there she was on the arm of her father, radiant behind her veil. Her white satin dress was trimmed with Irish lace, and her veil hung from a coronet of orange blossoms. She slowly descended, her long train billowing behind her. Her bouquet of orchids and lilies of the valley trembled slightly.

Tears filled his eyes.

Little Peter waved. "Hi, Julia."

Everyone laughed again.

Julia's smile shone through her veil as her eyes met his.

Her whole family was so dear. Sometimes he wished they would all move in so he could enjoy them all the time.

But no, he was going to fill it with children of his own.

The End

Author' Note

WOULD YOU LIKE to visit the Easterly House? You can.

In my Tour of Mansions series, you can actually visit the places I write about.

The Easterly House and gardens is really the Eastman Museum at 900 East Avenue, Rochester, New York. Check out the website for times, prices, and pictures: https://www.eastman.org/.

For more pictures of the George Eastman House visit my website at http://www.bethlivingston.net/

The Francis Parker School #23, 170 Barrington Street, dates from 1902. It is still in use today as a neighborhood school.

Miss Weston lived in an apartment at the rear of 123 Barrington Street.

The house I used as my model for the Bradshaw house is 245 Barrington Street.

You can drive by the Park Avenue Hospital at the corner of Park Avenue and Brunswick. It is now apartments and shops. The Park Avenue Hospital was built in 1894 as a private hospital, became a boys' school, and then opened again in 1907 as a hospital with forty beds, the smallest hospital in Rochester. In 1908 it also had a training school for nurses. It closed in 1975 and moved to the new Park Ridge Hospital.

Next door is the church I used as my model with its beautiful sanctuary upstairs and the fellowship hall downstairs.

Take a walk past the waterfall in downtown Rochester where Lee and Miss Weston met for lunch. It is High Falls on the Genesee River, seen from the Pont de Rennes Bridge on Platt Street in Brown's Race Historic District.

Ontario Beach Park which opened in 1884 was amazing in its heyday. The amusement park was torn down in 1920. All that is left now is the carousel and the long pier.

I hope you'll enjoy exploring all these places as much as I did.

Here is the recipe for Mr. Easterly's Lemon Meringue Pie.

Creamy Lemon Meringue Pie

1 cup plus 2 tablespoons sugar	4 egg yolks, slightly beaten
1/3 cup cornstarch	2 tablespoons butter
1/8 teaspoon salt	1/2 cup fresh lemon juice (about 2 lemons)
1 cup milk	2 drops yellow food coloring
2/3 cup water	9" baked pie shell

Heat oven to 400F. Mix sugar, cornstarch, and salt in saucepan. Stir in milk and water gradually. Cook over medium heat, stirring constantly, until mixture thickens and boils. Boil and stir 1 minute. Stir at least half of the hot mixture gradually into egg yolks; stir into hot mixture in pan. Boil and stir 1 minute; remove from heat.

Stir in butter, lemon juice, and food coloring. Pour into baked shell. Make Meringue. Spread over filling, carefully sealing to edge of crust. Bake until light brown, about 1 minutes. Cool.

Meringue
4 egg whites
1/4 teaspoon cream of tartar
1/2 cup sugar

Beat egg whites and cream of tartar until foamy. Beat in sugar, 1 tablespoon at a time; beat until stiff and glossy. Do not under beat.

If you need a recipe for pie crust, this is my favorite:

Never-Fail Vinegar Pie Crust

2 teaspoons apple cider vinegar	5 cups flour
1 egg	1 pound lard
water	1/4 cup plus 2 tablespoons shortening
2 teaspoons salt	

Put vinegar and egg into a measuring cup. Beat lightly. Add enough water to measure 1 cup of liquid. Mix salt and flour. Cut in lard and shortening with a pastry blender until mixture resembles coarse cornmeal. Add vinegar mixture gradually until mixture forms a dough. Makes 6 pie crusts. I usually form them in pie plates and freeze them until needed.

Acknowledgments

Thanks to Kathy Connor, the George Eastman Legacy Curator, for providing me with so many research materials and for giving me a behind-the-scenes tour of the cellar and servants' wing. Thanks also to Jesse Peers, Archivist of the George Eastman Legacy Collection.

Thanks to Amy Kinsey, Landscape Curator, for her wonderful garden tour and for sending me the historical pictures in her docent's file.

Thanks to Debbie Karr Goyette, an old childhood friend, who toured Ontario Beach Park with me, riding the carousel and walking the pier.

Thanks to Rhonda Morien, principal of Frances Parker School #23, for her tour of the school, especially of the kindergarten rooms.

Thanks to Christine Ridarsky, Historical Services Consultant of the Local History and Genealogy Division of the Central Library of Rochester and Monroe County, for finding helpful material on Francis Parker School #23 and the Park Avenue Hospital.

Thanks to Terrie Goeddertz for her memories of Francis Parker School and the Park Avenue Hospital.

Thanks to my son, David Livingston, and my sister, Karen Fisher, for their invaluable editing help. I couldn't do it without you.

Thanks to my critique team: Grace Hedges, Chris Haile, Vickie Mellody, and my daughter, Laura Gardner. Your insights were so helpful.

Thanks to Ben Larson for designing my cover and my website.

Thanks to Lindsey Feltz Quigley for providing her picture for my cover. Although we didn't use it, Lindsey became my inspiration for Julia Bradshaw.

Watch for the third book in the Tour of Mansions series, *Sunnyside Hill*, which takes place in Sonnenberg Gardens in Canandaigua, New York.

Check out my website at http://www.bethlivingston.net/ and "like" my Facebook page at https://www.facebook.com/authorbethlivingston/ for updates on all my books.

Made in the USA
Columbia, SC
06 November 2017